Also by Hilma Wolitzer:

ENDING
HEARTS
IN THE PALOMAR ARMS
SILVER*

*Published by Ivy Books

IN THE FLESH

Hilma Wolitzer

IVY BOOKS • NEW YORK

FOR

TED SOLOTAROFF

Library of Congress Catalog Card Number: 77-1704

ISBN 0-8041-0508-1

A portion of this book was originally published in *Esquire Magazine*.

Manufactured in the United States of America

First Ballantine Books Edition: August 1989

The author thanks the John Simon Guggenheim Memorial Foundation for its generous support and the Yaddo Corporation for a fine place to work.

Special thanks to Gordon Lish.

Oh futile tenderness
of touch in a world like this!
how much longer, dear child,
do you think sex will matter?
There might have been a wedding
that never was . . .

—from "The Demon Lover"
    by Adrienne Rich

1

WE WERE MARRIED IN 1957, IN THOSE DARK AGES BE- fore legalized abortion. I know that's no excuse. There were always illegal abortions. But my social circles were narrow and unsophisticated. The doctors in my life were of the old-fashioned tongue depressor variety. Their worst crimes were probably kickbacks on unnecessary, but lawful, hysterectomies.

I knew vaguely about worldlier women who flew down to Puerto Rico or other tropical places to have safe, painless surgery, and probably even had time to get in a little sun and dance the carioca. But I had never even been in an airplane. And the stories I knew by heart were about hapless girls in the back rooms of drugstores after hours, whose blood flowed in fountains, poor girls whose butchered parts were packaged and distributed among the trash cans of the city.

In those days, my mother, in her innocence, spoke with longing to her cronies about being a grandmother someday. It appeared to be her goal in life. I think she wanted to wear a gold charm bracelet dangling with symbols that commemorated the births of babies. She wanted a record of bright and precocious sayings and an accordion folder of photographs—that first-class ticket to the society of grandmothers.

I was her lone child, come late in life, "like a biblical miracle." She might have more appropriately named me Ruth or Leah, but instead she chose Paulette, after her favorite actress and after a distant cousin on my father's side. I believe she had a premonition that I was to be last as well

as first and so had used the female version of a masculine
name to cover all unfulfilled dreams. And she was right. My
birth had denied passage to any future brothers and sisters.
My mother claimed that one morning a few months later
everything had simply fallen out of her. As a young misin-
formed girl, I had pictured the worst: a giblet tangle of fal-
lopian tubes, ovaries, and the little pear-shaped uterus, all
lying useless on the bathroom floor. But first I had been born,
dropped in agony like an oversized egg from a disconsolate
chicken. Way behind schedule, my mother was impatient for
the natural order of the generations.

When I was twenty my goal was to lie entwined with Howard forever. We had met at a school dance in my second year
at N.Y.U. He was eight years older, a saxophonist with the
combo that was playing that night. I didn't want to dance at
all; I just stood against a wall and watched him and listened
to the music and felt that giddy sickness that would not go
away. "What's the *matter* with you?" my girl friends asked,
but I couldn't explain it then.

Sex, which I had discovered in the misery of childhood
(like everyone else), had finally reached the ultimate stage of
partnership. And what a partner I had! Even cramped in the
back seat of Howard's car, I recognized with awe all those
sensations we invented and that new voice that came from
the dark pit of my throat ("Don't . . . oh yes . . . oh God.")

Was it possible that my mother and father didn't know? In
their world there could be mingling without coupling, kisses
without tongues. When I came home, struck with experience, I tiptoed past their bedroom, and they yoo-hooed and
advised me to take some milk and cupcakes before I went to
bed.

Lying in bed, "in trouble" already, I used a wad of toilet
paper and a flashlight for undercover checking. Nothing.

There was probably still a chance that I was mistaken or
that my body was just giving me some punitive suspense. As
I had assured Howard, it was my *safe* time and our pleasure
didn't have to be deferred for the sake of caution. Of course
he had hardly waited anyway, had barely missed a stroke.

I checked again. Nothing.

During the past week I had looked around for heavy things to lift. Nothing seemed just right. Books were ridiculously light, and the refrigerator was stationary.

Howard and I even ran four laps around the Jamaica High School track and then collapsed panting in the tall grass behind it. There I found out that his own birth had been unplanned. It seemed like the saddest irony. "But how do you know that?" I asked.

"My mother told me," Howard said casually.

I was shocked. If there was a baby, or its meager beginnings inside me, that refused to be dislodged, if I actually *had* it and it grew up, I would always tell it how we planned its being, nurtured it, and then rejoiced in its arrival. Everyone is entitled to that.

But in the meantime, hot baths and strenuous exercise. Drifting into sleep, the flashlight locked between my knees, I thought about the slow passage of sperm, the mere *chance* of it, that rendezvous of sperm and egg like some nostalgic event.

I adored Howard's physical presence in a room, was willing to overlook ordinary frailties and even idiosyncratic turns in view of his special dark beauty. In my first stunned perception of him, he looked like a cross between Bugsy Siegel and Delmore Schwartz.

But he was a moody man, given to occasional depressions and frequent existential twinges. Sometimes he complained about a feeling of sinking or drowning, and I saw myself swimming tirelessly alongside him, his own personal Gertrude Ederle, buoying him up, keeping his spirits above water.

I was delighted to have an obsession. I dearly loved the intensity of that word, reminiscent of old Bette Davis movies, of thrilling historical passions.

No one approved. Howard had been married briefly before to a woman named Renee, a maniac of sorts. He still heard from her from time to time. My mother said that his loyalty would certainly be divided, and besides he had bedroom eyes. My father said that he was not ambitious. Sherry, a classmate with bohemian leanings, was never going to let herself be snared this way. When I told her about Howard and me, she was another prophet of doom. "What is he? Scorpio?" she said. "Uh-oh."

Howard's mother was convinced that our relationship was only a phase. She would probably say the same thing, if asked, about the human condition. His father jangled the change in his pockets and looked like he was making plans.

As our crisis mounted, Howard became more unsure about committing himself. I tried to be understanding, remembering what he had been through in his life so far. We sat in his car, parked on a dark street in a neutral neighborhood. There was no question of doubt anymore. All the evidence was in.

"What do *you* want to do?" he asked.

Fear had canceled some second thoughts. Now unreasonable love wiped out the rest. "You know," I said, trying to telegraph that love. "What about you?"

He sighed, his eyes shifted restlessly, and I imagined my mother's pride and joy, a slender gelatinous thread riding the sewer currents of Queens.

"Are you afraid, Paulie?" Howard said, and I knew then that *he* was.

I made him say it anyway. "Of what?" I asked, forcing his glance.

"Of . . . I don't know . . . of medical complications."

"Aren't you?" What a mess it could be! I concentrated, flashing terrible mental pictures at him, *Daily News* headlines, even threw in some war atrocities for good measure.

He shuddered, receiving my message. I couldn't help thinking that men whose mothers have established an early pattern of guilt in them are probably the easiest. Even in those green days I had a psychological bent.

"So that's it, I guess," Howard said, and we were engaged.

I threw my arms around him, sealing the bond with an ecstasy that was almost religious. "It will be wonderful," I promised. "We'll have a wonderful life together. We'll have terrific good luck. I can feel it."

He hugged me back, but all I could really feel were the doombeat of his heart and the collapsing walls of his will.

2

*T*HROUGH SOME MINOR POLITICAL INFLUENCE WE WERE given first refusal on an apartment on the nineteenth floor of a building in a large cluster of buildings in Forest Hills. We were assured that thirty other couples on legitimate waiting lists had been bypassed in our favor.

We went to see the apartment two weeks before the wedding. The couple who were moving out led the way through a maze of labeled cartons and crates. For some reason the man felt obliged to point out the obvious. "Well, here's the oven," he said, and we peered dutifully inside, as trusting as Hansel and Gretel. "And this is the refrigerator." An orange nestled against what appeared to be a urine specimen. There was the boiled egg smell of school lunchrooms.

Somewhere an infant cried, its wails muted and distant-sounding. Was it packed into one of the crates?

Howard poked around. He looked into closets and he examined sink stains as if they were hieroglyphics. "You folks going into the suburbs?" he asked. I could see he was getting ready to have one of those discussions about the merits of city life against those of the country. He smiled encouragement at the man who didn't smile back.

"We're splitting up," the wife said, and she threw a couple of pot covers into a carton where they clanged together like cymbals in mid-symphony.

My heart tilted. Premonitory signs meant a lot to Howard. I looked at him, but he didn't say anything. What could he

6

say anyway? Good luck? You can't win them all? He wandered away, wordless and troubled.

The apartment was small. Lilliputians might have lived there quite graciously. Footsteps, voices, even the resonance of thoughts, it seemed, clamored through those thin walls. It was hard to think in positive terms, of coziness and economy. But of course we took it. We pressed money and gratitude into the hands of our benefactor and certain designated middlemen. One of them was the superintendent of our building. He opened the door of his apartment slightly and then wedged himself in the opening, as if he believed we might force entry. When we introduced ourselves, he smirked, giving the impression he knew plenty about us already.

We were married in traditional June, as it turned out, all arrangements made in a desperate frenzy. There were some last-ditch attempts by others to foil our plans. Howard's father, who directed funerals in Rego Park, tried to convince me to call off the whole thing. Behind Howard's back he offered two hundred dollars and a side trip to the Virgin Islands. He was such a literal man. Did he think I might be restored to my former state there? A man in his business, I thought, should have been *uplifted* by the promise of new life, no matter what the circumstances.

An hour before the wedding, my mother, who had been bitterly silent all morning, said, "You had promise, Paulette. Teachers always said good things about you. With a little luck, you could have been somebody."

But I knew she was remembering her own dreams for me, those tap dancing classes, those elocution lessons, that futile but desperate desire to have mothered Shirley Temple instead of me. I felt sorry for her then and I stroked her arm in consolation. But she wasn't finished. "You used to write nice poems," she said.

I was startled. She had hardly ever acknowledged my poems before. "Oh, Ma," I said. "That was kid stuff. Adolescent mewling."

Which wasn't entirely true. I had intended to be a poet at

one time, could be one yet, for all I knew. I still kept copies of my best poems and all the rejection slips from *The New Yorker, The Atlantic Monthly*, and *Partisan Review*. They were standard rejection slips, not one with a personal note of encouragement or regret. I remember that I licked the first one to see if the signature was machine printed too, but the blue ink came off on my tongue. Sometimes I looked at the mastheads of those magazines for the names of the people who signed the slips, but they were never there.

"Say something nice to me now," I told my mother, fussing with the corsage that drooped tearoses on her breast. "It's my wedding day."

"Well, I guess you know what you're doing," she said. It was the best she could come up with under the circumstances. But at least she was calmer than she and my father had been when I first offered my news. A musician! They clapped their foreheads and beat their breasts. How to explain that his music was an essential part of Howard, a second voice full of yearning and declaration; that his saxophone was a golden extension of his body? Musicians were confused in their heads with gypsies and dope peddlers, with vagabonds and thieves. But weren't they right in a way? Didn't he look wicked with his dark, sleepy eyes, and that mobster's bulge in his trousers? Hadn't he come in a caravan disguised as a '52 Chevy, to steal me away?

"It's a bum's life," my father said. "It's not steady."

My father had worked for twenty-eight years in the Post Office, and he could respect only the pension-bound promise of a government job. In the thirties, he pointed out, civil-service employees still put bread on their families' tables and kept the nation running besides.

"But Howard is going to have a studio," I pointed out. "It will be a *business*. He'll rent time to other musicians who want to make recordings, and he'll give lessons on the saxophone and clarinet. And he's part of a nice little combo. They play club dates and weddings. Strictly union scale," I added, trying to speak my father's language. But it was all a threat to them: Howard's history, his handsomeness. Why hadn't he gone in with his father? Unpleasant work maybe, but definitely steady.

"He's an *artist*," I explained. "A sensitive man."

"A married man," my mother said.

"Divorced," I said, correcting her. "Annulled," I said, correcting myself. "They were hardly even married. It was only a little mistake."

Mistake! It was as trivial to them as my being only a little pregnant. Their X-ray eyes glanced in the direction of the *real* mistake, that furled fetus suspended below my heart.

Howard's married sister in Los Angeles sent a telegram: Every happiness. STOP. Wish we were there. STOP. Hope it's a bed of roses. STOP.

Howard assured me it was meant in ironic good humor, but he didn't even sound convinced himself.

No one cried at the ceremony. It was a small uneasy assemblage, but at least Howard's first wife didn't show up, as he had hinted she might.

My oldest friend Judy Miller and her husband stood up for us. Sherry interrupted her wild life in Greenwich Village to serve as another witness. Two musicians from Howard's combo wore dark glasses and drummed out nervous little melodies with their fingers on their folding chairs. They called everyone "man" regardless of gender. My mother wondered if they were blind. She wondered if they took opium.

Howard had a minor nosebleed, delaying things for a few minutes. But then it was done. Quickly, without pageantry, without epithalamiums.

A modest luncheon followed. The maraschino cherries oozed artificial color over the fruit cup. Lenny drank too much and told ethnic jokes and jokes about wedding nights, managing to offend everyone.

Howard and I moved into the apartment right after the wedding. On the first night, lamps without shades threw our crazy shadows everywhere. We turned off the lamps and went to bed. The windows were curtainless and filled with moonlight and the place smelled of new paint and insecticide. Above our heads strangers shouted and ran heavily across the floors.

This is our new life, I thought. So far, so good. The ghosts of the former tenants had left, were gone forever with their unresolved quarrels, their rumbles of discontent. I shut my eyes and tried to memorize the room and the furniture. My hand and Howard's crept toward union under the bedclothes. Everything that mattered seemed to be held in that joining. But was my grip stronger, more urgent than his?

My eyes opened and I looked at Howard lying next to me. I imagined him a fugitive from my will and determination, even from my love. His spirit moved without shadow across the unbroken paint of the walls. Away. Away.

And what if I could never write again after this? Fabled punishment for happiness; one pleasure in exchange for another. But what if all creative thought went into clothes-washing and cake-making and just keeping Howard there; if the baby lying mute and waiting absorbed *everything*, my language along with my calcium?

I gasped, struck with a kind of terrified joy. Howard mistook it for a cry of lust, and he moved over me. And when we finally moved together, thoughts, with the powdery substance of dreams, invaded me. This was the stuff then, this was the real thing: these arms, legs, flesh, these odors, gestures, this room, bed. Here were the poems, the unwritten words waiting coiled and crouched like loyal and patient beasts.

"Here it is," I told Howard, and I gave myself up.

3

Being born is something
like showing up without
cash in a small town.
Try pretending vagrancy
is only innocence.
Learn the local lingo
in a crash course,
and make one good friend.
PAULETTE F., *January 5, 1958*

I PLANNED TO GO ON A DIET RIGHT AFTER THE BABY WAS born. In the meantime I was growing, becoming bigger than life. I might have been a stand-in for the Russian Women's Decathlon Champ—a thing of beauty and power.

Howard assured me that he loved me this way, statuesque, he called it, a word borrowed from false novels. He claimed that I was the first woman he could really *sleep* with, in the literal sense of the word. Renee, his first wife, had been scrawny and pale, poor thing. The knobs of her hips and elbows had poked him abruptly from dreams, reminding him of the skeletal frame underneath.

"Everyone is big nowadays," my mother said, *her* hands and feet like tiny blunt instruments.

"Ah, beautiful," Howard murmured, in the sleepy voice of sex, as he burrowed in.

But I'm nobody's fool. On Sundays I saw him look through the magazine section of *The Times* and pause with wistful

11

concentration at those slender models in the brassiere ads. There is desire beyond mere lust in that, I thought. He might have looked at girls in centerfolds instead, at the opulent ones, who were there to inspire a different and simpler kind of longing.

If, in his secret heart, he wanted me to be slim and trim, I would be. The women's magazines were full of easy formulas I could follow: the thinking woman's diet, the drinking woman's diet, the shrinking woman's diet. It would be a cinch.

But there had always been more to me than meets the eye, more than can be seen on the wide screen. More than those breasts weighting their hammock or the frizzy-haired head ducking in doorways. Underneath there was a domestic heart with the modest beat of a ladies' wristwatch. And inside my bulk, the future me stepped daintily, waiting for release.

The baby grew too, floated in its confinement, pulsed and sounded its limits.

And Howard was madly in love with it. It was a romance he had never experienced before. He had been married once and of course he had always had women. They would have followed him from Hamelin without even a note. They still sought him out. I watched, narrow-eyed, as new ones came up, threatened and disappeared. Howard was inviolate, he was a family man now. When he embraced me, he said, "I feel as if I'm embracing the world."

Confident, a veritable monument to his new life, I stretched and sighed in his arms. "I'm going to diet when this is all over. Become très chic."

"No," he protested. "Don't."

I did a little pirouette. "This stuff is going to fall off like snakeskin."

"Don't lose my favorite parts," Howard warned.

We went to visit other couples who nested in their apartments. Judy and Lenny Miller had a little girl named Roberta. Her toys were always in evidence; a vaporizer was her constant bedside companion.

Howard and I tiptoed in to admire her. When she was awake she was a fresh kid, the kind who screams whenever she speaks, and who answers civil, friendly questions with "No, *silly*," or "No, *stupid*," a miserable kid who makes nose-picking a public pleasure.

But now the steam curled her hair into heartbreaking tendrils. The hiss of the vaporizer and the sweet rush of breath. We whispered in this shrine, made reverent by the miracle.

When we tiptoed back to the living room, I thought: Howard doesn't even feel trapped. He actually *wants* a baby, wants this whole homely scene for his own. And I hadn't really trapped him anyway, had I? Isn't the sperm the true aggressor, those little Weissmullers breaststroking to their destiny? Or is it the egg after all, waiting in ambush, ready to grab the first innocent stray? "Who really did this?" I once asked Howard. But he thought it was a theological poser. "God, I suppose, if you believe in Him," he said. "Or else the life-force of nature."

We sat in the Millers' living room among the debris and leavings of playtime. Howard rested a proprietary hand on my belly. All conversation came back to the inevitable subject.

"My doctor said he never saw anything like it," Judy said. "He had real tears in his eyes when he held Roberta up."

It might have been sweat, I thought. Judy tended to idealize things.

She was talking about the natural childbirth course they had taken, where she had learned to breathe the right way during labor, so that she was able to be an active member of the delivery team.

Lenny had been there too. Now he picked up a baby shoe and allowed us to observe the wonder of its size in the width of his palm. "It was a beautiful experience," he said. "Most of the time we're working against nature in the births of our children. It's hypocrisy to keep the father outside, a stranger at the gates, so to speak."

What a metaphor! Lenny, who was a teacher in the city school system, was a pushover for any innovation in education. I imagined him whispering tips to his unborn daughter on the phonic method of reading.

Now he advised Howard not to be that notorious slacker, the biological father who drops his seed and runs. Lenny had been right there, rubbing Judy's back, speaking encouragement, talking and stroking his child into the world. I could sense Howard's excitement.

Then Judy brought out the photographs. We had seen them before, of course, but it seemed particularly appropriate to see them once again. Lenny was careful to hand them to us in proper chronological sequence. Judy, huge, horizontal on the delivery table. Himself, the masked robber of innocence, smiling at her with his eyes. The doctor, glistening with sweat/tears, his hand upward and lost to view. Oh, God, what was I doing? The evidence was all there. Judy, grimacing, clenching, contracting, her every expression reflected in the other faces.

"See," Lenny pointed out. "*I* was in labor, too." Then, "Here she comes!" handing us the one with the emerging head, a small, bloodied, determined ball. Judy's own head was lifted in an effort to watch, and she was smiling.

Then triumph! The whole family united at last on this shore. Mortal, tender, exquisite.

They were winning photos, there was no denying that. Howard was speechless with emotion.

"I thought I was dying, that's all," my mother said. "You were ripping me to shreds."

My father left the room.

"He can't stand to hear about it," my mother whispered. "They feel guilty, you know."

"Howard and I are taking a course," I said.

"A course! What are they going to teach you—how to scream? *You* were feet first," she said accusingly.

But I wasn't put off by her. She had lied about everything else most of my life. "God helps those who help themselves," she used to say. And, "All cats are gray in the dark." That, about lovemaking!

Howard and I went to school where I learned to breathe. We saw films on the development of the embryo and the benefits of nursing. I could picture that small silvery fish already endowed with my genes and Howard's, already bound to us by far more than the nourishing cord. I continued to grow, stretching my skin to translucency, to a new iridescent glow. Howard fed me tidbits from his plate to support my image and keep up my strength, and I took a vitamin supplement that came in little pink and blue capsules.

I learned to pant, little doglike huffs and puffs for the last stages of labor. I practiced smiling into the bathroom mirror while I panted, in imitation of Judy's Madonna smile of the last photograph. She had looked radiant, more beautiful even than in her wedding pictures.

We had decided against delivery photographs for ourselves. Everything would be recorded perfectly in the darkroom of the heart.

Howard and I cherished our new vocabulary. *Term.* I was carrying to full *term. Dilation. Presentation. Lactation.* Gorgeous words from a superior language.

Our lovemaking took on the excitement of imposed restraint. "Are you all right?" Howard would ask. What a paradox!—to be so powerful and fragile at once.

We played with names for the baby, from the biblical to the historical to the mythical. Nothing seemed good enough or suitably original.

We waited. I went for monthly checkups. Other pregnant women in the doctor's waiting room and I smiled knowingly at one another. We found ourselves united in a vast and ancient sorority without the rituals of pledging. Reducing us to girlish dependence, Dr. Marvin Kramer called us by our first names. We called him Dr. Kramer.

Opening my legs on the examining table while his cheerless nurse laid a sheet across my knees for the sake of discretion, I could just make out the blond crown of his head, halo-lit by his miner's lamp. But I could hear his voice as it tunneled through me. "You're coming along fine, Paulette. Good girl, good girl."

"Well, if you can't be good, be careful." That wasn't one of my mother's chestnuts, though it could have been. But I had been carried away, lost forever to common sense and practical advice. In the back seat of a car, so many destinies irrevocably set. It was astonishing.

"I can hardly move anymore," I complained to Howard one day. He crawled to a corner of the bed and folded himself to give me the most possible room.

The gestation of an elephant is almost two years. Mindless hamsters pop out in sixteen days.

"It will be over soon, love," Howard said, and he reached across the bed and touched my hair.

Then what? I wondered. Was that when my magic would lose its potency?

"Do the breathing," Howard suggested.

"Take gas when the time comes," my mother said. "I wouldn't lead you astray."

Judy and Lenny came to visit with Roberta, who whined and tap-danced on our coffee table.

"I'm going on five hundred calories a day," I said, "as soon as I drop this load."

"Try to sound more maternal," Howard whispered.

"Short skirts are coming back," I said in a threatening voice. "And those skimpy little blouses."

"Oh, just breathe," he begged.

"I'm sick of breathing," I said.

Labor began in the afternoon. It was a dispirited Sunday and we were listening to a melancholy Ethical Culture sermon on the radio.

The elevator stopped five times for other passengers on our way down to the lobby of our building. Neighbors smiled at us and looked away, pretending they didn't know where we were going with my swollen belly and little overnight case. Inside their pockets they counted on their fingers and were satisfied.

When we came to the hospital, Howard immediately notified the admitting secretary that he was a Participating Father, and that he was going up with me.

She laughed out loud and continued to type information on the insurance forms.

"It's not too bad, so far," I told Howard, wondering why my mother had to dramatize everything.

"I'll be with you," Howard promised.

They made him wait downstairs, despite his protests. "We won't be needing *you* for a while," the secretary told him, and she winked at me.

"Good-bye," I said at the elevator. I wished we had decided in favor of pictures, after all. I would have started right there with a record of his poor face as the elevator doors slid shut and the nurse and I went up.

"Primapara!" she shouted to someone I couldn't see, as soon as we left the elevator.

Well, *that* sounds nice, I thought. Like prima donna or prima ballerina. We went swiftly down a corridor past little rooms. Other women looked out at me.

What's all this? I wondered, everything unlearned in that first bolt of fear.

I had my own room. A Room of One's Own, I thought. But *this* certainly wasn't what Woolf had meant. The minute this was over, the first chance I could get to concentrate, I would start writing again. It was only a biological pause; just so much psychic energy to go around, one thing at a time. I climbed into the high bed like a tired and obedient child.

The new doctors who came to examine me all seemed so short. And they smiled as they dug in and announced their findings. "Two fingers. Three fingers."

Why didn't they use some secret medical jargon for what they were doing? It sounded suspiciously like a juvenile sex game to me, as if they were only *playing* doctor.

It was such a quiet place. There was none of my mother's

famous screaming. Things must have changed, I decided, since her day.

After a while I was shaved, for collaborating with the enemy, I supposed. More silence. Then a shriek! I sat up, alerted, but it was only some horseplay among the nurses.

"What's going on?" I asked someone who came in and went out again without answering. "Hello?"

It was lonely. Where was Howard anyway?

And then he was there. When had he grown that shadowed jowl? And why were his eyes so dark with sympathy?

"It's nothing," I said severely. "Stop looking like that." Lenny had seemed magnificent. Howard only looked mournful and terrified. So *this* was where his life had led him.

Things didn't get better. Howard rubbed my back and jerked me from the haven of short dozes with his murmurs, his restlessness. There were noises now from other rooms as well. Voices rose in wails of protest.

But I had my own troubles. The contractions were coming so damn fast. I was thirsty, but water wasn't permitted—only the rough swipe of the washcloth across my tongue. I caught it with my teeth and tried to suck on it, cheating.

There was no discreet examination sheet in this place. Strangers peered at me in full view. They measured, probed and went away. A nurse pushed a hypodermic into my thigh when I wasn't looking.

"Hey, what's that?" I demanded. "I'm not supposed to have anything. This is a *natural* case, you know."

"Dr. Kramer is on his way," she said, evading the issue.

"Taking his own sweet time," I snarled.

Howard seemed shocked by my rudeness and the abrupt shift of mood.

"This is getting *bad*," I told him, but it wasn't what he wanted to hear. In the distance a Greek chorus warned—too late, too late.

They wheeled me dizzyingly fast to the delivery room.

Howard ran alongside like a winded trainer trying to keep up with his fighter. "Almost there," he said, breathless.

How would *he* know? It was miles and miles.

Despite everything, they strapped me down. "This is barbaric!" I shouted. "Women in primitive places squat in the fields!"

"Oh God, *that* bullshit again," a black nurse said.

"You trapped me into this," I told Howard. "I'll never forgive you. Never!"

He was wearing a green surgical mask and now he stood as poised and eager as an outfielder waiting for the long ball.

"Imposter!" I cried.

"Paulette!" Dr. Kramer called. "How is my big girl?"

"Just tell me what to do," Howard said.

"Why don't you hold her? There. Lift her a little and support her sternum."

Sternum, sternum, what were they *talking* about?

I yowled and Howard said, "My love, I'm here!" His eyes were brilliant with tears.

The whole room shuddered with pain. And I was the center of it, the spotlit star of the universe. Who was trying to be born here anyway—Moby Dick?

Oh, all the good, wise things I had done in my life. I might have done anything and still come to this. In school that teacher rolled down charts on nutrition. We saw the protein groups, the grain groups. Green leafy vegetables. Lack of vitamin C leads to scurvy.

Liars! The charts ought to show *this*, the extraordinary violence of birth, worse than mob violence, worse than murder. FUCKING LEADS TO THIS! those charts ought to say.

"A few more pushes and you'll have your baby," Dr. Kramer said.

Ah, who wanted a baby? For once in her whole rotten life, my mother was right. "Dr. Kramer! Marvin! Give me gas!" I cried, using his first name for equal footing.

But instead he caught the baby who had shouldered through in the excitement.

And I had forgotten to smile, had greeted my child with the face of a madwoman.

Somewhere else in the room, a nurse pressed Howard's head down between his knees.

"No pictures. No pictures," I said.

4

Stop me if you've
heard this one.
It's about R. and
his wife, B.
locked in love or
a murderous hold.
Or maybe it was
someone else I
used to know at
another time.
The main thing is
the way it's told.

April 27, 1958

WE WENT TO THE SUPERMARKET TOGETHER ON SATURDAY to gather our weekly needs. Howard pushed the shopping cart with the baby asleep in the blanket-lined seat, and I walked alongside, pulling boxes and cans from the shelves. Anyone who saw us like this, strolling under that canopy of signs, SPECIAL!, FAMILY PAK!, SAVE!; under that photograph of a couple toasting one another with glasses of milk, must have thought we were an ordinary family. But was there such a thing? It seemed so extraordinary to be us, Howard and Paulette, transformed miraculously into these new people: husband, wife, father, mother, titles for greeting cards and tombstones.

What was Howard thinking as we rolled past the pyramids

of fruit, the obvious seductions of the appetizer counter? Men have always been consoled on their loss of freedom. Howard had been given a bachelor party by his friends to ease the transition, a drunken affair with a great deal of sexual innuendo and half-joking warnings about the imminent end of his liberty.

I was given a bridal shower instead, a celebration of this next inevitable step in my career as a woman. I was encouraged by pot holders and nightgowns, the paradoxical equipment of wifehood.

But Howard wasn't thinking bad thoughts. He wasn't eying those carefree young men at the Speedy Checkout, who were buying porterhouse steaks and a bottle of grenadine. In my purse was the shopping list, the items I had forgotten written in at the bottom in his own touchingly broad and childish hand. *Light bulbs, Drano, soap.* And then, *Do you know I love you?* I would tear that part off later and preserve it between the pages of a book.

He hummed and whistled to the awful piped-in music as if it didn't assault his professional ear. We worked like a relay team, passing the items from the cart to the rolling counter, carrying the bags and the baby to the car, where Howard took my hand on an impulse of love and pressed it against his face.

And yet there can never be enough proof, enough assurance. "Do you love me?" I found myself asking Howard on Monday morning. I felt a little guilty even as I said it. It wasn't original or witty, two of the things I had promised myself I'd be. But Howard didn't mind. He rolled against me in bed, and I arranged myself to his contours—a perfect fit! Anyway, it was impossible to be more creative so early in the day, and not to speak in the smug, familiar rhetoric of lovers. "Do you love me? When did you first know? Am I really beautiful?"

In a few minutes he would have to get up and go to work. But in the meantime it was enough to just lie there, delivered from sleep, and repeat our ritual of homage. It worked both

ways, that was the wonderful thing. I was the best and Howard was the best. We outdid one another in the generosity of
our praise. Who could have invented better lovers, a sweeter
cock, a more warming fire? Ah, love, its saintly tolerance
for imperfection!

Our baby (who was sleeping later than usual this morning)
wasn't so perfect either. In the first spring of his life, he had
developed a crusty eczema in his hairline. Nothing in itself,
we were told, but sometimes the precursor of other things:
severe allergies, even asthma. After breast-feeding, we ex-
perimented with goat's milk and exotic mixtures of soybeans
and green bananas, until things began to look better.

But that was only the beginning. A few months later we
noticed that Jason's feet turned out, like Chaplin's. An or-
thopedic device called a Brownie Bar was prescribed for night
use. It was a straight metal strip welded to a pair of open-
toed baby shoes, and it was guaranteed to train Jason's feet
in the right path.

What next? we wondered, and we didn't have to wait long
to find out. One navy-blue eye began to slide furtively out of
focus, moving restlessly toward his nose and back again.
Howard was very upset, even after the doctor promised that
it would correct itself eventually, that there were exercises to
speed up correction, that it was only a weak muscle. The
idea of an additional weakness in someone already so vulnerable was staggering. Who had passed on this weakness
anyway? For which of his own sins was Howard being so
deviously repaid? For car-fucking? For pubescent lust for his
own sister? For eating bad hot dogs at ballgames? For not
remembering dead grandparents who had predicted on
deathbeds that they would not be remembered? Suddenly
there was only human responsibility for everything that happens.

"We never had those things in our family," my mother
said.

* * *

"Listen, it's nothing to worry about," I told Howard, about Jason's latest flaw, but I wasn't so crazy about it myself, and preferred to admire him asleep or turned to favor his better profile.

And now he *was* asleep in the next room, which had easily been converted from a junior dinette to a cozy nursery. Howard made the first tentative signs of leaving the bed.

"Don't go," I said, holding on with a stranglehold, pinning him down with my weight.

"I have to," he murmured, but he didn't move any farther.

My hand explored under the covers and found him. "Ah, Dr. Livingstone!" I said. "I would know you anywhere."

"Don't start that now," Howard said without conviction. "You know I have to go to work."

"Think of *this* as your work," I said.

"It's getting late," he warned, but his body betrayed him and his voice was heavy with desire.

We moved in concert to the center of the bed, locked together like Peabody dancers. Oh, my mother was all wrong; the first flush of passion doesn't die like a vampire in a blaze of sunlight. This bed was an even more magical vehicle than a car. And the magic of anatomy—that rosy rising, tongues seeking refuge, all the oiled and meshing gears of pleasure.

Afterward, we lay like the dazed victims of a train wreck until Howard stirred.

"Don't move. Stay here for just a minute."

"Sweet love, I have to."

"*Half* a minute, then."

"My beautiful white valley," Howard murmured, his voice coming muffled.

"My little stand-up comic," I said to the creature retreating now into its dark nest of hair.

After a while, Howard lifted my arms gently to release himself, softening the shock of separation with a series of light kisses. "I'll check the baby," he said, and I smiled, poised on the edge of sleep as he left the bed. Oh, that goodness of his, that dogged loyalty. I dozed.

But what if all his relationships earned that kind of devotion? I thought of Renee, Howard's first wife, and my eyes opened. She was certainly still in our lives, calling up to ask advice or just to say hello. How could he ever have become attracted to her in the first place? It could only have been her pathos, I decided, because Renee isn't Howard's type at all. She's little, her flesh is stringy and pale. She has large, light freckles everywhere, as if she can't decide to be one color or another. But he had married her anyway, hadn't he?

And his mother still lived on the unguarded border of our neighborhood. She loved him with an unnatural love. Those were her very words. On another occasion she said that he was her whole life. What was I supposed to say to that? She was his mother, after all, and this was Queens, N.Y., in broad modern daylight, not the portentous gloom of Greek tragedy. His mother was little too. Howard could lift her with one hand, something she demanded he do from time to time to demonstrate that phenomenon of the child outgrowing the parent. Howard was clearly embarrassed, but his mother insisted. Alley-oop! And she was in midair, smiling professionally and with her arms outstretched like Sonja Henie's. Defying gravity and all the laws of decency.

God, there were so many threats. And far outside our own harmony, there was discord and violence. Every morning we read the newspaper and discovered terrible brutal acts had been committed while we slept, during our very dreams. Even in our building, people wrote obscene threats on the elevator walls. Women quarreled about whose turn it was in the bakery, and children tried to bury one another in the sandbox.

The couple next door were always fighting. The walls were so porous that their battles sifted into our living room. The paintings trembled and shifted, lampshades danced, and glassware chimed in the cupboards. It was like listening to the radio when we were children, to the Lux Radio Theater of the Air, when the visual part was always left to the imagination.

Howard and I were so glad to be alone together in the evening after the baby was asleep, but our neighbors' voices insisted on our attention, demanded we be the audience to their drama. "You bastard, you're ruining my life!" the woman next door shouted.

Howard would go to the adjoining wall and bang a warning with his fist. "There's a baby asleep in here!" he'd say, and there would be a small silent pause before they would begin again.

I couldn't understand it. Why did they stay together? They didn't even have children to bind them. And they were older than we were: was this a little preview of what was to come? I wondered if they had ever been like Howard and me. How close was passion to violence anyway? If I heard that couple cry out in climax, would I be able to tell the difference? "I'm scared," I told Howard, feeling like a small, unarmed country.

Howard turned up the volume of the stereo, canceling out our neighbors' war cries with love songs. "Don't listen," he said, and we danced in a close reassuring embrace, thinking, it's all right, it can't happen here.

Now I could hear Howard moving and singing in the nursery. I padded inside. The baby was on his dressing table and he crowed with happiness at the sight of our faces bobbing and looming into his tenuous field of vision. Mommy and Daddy, those two good giants.

The small room stank of urine and spit-up milk. Howard was unpinning a soaked diaper, while Jason kicked his locked feet high, the Brownie Bar catching fire from an arrow of sunlight.

"See, he's *happy*," I said. "Stop looking at him as if he's the man in the iron mask."

"Hey there," Howard said, wiggling Gulliver's finger until it was taken in the astonishing grasp of that tiny fist, and held.

I touched each of them with one of my own hands, so that we formed a small, imperishable circle.

5

*S*HERRY CAME TO VISIT IN THE AFTERNOON. *SHE BROUGHT* a toy for the baby that had been made by an artist friend of hers in the Village. It had sharp edges and the paint looked like the kind that would flake right off. I made some insincere remarks and then I put it on a high shelf in Jason's room.

"God, I *love* it in here," she said, taking in the Boy-Blue night-light, the Disney decals, and the newly folded stack of tiny garments.

Did she mean it? Sherry had always insisted that the only worthwhile aspects of human existence were adventure and mystery. "We know how it all ends," she said. "So we need the uncertainty of day-to-day experience to distract us." That philosophy certainly precluded marriage with its built-in pre-dictability. She was going to try everything else once, and hardly anything twice, if she could help it. Right before Jason was born, Sherry had a life-threatening abortion in Havana. Now she had obtained a couple of guaranteed local contacts, one in New York and the other in New Hope, Pennsylvania. It was hard for me to imagine her decorating a nursery corner in her apartment with its floor pillows and beaded curtains and death-wish colors. It was even harder for me to imagine maternal longings in that narrow, armored breast. Every-thing about her spoke against it: the long, protective finger-nails, for instance, all that heavy, aggressive-looking jewelry she wore, and her bang-shadowed eyes that always seemed troubled with ingrown thoughts. A child of hers might have to settle for Purina Cat Chow instead of Gerber's lamb and macaroni dinner. When the kid passed away from malnutrition or began to grow fur and whiskers, Sherry would be dragged off to jail, with her mother in the background wailing, "*I* don't know how this happened. I raised her to be a good mother."

But Sherry didn't even really like children. Right now she wasn't looking at the sleeping Jason himself, only at the *things* in his environment. I chose to believe her anyway and to encourage her admiration and envy of us. After all, wasn't this far better than *her* life in that tiny, dark studio room shared from time to time with a restive lover?

Sherry always hinted at bizarre goings-on out there, of new dimensions of pleasure forbidden to ordinary housewives, of brand-new sexual acts, involving rubber bands or ice cubes, that were being invented on the hour. Didn't I want to know? But I felt too complacent about my own capacity for invention, about Howard's, to pay much attention. And besides, Sherry tended to exaggerate. The "terrific apartments" she always found for herself or for friends were usually dismal, roach-infested firetraps. And the men she bragged about sounded much better than they turned out to be: dark-eyed poets who read with the resonance of Dylan Thomas but who couldn't publish, distinguished-looking married executives who wanted to have it both ways, and unemployed actors, for whom she washed underwear and socks. Her mother was desperate for Sherry to settle down and in her anxiety even used me as a dubious example of good behavior. She would have preferred marriage and *then* pregnancy, in that orthodox order, but at least I was more normal than her own crazy daughter. Strange men answered Sherry's telephone during the day when her mother called; men with names as blunt and short as their capacity for allegiance: Max, Jake, Al. Her mother always hung up, stunned and disheartened. But what could she expect from a girl who believed in the influence of the stars more than in the conventions of society—who chose men because they were Taurus with Scorpio rising, rather than because they were eligible and gainfully employed?

Sherry had offered to do my horoscope. Given the time and place of my birth, she would be able to tell me what was in store for me, how things were being predetermined in the dark reaches of the universe while I was innocently sleeping or eating or making love. But I didn't believe in astrology, or phrenology, or Tarot cards; only in my own ability to control my own destiny.

Poor Sherry. Once I might have envied her, the way one envies George Sand or Isadora Duncan or other doomed but independent women.

Now I was delirious with domesticity. I was like Sherry's mother, my soul sparkling with silver polish, my pride stiffened with laundry starch. Everything here spoke of stability and trust. Everything in Sherry's life was shifting, transient. She didn't even have a permanent job for fear of losing some of her precious freedom. She could have worked as a school-teacher, she was licensed, but instead she went out on calls from an employment agency that specialized in temporary office work, and she did horoscope readings on the side.

I made a tunafish salad for lunch, and I decorated it with radish roses and carrot curls from instructions in the August issue of *Family Circle*. I threw a batch of homemade cookies into the oven too, but Sherry, used to the poison of pickup meals and cafeteria browsing, hardly noticed. She was one of those people who only played with food. Now she made fork ridges in the tuna and tidy anthills of crumbs with her roll.

But I ate everything on my plate, starting with polite nibbles, then plunging in because it was delicious and because eating was so pleasurable.

Some days I woke with an absolute determination to diet, with a head full of cottage cheese and calorie counts. I'd weigh myself ten times in the morning, shifting from one foot to another to give myself the benefit of the doubt. And then, halfway through the day, I'd go under, gobbling up the little pieces of finger food that Jason moved around on his high chair tray like chess pieces. Waste not, want not. On to the refrigerator, where temptation waited with frosty patience. EAT ME, the food said, and I did, growing bigger, just like Alice. Which only proved that eating had almost nothing to do with frustration or unhappiness: I would never have defiant little hips like Sherry's anyway, even if I starved to death, and, God knows, I needed my strength. Look what I had accomplished already that day and it wasn't even two o'clock.

Sherry grew dreamy over coffee. "I don't know," she said. "Maybe you have the right idea, after all. Maybe everything else is only marking time. One love. Financial security. A beautiful child. *That's reality*."

"It's nice," I said modestly. "But it doesn't have the suspense of your life." I felt I could afford to be generous.

"That's true," Sherry admitted. Only last week a painter had moved in with her, just until he could find a decent studio at a reasonable rent. He was beautiful, she said, a della Robbia cherub, fully grown. He smelled deliciously of turpentine and linseed oil, and his brow was folded with the importance of abstract thought.

I was taken in by the romantic sound of it. And it wasn't simply promiscuity if there was only one man at a time, and if it *felt* like love while it lasted.

Sherry told me that she posed for her artist sometimes, as an added service. "But you know how *that* usually ends up," she said. "Hey, Paulie, that's something you could do, if you ever want to earn some extra money. At the Brooklyn Museum or the Art Students' League. They'd love those Mother Earth curves of yours."

"Oh, I'd never!" I said, and I felt myself blush.

Sherry laughed. "Wow, Paulie, you really *are* into it, aren't you?"

"Of course I'm into it," I said. "What do you mean? Do you think you can have this kind of relationship without absolute commitment?" Did she think I was only playing house?

"And does Howard feel the same way?" she wanted to know. What kind of question was that? If it had come from anyone else, I would have thought it born of malicious envy.

But Sherry wasn't like that. If she was outspoken sometimes, it was because she believed it was in the service of Truth.

Of course Howard felt the same way. She should have been there that morning, or any morning so far in our marriage. She should have been there at night, when I hung out the window, precariously balanced, waiting for Howard to come home. She should see him *running*, not walking, across the traffic on 108th Street, just to get back to Jason and me as fast as he could.

"I only mean it's difficult for men, I think. They tend to be you know . . . more . . . *restless*."

"You can't generalize like that!" I said. "You're only speaking from your own experience, with the kind of men you know."

"Some of them are married," she said.

How had the conversation turned this way, with me defending the life-style she had seemed to covet only a few minutes before? What did she know about marriage anyway, someone whose heart was probably as empty as her refrigerator, someone who could bring a potentially deadly weapon as a gift for a helpless little baby?

"Especially musicians," Sherry was saying.

"What?"

"Musicians have a special kind of sensuality. For heaven's sake, Paulie. *You* know what I mean. It's one of the first things you said you liked about Howard yourself. And women have been attracted to musicians since the time of King David."

"So what?"

"So, nothing. What's happening here, anyway? I'm not saying anything about Howard. But have you ever gone with him on one of his club dates, or to those weddings and bar mitzvahs he plays?"

They called themselves the Fantasy Five. There were more conventional groups around, the ones who blasted the unfortunate wedding guests seated at tables close to the bandstand with old favorites, updated by a Latin beat; the ones who provided shipboard games at bar mitzvahs, where all the guests got to move around the dance floor in an attached line or to pass a balloon among themselves without using hands. The old people still moved to their own drummers in Harvest Moon Ball routines and diagramed two-steps, no matter what the beat, no matter what the message. But more and more young couples liked the sounds of Howard's combo, those jazzed-up arrangements that cut the sentimentality of old love songs, like "Deep Purple" or "Stardust," and left in the seduction. It was the music I loved best because it was Howard's and because it was loaded with the ache of wanting.

I pictured Howard getting ready to leave, freshly shaven, in his tuxedo and blue-studded shirt. Me saying good-bye in my stay-at-home peach bathrobe.

"There are always women on the make in those places," Sherry said. "All dolled-up and cha cha cha. They're either divorced or single or married to the asshole dancing around with a flower in his teeth." She even knew a story about a bride who ran off with the bass player minutes after the ceremony.

I crossed my arms in defiance. "Sometimes you have to take risks in this life." It seemed a strange thing for me to be telling someone who usually carried a diaphragm and a toothbrush in her pocketbook, just in case.

"If I were you, I'd take out a little insurance," she said. "Why don't you just go along from time to time?"

"Do you mean as a watchdog? As a *spy*?"

She shrugged. "Well, you could always make yourself useful."

"How? By turning the music? By carrying the drums? Sherry, they don't need me."

"I don't know." She was thoughtful. "Maybe you could be the vocalist."

"Are you crazy? I can't sing. Tap dancing was my specialty, remember? And there isn't much call for that these days."

"I'd think of something if I were you," she said. "Shake the maracas or something, like what's-her-name, with Cugat."

"Howard has a *jazz* combo," I said. "And anyway this whole conversation is stupid. A very important part of the marriage bond is mutual trust and respect. I trust Howard and he trusts me."

Then Jason started screaming from the other room, letting me have the triumph of the last word.

It was Sherry's cue to leave. A screeching, soiled infant was more "reality" than she could handle at the time.

I walked her to the door where we embraced in a shaky truce, her African warrior's neck-piece nicking my throat. "Are you still writing much poetry?" she asked, getting the last word in after all. I listened to her footsteps from behind the closed door, as she walked quickly back to uncertainty and loneliness, cha cha cha.

6

> Later, ambition will wake
> and rouse the other hungers
> and light the lamps in
> all the chambers of the night.
> You'll want more; something
> never satisfied by voice or touch
> but now love's heart-knock is enough.
>
> *May 16, 1958*

AFTER SUPPER, AFTER JASON WAS PUT TO BED, TALCUM-sweet and overkissed, Howard and I staggered into the living room to talk. This was the best time of the day. We couldn't afford real analysis, so we did one another instead. I was quite classical in my approach; I went back to childhood, digging up traumas, but Howard liked to deal with the recent past. He took his first marriage out like a stamp collection, and we looked at it together. Howard talked about that time as if he were just begun then himself, as if he expected me to feel some nostalgia or regret for the poverty of their relationship. Grudgingly, I did. I saw them in their marriage bed, ill-fitting like two parts of different jigsaw puzzles. I listened to Renee talk him out of sleep, pry him from dreams with the wrench of her voice. "Is this mole getting darker? Listen, Howard, is this a *lump*?"

She was always a hypochondriac, and Howard, who had such a tragic sense of life, easily became one too. By the time I met him, he was dying from a thousand diseases. I laughed at all of them. "Are you kidding?" I said.

He was skeptical but hopeful. "How do you know? *You're* not a doctor."

But I wouldn't allow him a single internal mystery, and in time he was cured. The laying on of hands, I called it, covering him with my own healing flesh. "Oh, you don't know!" Howard cried, but I did, and he was cured of palpitations and bruises and fears of castration.

Now we lay in an embrace on the living room sofa, settling in for our evening talk. "You first this time," Howard offered, and I went spinning back. One of my earliest memories is of myself tap-dancing on the shining surface of the kitchen table while my mother clapped in rhythm from the sink. Shirley Temple had invaded her heart and her brain, and she could hardly think of anything else. This miracle of her own battered womb, dimpled and brown-eyed, and sort of dirty blond, might turn out to be another Shirley Temple. And who was Shirley Temple anyway? Just a lucky little kid, or maybe only an ambitious midget.

"What did your father think?" Howard asked.

"My father didn't want any part of it. He had his job in the Post Office; man's work, the stuff that kept our nation number one in the world. He stayed out of things at home, out of my mother's way. Fantasy and dreams of glory were *woman's* work."

I told Howard how my mother used to lie in bed, restless with aspiration, and make up stage names for me: Tiny Starr, Merry Bright, Dolly Sweet. She would get up finally and roam through the house, wringing her hands because it was the middle of the night and she was in Brooklyn where nothing would ever happen. In the morning she would be serene again, willing to wait through dancing lessons and elocution lessons for the talent scout who would scoop me up and take us all off to Hollywood.

"She bought a little wooden platform for me," I said. "And she invested in an electric curling iron. She always

singed my hair, so that the ends looked gray and smelled like
burnt chicken feathers.

The elocution lessons were given by a Miss Peel. We, the
undiscovered, called her Miss Banana or Miss Lemon within
our limited capacity for revenge. She taught us to recite "The
Midnight Ride of Paul Revere" and "Miniver Cheevy."
Then she taught us some original numbers that included Irish
dialect—"And the top o' the mornin' to you, too, Mrs.
O'Grady"—and German—"Ve must give ze boy lessons,
Mama. Little Ludvig has musical talent!" There was a
pseudo-oriental thing too, for which I had worn a kimono
and had to bow a lot, saying, "Velly, velly good."

"Stop laughing," I told Howard, pinching his arm. "It
was serious. If I made good, I'd have a walk-in dollhouse
and a canopy bed. I could quit school, which I hated, and
have a private tutor played by Mischa Auer who would make
learning fun. You should have seen me as a butterfly, ever so
lightly kissing the flowers, or as a spastic old woman being
sent by ungrateful children to the poorhouse. There wasn't a
dry eye. I would have broken your heart. But I always loved
the dancing best. I was going to dance on the steps with Bill
Robinson, just like Shirley."

"Show me," Howard said.

"Do you mean now? I can't. I don't remember. I don't
have shoes."

But he urged me with his eyes, with his hands, until I got
up from the sofa and stood in the center of the living room.
I began to turn slowly in time to the music inside my head.
I imagined a baby spotlight hitting the drapes behind me and
two pink ones fused into a heart shape and lighting my face.

Smile, baby, smile. Brush, step, brush, step, dah, dah,
remember to smile always because a smile makes them forget
their troubles. Smile, one two, their troubles dropping like
flies in the aisles.

God, I remembered almost everything and it felt so nice,
turn and spot and turn with my hair gently slapping my face.
Ah, Bill, will you take my hand and show me how, will you
dance with me with your tippy tappy toes? Didn't my mother

say he was one of a kind, the only colored man she had ever trusted? And I put my hand in that worn pink palm and came down a step at a time, every step a separate little stage and that spot bouncing after us like a playful pup at our heels. Taking my cue from Bill who smiled, smiled, a credit to his people and to 20th Century-Fox and I was a credit to everyone, a credit and a joy to Jack Oakie and C. Aubrey Smith and Jimmy Dunn and Jane Darwell and Mommy and Miss Peel, who would get a special seat onstage—

I was out of breath and a little dizzy and the neighbor downstairs was banging on her ceiling with a broomhandle.

"Jesus," Howard said. "No wonder you didn't make it."

"Was I awful?" I asked happily. But I could see that he was touched.

"No, you were beautiful in a way. But Bill Robinson would have shoved you down those stairs." Howard brushed the hair back from my flushed cheek with one hand.

"Yeah," I said dreamily, snuggling up again. "My mother cried like a baby when he died. As if the dream finally ended there. Although it already had, a long time before."

"What happened?"

"Nothing really. No talent scout ever showed up. My curls drooped and my hair got darker. Lemon rinses didn't work. And I began to grow, faster and faster. I burst out of those tutus, popped the seams of the kimono. That was it, folks. The End."

"I don't think your mother ever got over it," Howard said.

It was true. Whenever she saw an old Shirley Temple movie on television, whenever she saw that curly-headed moppet singing her way out of an orphanage and into the hearts of America, she'd have to take a couple of Bromo Seltzers before she felt calm again.

Later, Howard and I went into the bedroom where he undressed me and I undressed him. Where was Shirley Temple at that very moment?

In the morning when I went to the bathroom, there was a message taped across the mirror: *A Star Is Born.*

7

"*Tell me about it, Sweetheart,*" I said. "*You'll* feel better." I propped an extra pillow behind his head and lay down again.

Howard was doubtful. All his life, he had been the victim of seduction, and he didn't think talking about it would help at all. The minute his mother first saw him, ether-dazed and slick from the birth canal, she fell wildly in love and threw his father over in Howard's favor. Subsequently, grandmothers, aunts, neighbors and teachers were crazy about him. Sometimes when we'd visit, his mother would drag out old photo albums to document his history and remind me of my privileged position. There was Howard as a small boy, ducking his head, smiling with that heartbreaking appeal, between the skirts of his mother and sister. There was Howard in adolescence, the tall, dark center of a bouquet of girls. He was thinner then, he looked shy, and with a shining promise of the beauty yet to come. Some of the girls had signed the photo. *To Howie, with all my love forever. Don't forget to write.* Marilyn, Roz, Lucille, and Janet, who had added an open-mouthed lip print in indelible Tangee Coral. What had happened to all those girls?

He had a summer job when he was in high school, at a place called Kaplan's Kabins, a colony of small bungalows in the Catskills, with a gnat-studded casino for weekend entertainment. He and a couple of other boys, a trumpet player and a drummer who doubled on the piano, formed a pickup band. They hardly had time to tune up before they left for the mountains with their instruments, and their wallets bulging with condoms, enough to last them into the Afterlife.

The married women went after him too, the ones who couldn't seem to wait for their husbands' Friday night pilgrimages from the city. Howard was educated on squeaking bedsprings that stilled the singing crickets outside those screened rooms. Babies slept close by in mosquito-netted cribs. The women smelled of suntan lotion and the moist fragrance of lust. He was such a romantic boy, he tried hard to be in love, but there was always too much variety and never enough time.

"Now tell me everything," I said, wondering if I actually wanted to know. It was the main purpose of our night talks. We would be each other's personal historian. Confession would work as a catharsis, leaving us clean again for one another. At first Howard was reluctant, sticking close to the recent past, to Renee, who hardly counted in a narrative of passion.

But then we went gently back in time, back through early fantasy, through tender crushes, to first infantile fingering and revelation. We probed at early memory in search of connections. "Oh, you felt that way. But so did I!"

We had grown up at different times in similar neighborhoods. I loved to think that Howard was a schoolboy when I was still an infant, that he might have wheeled me in my stroller or held my hand crossing a street.

I had been lonely in school. Howard had broken his arm on three occasions. We had both stolen money when we were young. I had stood on a boy's dime for an hour, pivoting slowly in place, pretending sympathy, pretending to help him look, until the streetlights came on and mothers called us home to supper, when I pocketed the dime and ran. My confession encouraged Howard's own. He had once taken money from his mother's purse and, sin upon sin, had spent it on a book purchased from an older boy in school. It was "The Adventures of Mutt and Jeff," as never seen in the Sunday supplements; a well-worn edition, dog-eared and stained by the sweat of other hands and God knows what else.

He only had it about a week when his older sister Beverly found it on the floor of his closet, under old toys and real comic books. He tried to remember what she was doing in there in the first place. Had he wanted her to find the book? We didn't go into that. We were cautious, shying away from being too analytical—it slowed the progress of our stories, and besides, Howard didn't believe in it.

"Disgusting," Beverly had said. "*This* is disgusting and *you're* disgusting." And Howard, who could find no other rationale for the wild ecstasy of his feelings, had been convinced. Beverly had threatened to tell those proper authorities, their mother and father, and Howard knew he would soon be the object of everyone's disgust. Even his mother, who defended him in all family arguments, who allowed only him the luxury of bad moods, would be made to see the revolting truth. He pleaded with his sister not to tell, and finally she agreed, keeping the offending book in her adjoining room in a nervous settlement.

And Howard, who can't remember how he knew what was expected of him, scratched an infinitesimal peephole in the painted French door between their rooms.

His sister is married now and has three children. They live in Los Angeles, and she sends photos of herself and her family posed around their backyard swimming pool. Her bathing suit is a one-piece affair with a skirt. I can see she is an ordinary suburban matron, smiling and squinting into the sunlight.

But secretly I always think of her as The Stripper, that long-haired, sly-eyed girl removing the clinical-looking underwear girls wore in those days, in a slow, calculated rhythm, guaranteed to disturb her brother's pulses. Her bedside lamp had a green towel draped over the shade, giving everything an eerie and theatrical glow.

He never touched her, except for the wild scenes that passed through his head like landscape seen through a train window. In reality the glass door stayed between them, a board between bundlers. But, oh, she knew he was watching, and he knew that she knew, increasing the excitement on both sides, pushing the experience far beyond the two-dimensional cut-ups of Mutt and Jeff.

"She told anyway," Howard said.

"Wow," I said. "What did you do?"

"Denied everything, of course. I said she was crazy. Her brain must have gone soft from those curlers she wore. I said she had scratched that hole herself—how did *I* know why it was on my side? When she wasn't home I shredded Mutt and Jeff until I could flush the pieces. I pretended a passionate interest in Hebrew school. If they started up with me, I pretended to be praying. I planned her execution."

The family moved to another apartment, this one with real wooden doors. Howard's father inspected them monthly for boreholes.

Things were not good after that between Howard's mother and his sister. They quarreled over surrogate issues, about messy rooms, about doing the dishes, about hair in the sink drain. Beverly called him names; she grew long fingernails like the Dragon Lady's and she raked him in passing. If he was in the bathroom for more than a few minutes, she hammered on the door. His mother and sister screamed. His father banged on the table for peace.

Then Beverly fell in love with an outsider, breaking the incestuous chain. Howard's mother became calm again, planned an engagement party and a trousseau, and Howard was restored to his favored position. Even Beverly grew tolerant of him. She no longer called him "the animal." Instead she referred to him as her "little" kid brother, with teasing affection, when other people were around. Finally she married and moved out.

"But I'm *glad* you got started early," I said. "You've had all this time to get so accomplished." Privately, I wished it had been me starting him off. I wished I could have erased all of those girls and women from his memory and from his life. "Does it all still bother you?" I asked Howard, ready to offer consolation.

"No, no, of course not," he said. "I was only a kid."

But I think he was left with the burden of guilt anyway. Despite what Howard says, you can't go too far back for things like that. Why else would he have married Renee, whose body promised nothing but terrifying cell changes? Of course she was down and out at the time; between jobs, between dress sizes. And Howard, raised on Superman and the Green Hornet, believed in heroism and the miracle of transformation. Renee took off her eyeglasses and unpinned her hair. *Ta-da!* But blinded, she only careened into furniture, and her shoulders blossomed with dandruff. Someone else would only have befriended her, lent her money perhaps, and a sympathetic ear. But Howard, gallant and optimistic, had gone all the way. They lasted only seven months. Later, he helped her move into another apartment, carrying cartons up three flights, hanging pictures, setting mousetraps under the sink.

I felt sad after we talked, the price of counter-transference, I supposed, but I could see that Howard felt better. He went inside and brought back his saxophone. He rolled up his shirtsleeves and he played thrilling and melancholy numbers from an earlier time. He played "Laura" and "Dream" and "Body and Soul," holding some notes in a long, breathless embrace. His cheeks billowed and dimpled and I could hear the gentle sibilance of his spit on the reed.

8

*M*ANNY CAME OVER ONE EVENING AFTER SUPPER TO
sell Howard some life insurance. He was a musician too, a
drummer with a group Howard had known for years, but on
certain nights Manny turned into an insurance salesman.

Howard had grown up with an awareness of mortality,
with conversations about it at breakfast. After all, his father
was a funeral director. The whole family knew that those
platitudes of consolation he recited were only a commercial
front for the worst possible knowledge. Those were dead
people being prepared and then buried, and it was for ever
and ever.

Still, it hadn't struck Howard until he was ten or so, am-
bling along in his schoolboy innocence, tossing a ball in the
air, thinking of baseball cards, of the candy in his pocket, of
nothing. Boom! He had been assaulted with the truth! That
was *him* in those polished boxes, draped with flags and flowers. That was *him* shut in the darkness of the earth. No matter
how deep you dug there would be no smiling Chinaman waiting with colored lanterns and bowls of rice. There would not
be a living soul. Howard was stunned by the revelation. He
staggered like a drunkard around the street. He didn't want
to believe it, but it was certainly true. Everyone dies, even
handsome boys who are loved. His own father's gloominess
was simply a hot tip from a man with inside information.

It was a delayed reaction. His father had taken him to the
funeral home the week before, despite his mother's protests
that he wasn't old enough yet to know what was what. But

43

his father had an eye on the future. Howard was an only son and it couldn't be denied, undertaking was steady work. An uncle had a repertoire of nervous jokes. See the cemetery, kid? Everyone's dying to get in.

What did Howard want to be when he grew up? He wanted to be Tom Mix or Joe DiMaggio. He wanted to live in an apartment house where dogs were permitted. He wanted the leisure to reread every comic book he had ever owned.

There was a funeral service in progress when Howard and his father got there. "Lift your feet," his father said. "Fix your tie."

Outside a train of long, black cars waited, their motors humming in hymn-like harmony. Inside it was dark and dreary, like assembly on a rainy day at school, like the movie theater just before the lights go on again after the main attraction.

The main attraction here was the coffin. Of course Howard had seen coffins before, had even been to the display room where the bereaved made their final selection. But then there were no bodies, no ghosts, and seeing a variety of coffins like that made it difficult to associate them with the tragedy of a single death. Howard wasn't interested in death anyway. No one had died in his family during his time, except for distant relatives, who were now only more distant. Tennessee, Chicago, or hell, it didn't make much difference to a dreaming boy. Seeing a stage set without the actors, without the play itself, has no real impact. You can tell it's only theater, only make-believe.

But now there was everything! The leading actors, those mourners, swaying and murmuring in the front rows; the chorus of interested parties in the other rows, men in dark suits, everyone in hats, women wearing gloves. And the coffin! A single chosen box in which, his father told him, the shrouded body of an old woman reposed. Would his father fool him? It was possible. Over the years he had threatened bogeymen for bad behavior, explained thunder as God's rolling of pickle barrels, and Howard's penis as something to be left strictly alone.

What Howard would have given for a quick peek inside! He imagined the coffin opened, and the woman popping up like a jack-in-the-box. Boy, those people would all be surprised. How did they know she was dead anyway? Could you die if you didn't want to, if you breathed in-out, in-out without a stop?

Children died too. He knew that because his parents sometimes whispered together when his father came home, his mother rolling her eyes and wringing her hands and then knocking on wood for good luck. Howard would go to the window and look upward for the Angel of Death. But he was nowhere to be seen. He was still in that other neighborhood, where some other poor boy had drowned or succumbed to a childhood disease.

But most of the corpses were old. It was impossible to imagine their great age, what it was like to live inside the shirred skin, to take little slow steps like a windup toy running out. They were *them* and Howard was *himself*, sleek as summer fruit, bouncy as a new Spalding. If he breathed on a mirror, there was evidence. If he peed into snow it would melt.

The rabbi spoke about the deceased. He said she was a wife and a mother and a grandmother, bringing a ruffle of response from the first row. He said she had been a simple woman, had come to this country as a young immigrant girl without a family, without a dime. More murmurs, a few sobs. She had married young and raised a family. She had worked side by side with her dear husband, may he rest in peace, in his bakery where rolls were sold two for a penny, imagine! She had nothing to regret, not those children: doctor, accountant, high school teacher, whose heads bobbed now in acknowledgement of their names like flowers in a breeze. Not those devoted grandchildren who squirmed in their seats, looking to the back of the room and past Howard, to the doors marked EXIT.

His father wore his solemn face and a neat three-pointed handkerchief in his breast pocket. The mourners rose and sat, listened and wept until it was all over. Then a side door was opened, letting in a dizzying blaze of sunlight, the real life of traffic and birds.

A week later Howard knew everything in a terrifying on-slaught of knowledge. There *was* an old woman in that box, but there was a young girl in there too, and maybe even a baby, cradled in Russia, waiting to grow up and come to America and sell rolls two for a penny. Oh!

Well, at least you could buy insurance. At least you could provide for the loved ones left behind. At first the two men had talked shop. It was so nice, sitting in the lamplight with Howard and his friend, hearing words like "riff" and "ride," "set" and "arrangement." I almost forgot why Manny had come. But then he cleared his throat and took his briefcase from behind the chair.

Now we were into a new language. Manny put on a pair of horn-rimmed eyeglasses that looked like a disguise from a kid's spy set. "Actuary charts," he said. "Premium rates." "Term." "Straight life." He opened brochures across the table and he and Howard bent over them, navigators charting a perilous course.

"I'm taking twenty in straight life," Howard announced, after I brought some coffee in.

"How about a policy on me?" I said, but Howard wouldn't think of it. *His* death was the issue here. Term dwindles, he explained, if you live long enough. Lots of the policies had titles that were only euphemisms for term insurance. "I have responsibilities now," Howard said. "The ten thousand from the V.A. is only peanuts." He wanted Jason to go to college, to medical school too, if that was what he wanted. I imagined Jason in a cap and gown, a Brownie Bar still nailing his feet together.

"That's that," Howard said, after Manny left. "Just a physical exam and everything will be arranged. You're taken care of."

"Stop talking about it," I said.

"Don't act like a kid. You have to face facts." He paced, a cigarette suspended from his lip, his eyes squinted against the smoke. He went to the refrigerator, looked inside and then shut it again.

"All right," I said, "but stop talking about it."

We went to bed, but neither of us could fall asleep. We turned from side to side in a restless ballet. "Stop *thinking* about it," I hissed.

In the middle of the night, I found Howard sprawled near the foot of the bed, naked, uncovered. His body hair was damp and curling. His feet and genitals looked as pale as a saint's. I drew the covers around him and put my mouth against his ear. "I won't let you," I whispered.

9

SHERRY WAS RIGHT ABOUT ONE THING AT LEAST. THE writing wasn't going well at all. There had been only a few poems since Howard and I were married, and it wasn't as if I hadn't tried. Sometimes there were just beginnings: one or two aborted lines. After lovemaking, I would feel myself *ready* for a poem, as if I had been transfused with inspiration. But then nothing followed except for a dreaming stupor that finally became sleep. I supposed I was too tired, that I had to adjust to the hectic pace of married life and motherhood.

I kept books of poetry on my night table for encouragement and comfort. I could open Oscar Williams' *Little Treasury of Modern Poetry* to almost any page and be soothed by Auden or Frost, Hopkins or Elizabeth Bishop. I thought of that dry spell as a refueling period, a time to gather new experience for distillation. It doesn't matter, I consoled myself. Soon the poems would come unbidden, if I only had patience. But it's well known that you should write something every day to keep your hand in. It's known that there are poems everywhere, that they perish in the streets for want of a poet. I looked in the growing clutter of Jason's toys. I watched water escape from my cupped hand held over the washbasin. I sifted carefully through the dust mice under the beds, but there were no poems anywhere.

It was impossible to write in the morning. I sat on the edge of my bed, bladder bloated and teeth furred, waiting for my turn in the bathroom. Then I went into the kitchen to prepare breakfast, to squeeze orange juice and to shake weightless crystals into bowls. When I cracked the crown of Howard's egg, I discovered it wasn't cooked enough, that the white was a translucent amoeba and had to be disguised with bread. Howard, in love, didn't notice, or didn't say.

When he was gone to his studio for the day, I took out my writer's box. It was once the container for Jason's baby blanket and there was still some blue fuzz lining the sides. I carried the box back to bed and examined those beginning lines as if I had expected them to continue themselves when I wasn't looking. Then I changed the clerical order of the old rejection slips from chronological to alphabetical. Now *The Antioch Review* was on top, and for some reason this made me feel better.

I dressed Jason and myself warmly because it was early winter and we went down in the elevator. I had an appointment with my dentist Dr. Sussman, and I had to do my weekly marketing. A woman in the building who did baby-sitting would meet us in the playground. As soon as I stepped outside, it began to snow. I put Jason in the sandbox next to other small children and I sat on one of the benches nearby. It was time for him to begin a social life of his own. I watched the children sitting in the sandbox with snow falling on their heads. "I shouldn't really be here," I confided to the woman sitting next to me. "I should be upstairs writing my head off."

"Yes," she said. "I should be upstairs cutting out a dress pattern. It's all over the kitchen table. It's all pinned and everything."

I smiled fiercely at her. "A writer isn't worth a damn without self-discipline. I bet Norman Mailer is somewhere right now banging away. On his typewriter."

She was a little brown winter bird of a woman. She wore navy-blue shoes. For a while she didn't say anything at all, and then she put her arm through mine, establishing a bond between us. She leaned her little bird face closer and she said, "Could you use a good story?" Before I could explain that I wasn't that kind of writer, she trapped my arm with the pressure of hers and began: "I was raised in a foster home," she said. "My Mom and Dad were very fine people. They treated me as if I was their natural child. Mom always said, 'God gave you to us and you are our very own.' And that's how I was treated. And yet I began to wonder about my natural mother, who she was, who *I* was. I don't like to say my 'real' mother because the person who raises you should have that honor. Well, this business of my natural mother began to drive my crazy. Mom and Dad didn't like for me to ask them, but many times I thought when I grow up I will look for her and find out the whole story of why she gave me up."

Oh God, I thought. My baby-sitter had come and taken Jason, waving to me as she left the playground. The snow was heavier now and the other mothers took their children from the sandbox.

But the woman in the brown coat continued. She told me that she was married at nineteen to a good man and that they had three children together. "To make a long story short," she said, patting my impatient arm, "one night my husband and I went to see a show. At the intermission we were standing around getting a breath of air when I turned around and saw this woman. Something about her made my hair stand up and my spine tingle. Do you know that feeling? I grabbed my husband's arms and I said, 'Joe, look at that woman over there in the blue dress.' When I pointed her out he said, 'Yeah, what about her?' and I said, 'Joe, take a *good* look.' It was scary because she had my exact nose and this thing here over my lip and Joe said, 'Jesus.' I said, 'Joe, what should I do?' Just then the woman looked over our way, but she didn't notice us or anything, you know? The lights started to go off and on to tell you to go back to your seats, and I got real nervous. I said, 'Joe, what should I do?' The crowd began to move back into the theater and we both just stood there and the woman got lost in the crowd."

All the children and mothers were gone from the playground and the woman and I sat on the bench, our laps filling with snow.

"Did you find her?" I asked wearily. "Was it your real mother?"

"My *natural* mother," she corrected. "That's the thing. I couldn't find her again. We looked all over the theater and then Joe said it was crazy because I was born in the midwest and things like that don't happen in real life."

I sighed and she looked at me anxiously. "Listen," she said, "if you don't like the ending, you can change it. I know that all the world likes a happy ending."

"It's not that," I said.

"I felt, that as a writer, you would appreciate it."

"It's not that," I said again.

Her mouth formed a narrow bitter line. "Nobody is interested in what happens to the little people in this world."

I didn't say anything.

We sat there in silence for a moment and then she said, "Perhaps you would prefer an anecdote. Everybody loves a good laugh. The most marvelous zany things keep happening to me. Lucille Ball makes a mint out of stuff like this. Listen, I once baked my wedding ring into a meat loaf. Wait, that's not all. My sister-in-law swallowed it!" She began to laugh. "It was a riot when it happened. Right out of the Lucy show. Ha ha. I once set fire to my apron carrying in a birthday cake." She laughed louder. "I have a wonderful funny life!" she shouted.

I stood up in my wet shoes and I walked out of the playground to the bus stop.

Dr. Sussman's office is in a new medical building. He looks out of place in these surroundings of chrome and glass, because he is a melancholy man and his mustache is wild and drooping. "You're soaking wet," he said sadly, and then, "Open wide." He found a big cavity on the upper right. "Almost nothing left here. We'll try to save it," he said. After an injection of novocaine, I watched him assemble his tools on the little round tray.

The white paper bib on my chest reduced me to an old

helplessness. I waited for the novocaine to take effect. "I'm suffering from writer's block," I said.

"Whazzat?" He opened my mouth and peered inside.

"No no. *Writer's block.* I'm a writer."

He was very interested. He listened to the story of my block and all the rejection slips. He clucked his tongue on the roof of his mouth. Then the weight of numbness began to set in and he started to work on the cavity. Tools passed in silver lines. "Can you feel this? No?" Water ran inside my head. While he drilled, Dr. Sussman confessed that he was a poet too. He had been writing poetry for twenty years, but he never sent it anywhere. We stared into one another's eyes and then he shut his. "Pigeons," he began in a husky voice.

He began to recite from memory his poem about pigeons. It was a very long poem and it had words like lancinate and panoplied and isotropy. The recitation seemed to leave him more melancholy than ever. A bead of moisture hung in his mustache. "What do you think?" he asked.

I tried to speak and gagged on some cotton wadding. He removed it and I said, "Oh, the language. Yes."

He smiled. "Lay off the sweets," he said. He squeezed my shoulder.

When I left his office, pigeons still passed before me in a dreary gray file. My mouth was lifted in a snarl. Outside the snow had stopped. I rode the bus to the supermarket near our complex. There were no poems in the street. There was nothing anywhere. Steam piped up under my feet. I thought: lamb chops, yams, shelving paper.

The checkout girl in the supermarket was one of those pale, pretty teenagers. I pulled the groceries from my cart and put them on the moving counter. They began to roll past me. Lamb chops. Jell-O.

"I spend half my life in the supermarket," I told the girl.

She smiled, ringing it up.

"I just try to get out of writing, I guess."

Her hand paused on the shelving paper. "You a writer?" she asked.

"Yes." My mouth stiffened in defense and my jaw ached where the needle had entered. Beneath a fringe of hair her eyes were thoughtful. Was this still another poet? Were *her* perceptions and dreams scribbled on reams of register tape? But then her eyes cleared and her foot tapped the pedal that set the counter rolling again.

"That's nice," she said at last. She put my groceries in two paper bags and they seemed an incredible weight in my arms. It was difficult to breathe. "Well, good-bye," I gasped.

"So long. Keep plugging, you hear?" She waved me through the electric eye door.

The elevator took me back to the nineteenth floor of Building A. After I put my groceries away, I made black raspberry Jell-O and at the last minute I sliced two bananas into the mixture. They drifted like stones to the bottom of the bowl.

In a little while the baby-sitter brought Jason home. I put him into his playpen and put the television set on to keep him company. He had liked to watch it right from the beginning, giving equal attention to Captain Kangaroo and the 6 o'clock news.

I sat down at the kitchen table and looked through the window at the gray winter sky. I stared at the sky, expecting it to break up into images, erupt into ideas, but there was no change at all.

The telephone rang. It was my mother and father. They always call together because my father is retired from the Post Office and because they have an extra telephone extension in their apartment. "Hello," they chorused. My mother uses the kitchen phone and my father lies on their bed. He takes off his shoes and his feet in their black nylon socks form a vee that he looks through while he talks. "How are tricks?" he asked, and I rustled up what sounded like a chuckle.

"So-so," I told him. "I'm having a little trouble with my poetry."

"Did that queen-size sheet fit the bed?" my mother asked.

"What sheet?" my father demanded. Since his retirement, he tries to keep up with all the domestic issues. "Did you send the children a sheet?"

"Don't you remember?" my mother said impatiently.

I said, "I can't seem to just sit down and *write* anymore."

"What are you having for dinner?" my mother asked.

"We're having veal cutlets," my father said. "Your mother is going to bake them. I just scrubbed the potatoes."

"Your father likes to eat the skin."

After we said good-bye and hung up, I set the table. I noticed that the patch of sky had grown darker. There still wasn't a poem in sight. Ezra Pound said to "make it new." Oh, easy for him, I thought. *He* never lived in Queens.

Soon I heard the whine of the elevator and Howard was home. "And how is Emily Dickinson doing today?" he asked. I knew it was only meant as a playful and goodhearted greeting.

But then I said, "It's all well and good for you to ask how I am. It's just terrific. Why don't you fix that faucet in the bathroom instead? Drip, drip, drip! It's driving me crazy. And for six months I have *begged* you to clean that crap out of the hall closet. You never do anything I ask you! You never do anything! We'll rot in this stupid apartment!"

Jason began to wail. "My God!" Howard said. "What's wrong?" He kissed me on the neck and wrists and on my breasts through the apron, to soothe me. I sat on his lap and told him about the day, about the lost poems.

Then he carried the baby to his high chair and we sat down at the table and ate the lamb chops and yams. When I brought out the Jell-O shimmering in its bowl, Howard exclaimed over the bananas as if they were glittering coins discovered at the bottom of the sea.

After supper he said he would go to the hardware store and get a washer to fix the leaking faucet. But I wouldn't let him. I would get after the superintendent to fix it tomorrow. Instead we put Jason to bed and we washed the dishes. Then we lay down together for our nightly ritual. He talked this time, and I listened in silent penance, to another episode in his marriage to poor, confused Renee. Then we made love, starting right there, but finishing under the rough white sky of the bedroom ceiling, and Annie was conceived.

10

*M*Y FATHER-IN-LAW HAD CHEST PAINS, AND HE AND Howard's mother decided to move to Florida. "He'll bake it out down there," she said. "He'll be all right. We're going to start fresh with new furniture and new dishes." She promised to give us all the stuff they couldn't sell.

"They die like flies down there," my mother said. "The ambulances come in the night to the back doors, without sirens. They cart you away, dead or alive."

One down and one to go, I thought, remembering Renee. I was so happy to see them leave that I didn't even mind the discards: the china that was missing cups, the silverware without tablespoons. "Who eats soup anymore?" Howard's mother said, pressing them on us.

Howard went back and forth with the car, stocking up. Our apartment was becoming a museum to their lives. Things didn't match: odd curtains, one-of-a-kind table napkins. "Why did you take this?" I asked. But I was being too demanding. Who said I had to live in a world of symmetry? They were going, *that* was what mattered.

"Take the lusterware vase on the hall table," my mother advised.

"I've always hated it."

"But lusterware's on the way back."

* * *

"We'll be scattered like refugees," Howard's mother said, on the eve of departure. "My son all the way up here, my daughter on the other coast. If it wasn't for *him*, I'd never go. I've had to buy six pairs of white shoes."

"This is the jet age," Howard said. "We could be together in minutes."

"God forbid," his mother said.

"A hundred and twenty in the shade," my mother whispered. "They turn to shoe leather. Skin cancer is treated in drugstores."

Howard's father had chest pains. "It's that pie," Howard's mother said. "That pie didn't look fresh to me. I told you not to eat that pie."

"Don't give me the canister set," I said. "Don't give me the shepherd and shepherdess lamps. Send them to Beverly in California. They may have sentimental value."

Howard's mother looked at the baby critically as if *he* was the one going to Florida. "His eye looks worse," she said.

Howard's father was short of breath at the airport. "He'll feel better down there," Howard's mother said. "He'll get himself in shape. Like you, Howie. *He's* like an ox, this kid." Then she said, "Give me a boost, hon. Once more for old time's sake. One hand only. I am still my bridal weight."

"They can have Florida," my mother said. "They can keep it. They can give it back to the Indians."

My father looked at girlie magazines. When he saw me, he moved to the paperbacks. "I'm keeping out of the way," he said.

"Do you have your tickets?" Howard asked. "Do you have your Dramamine?"

The grandparents passed the baby around like a volleyball.

* * *

We went to the Ladies' Room. There was no paper in my mother's booth. "Yoo hoo," she said, and her wriggling hand appeared near my feet.

"Takeoff is going to be delayed," Howard said, reading the arrivals and departures board.

.A flight from Arizona came in. Men marched down the ramp wearing cowboy hats and string ties, their tans fading fast.

We all walked together to Gate 6. The plane was taxiing into position. My father eyed the gilded wings on the lapel of a reservations clerk. "You fellows must have nerves of steel, taking those babies up," my father said.

Howard's mother gripped Howard in a half nelson. "It's so final!" she cried.

"The Indians wouldn't take it either," my mother said.

"Do you have everything? Do you have your boarding passes?"

"Nobody applies for senior citizenship," my father said.

Good-bye, Good-bye, for heaven's sake. I waved the baby's little hand as they were sucked into the funnel.

"Who's got the lusterware vase?" my mother asked.

11

IN ONE OF OUR NIGHT TALKS, HOWARD TOLD ME THAT HE had first met Renee at the shoemaker's. She was sitting in one of those little booths, waiting to have a loosened heel glued back onto her shoe. She had been thinking about suicide that day, she told him later. He had come from an all-night jam session, feeling elated but rocky with fatigue.

Howard sat down in the booth next to hers. He was going to have his shoes resoled, thinking he'd have a short snooze while he waited. She looked so pathetic sitting there, her hands in her lap, her bare feet resting one on top of the other on the little plush stool. At first he thought she was a child, a war waif perhaps who might break her clouded face with a smile any moment and say, "Chocolate, soldier?"

He shut his eyes, but he thought he could feel her staring at him. He was right. As soon as he looked back, her own eyes glanced away, and she blushed and let her fingers flutter around her face. Her feet looked blue. "Are your feet cold?" Howard asked.

"No," she said. "Maybe. I don't know. They're always that color."

Howard wanted to rub them, to buy her chocolate and new shoes. But he couldn't stay awake. He smiled an apology, folded his arms and dozed. When he woke, his shoes were ready and the girl in the other booth was gone. He remembered her blue feet, how thin she was.

A few days later he met her at the supermarket. Her basket was almost empty. She was buying brewer's yeast and Postum and a can of sardines. The few items in her cart rattled pathetically. As Howard walked behind her, he assessed her. She looked half-starved. Her eyeglasses, which were taped together at the hinge, slipped down her nose. He wondered idly how she'd look if she gained a few pounds, if she'd let her hair down. Her clothes seemed to belong to someone else.

He took her out for lunch and she told him about her suicide plans. She bit into her sandwich, sipped her malted noisily, and said she was thinking of ending it all.

"But why?" Howard asked.

Well, she was probably dying of cancer anyway.

He was horrified. No wonder she was so thin, no wonder her feet had been so blue! "Have you seen a doctor?" Howard asked.

Oh, *doctors*! She waved them away with one hand while she licked mayonnaise from the fingers of the other. What did they know? When Renee's mother had first been pregnant with her, a doctor had diagnosed a thyroid condition. Doctors killed more people than they saved—didn't he know that—and the A.M.A. covered it up. But yes, she had been to a doctor and he said there was nothing wrong with her, except maybe her diet. But how could she eat better if she was dying of cancer? And besides, she was running out of money. She had come to New York from Baltimore to go to secretarial school. She had learned to take dictation in those little squiggly symbols. She had learned to type sixty words per minute. As promised, the school had arranged jobs for all the graduates. But something always went wrong. She typed fast, but she made a lot of mistakes. Dear Sri, she typed. Yours Turly. People were crazy in New York, they were so fussy. Everyone was in such a hurry. She was almost hit by a car every time she crossed the street. She coughed into her paper napkin. Howard looked at it, surreptitiously, thinking he might see blood.

"How were you going to do it?" he asked.

She shrugged. She had trouble swallowing pills—a tricky gag reflex. She supposed she could always chew up a few bottles of those orange- or cherry-flavored ones for kids. Or take gas, maybe. If it wasn't disconnected for nonpayment. She could jump off the roof, but with her luck she'd probably be mugged on the way up.

"How come she was having her shoe fixed if she was planning on killing herself?" I asked.

Howard didn't know. He'd offered to buy her another sandwich. He took her back to his place and she wore his bathrobe for three days, her arms lost halfway up the sleeves, its hem trailing behind her like a bridal train.

"You're so good to me," she said. "You've saved my life. I would have had to do something drastic or maybe even go back to Baltimore. But I'm not going to get in your way."

So he married her.

12

*T*HERE WAS NO QUESTION ABOUT IT. HOWARD WAS THE beauty in our family. I didn't mind. What's wrong, I told myself, with a little role reversal? What's so bad about a male sex object, for a change? That ability to sprout hair like dark fountains, the flat, tapering planes of their buttocks and hips, and oh, those *hands*, and erections pointing the way to bed like road markers.

Besides, I had my own good points, not the least of them my disposition. Sunny and radiant, I woke with the same dumb abundance of hope every day. The bed always seemed too small to contain both me and the expansion of joy.

Sometimes Howard was depressed. It had nothing to do with me, with us, he said. It was just the way he was. But I did the best I could to cheer him up anyway, to tease and love him out of it. On some sad Sundays we drove out to Westchester or Long Island to look at model homes. It wasn't that *we* wanted to live in the suburbs, in that awful sterile sameness. How we laughed and poked one another at the roped-off bedrooms hung in velvet, at the plastic chickens roosting in warm refrigerators. But for some reason we believed that the long drive out of the city, the ordered march through un-lived-in rooms, restored him. Finally it became standard treatment for Howard's depression. Places like that only confirmed our confidence in our own choices.

Lenny and Judy Miller had moved to the suburbs, to a hi-ranch house in Port Washington, and one Saturday afternoon we were invited to a barbecue. Our second baby, unmarked by anybody's sins, was in Jason's old car bed on the back seat. And Jason, a tragic deposed king, stood alongside her, peering out the window. His feet had been corrected and his eye hardly turned in anymore, except when he was tired. But now he was newly cursed with this gorgeous intruder who was his sister and his roommate through no design of his own. I thought I knew how Jason felt; Annie had turned us into a *ménage à trois*, Howard and I having been a single love object for so long. Jason was being forced to grow up quickly or else, to make room for someone even rosier and sweeter than himself. He watched as I bathed Annie, his gaze focused where her missing parts should have been. Was he next?

"Do you love the new baby?" people asked, and poor Jason smiled and hid his murderous rage and fear. Howard tried to give him extra attention. They went around like primates; Jason curled on Howard's neck, his legs wound around his father's chest, his glance sly with pleasure.

We were a family of four now, encapsulated against the world, riding in our blue car on the Long Island Expressway.

Judy and Lenny had had a second daughter, a toddler now, and she and Roberta were waiting on the front lawn for us. As our car pulled into their driveway, they ran screaming our arrival to their parents.

Then they were all standing together in front of their house, like the people in one of those ads for mortgage insurance. (If something happened to you, could they still live like this?) There was even a large, shaggy dog, dancing and barking his frantic joy at their feet.

We were given the guided tour. Each of the little girls had her own bedroom. And there was a den besides, with a large television set overseeing the room from one corner. Judy had a row of shining new appliances and she opened them quickly, one after another, for our inspection. All I saw was a dazzle of light and chrome and color.

We couldn't walk in their backyard yet. The lawn had just been seeded, and the dark earth freshly turned. The barbecue was set up on the other side of the house, and just a few yards away the family next door was setting up theirs, the other husband aproned like Lenny. The two men waved to one another, and the thin stream of smoke rising from each barbecue seemed like another friendly salute between neighboring tribes.

I had to admit to myself that it was nice out there, in a pastoral sense. You can't hate nature, after all; not those sweet flower faces and the benevolent shade of the few old trees the builder had left.

Lenny was turning the hamburgers and steak and explaining the benefits of owning a house, in much the same way he had urged natural childbirth on us only a few years ago. We were always one step behind them in our social development, and I knew they relished this role of leadership.

"Equity," Lenny said. "That's the key word. It's like money in the bank. Real estate can only rise in value."

"But it's the bank that actually *owns* the house, isn't it?" I asked.

"Only the mortgage," Lenny explained. "It gets reduced over the years, while the house increases in resale value. No fat landlord is going to get rich on me anymore."

I looked at Howard, and saw that he had that glazed look he gets sometimes in the presence of salesmen. Judy ran in and out with platters of food, declining help from everyone. The children eyed one another.

"Show Jason your toys," Judy instructed Roberta, who ran immediately to the other side of the house. *"Mine,"* their baby announced, grabbing a ravaged doll from the ground, and clutching it to her chest.

Jason blinked, moving closer to Howard.

Judy whispered, gesturing toward her neighbors. "He's an orthodontist. She's a reading specialist. *Very* nice family."

The orthodontist turned his hamburgers; his wife shooed flies from the salad.

"It's so peaceful here," Lenny said. "And the crime rate is zero. Could you imagine unlocked doors? No elevators to break down? No pollution? No muggings?"

I looked at Howard again, wanting to exchange a glance of trust with him against the seduction of Lenny's pitch. But he was gently trying to release Jason's prehensile hold on his leg. "Play with Roberta," he said, but Roberta was nowhere in sight.

It was peaceful all right; only the birds and a distant song of trucks from the parkway. No sirens, no slamming doors, no screams. The hamburgers were delicious, smoky and juicy, and we sat in dappled sunlight to eat them. Jason had taken off his shoes and was running barefoot now with other children who had gathered on the new grass in front of the house. The baby, who usually had to be rocked into oblivion, slept in that pure air as if she had been drugged.

"See?" Judy said.

Yet I felt an invasion of sadness. It was as if I had suddenly gone deaf or senseless, as if I had been cruelly cut off from the mainstream of life. I didn't want any drastic changes yet, no further threat to the unit that was us, in our city tower among towers. I didn't want to grow old, either, or to die, and there was a lurking specter of death in all this silence and safety and sunshine. It was the same reassuring lie of manicured cemeteries without markers.

Howard would know about that intuitively, I thought. But he and Lenny were heading for the basement where Howard would be instructed in the mechanical workings of the house. Pipes and valves and current boxes, those lures that could be traced back to his first erector set, and extravagant maternal praise.

When they came upstairs again, the men were leaning toward one another and whispering in what looked like collusion to me. But then the children's playful shrieks reached a new imperative level, and a couple of minutes later Jason came sobbing into his father's arms.

"What is it?" Howard asked, frisking him for possible injuries, and we were finally led by a shuddering and barefoot Jason to the front of the house. On the lawn, Roberta and the other children were dancing in a mad circle like witches. Jason's shoes were scattered, one near a lamppost, the other in the driveway, and the children were chanting in high voices: ''Get-off-my-property, get-off-my-property!''

Of course they were chastised for being unfriendly, for not sharing graciously what they were so fortunate to have. Jason's shoes were retrieved, put back on and double-knotted for security. All of them were sent inside to watch television with a reward of ice cream for the effected truce.

But it was exactly the right incident, come just in the nick of time. Over their heads, Howard and I finally looked at one another in acknowledgment. He smiled and winked broadly and we were saved.

13

The operator brings us together.
Do you take this woman
this call?
Other voices rest on our line.
Out of town birds say
Hello? Hello? before
flying off.
Prairies, mountains, cities
make me deaf
make me shout
until your voice, warmed
to life in a nest of
wires, tells my name.
                              November 30, 1960

DOWN IN FLORIDA, HOWARD'S FATHER DIED IN HIS SLEEP,
moving Howard up one generation and canceling forever his
coming attractions of life. His father had been such a gloomy
man, given to terrible bulletins of what it was like to be forty
or fifty or sixty.

Howard has early gray hairs and he's always been worried
about growing old. Promises of pensions, matured insurance
policies and senior citizen discounts didn't cheer him at all.
"Distinguished one minute, extinguished the next," he said,
and I couldn't argue with that.

I encouraged him to do exercises in the morning. Slowly,
slowly, like Lazarus, he rose into situps, pulling his pros-

pects into shape. I bought sunflower seeds and he nibbled on them, sowing them into furrows under the sofa cushions. He said he couldn't in good conscience eat butter anymore. Instead he ate honey and wheat germ and remarked on the early deaths of famous nutritionists. They die the same ways we do, he said, even in car wrecks and floods.

Now his own father was dead of natural causes. I helped Howard to pack a suitcase so that he could visit his mother in Florida for a few days and prepare her for survival.

"Why are you packing *these*?" he demanded, pulling out his bathing trunks and the T-shirt with crossed tennis rackets on the pocket.

"It's hot down there," I said. "You're going to *Florida*."

"I'm not going for fun, you know." He crammed other things into the suitcase instead: gray scratchy sweaters, dark socks for the sober business of mourning; forcing New York and winter, the gloom of subways and museums, in with his underwear.

"Listen, my love," he said, when he was all packed. "You know I hate to leave you like this. But we'll keep in constant touch."

The children and I stayed in the airlines terminal until the plane lifted him away.

Back in the apartment again, things weren't so bad. I made a baked eggplant for supper, something I like that Howard hates. I slept in the middle of the bed, using both pillows. I kept all the lights on, a childhood luxury.

Still, Howard was everywhere: his fingerprints in crazy profusion on the furniture, his Gouda cheese gathering mold in the refrigerator, the memory of his sleeping hand on my hip. All night I was a sentry waiting for morning, while the children breathed softly on the other side of the wall.

In the daytime I sat with the other mothers in the playground. The baby slept under cold sweet blankets in her carriage, and I rocked her in an unbroken rhythm, like a tic. Jason was in the sandbox, among friends. They poured sand into his cupped hands and it slid down the front of his nylon snowsuit.

All around me, my potential friends sat on benches. On the bench facing me there were two black women in bright winter coats and scarves. Every once in a while their voices came toward me on the wind, deep and resonant, as if they were speaking all the songs from *Porgy and Bess*. I thought I could fall asleep listening to their voices, feeling as peaceful and drugged as I did when Howard combed my hair.

I looked up and found our kitchen window nineteen stories up. I marked it with a mental X the way vacationers mark their hotel rooms on postcards. Having a terrible time. Wish you were here.

In the laundry room the man from apartment 16J was waiting for his wash to be finished. There was something intimate in our sitting together like that, watching his sheets tangled and thrashing like lovers in the machine. Pajamas, nightgowns, towels, mingling, drowning.

We smiled at one another but we didn't speak. His wife, I'd heard, was a forbidding woman. Wretched hair, folded arms, a masculine swagger.

But he looked like a passionate man. You can tell sometimes by the urgency of gestures and by the eyes. His wife went to work and he was home alone all day because of some on-the-job compensation case. He jammed his laundry, still damp and unfolded, into a pillow case and he left.

What part of him was wounded or damaged?

That night Howard called from Florida. We shouted to one another over the distance of rooftops and highways.

"I'm lonely," I said.

"Me too," he answered.

"How is your mother?" I asked.

"It's very sad down here," he said.

His mother pulled the phone from his hand. "Your husband is your best friend in the whole world!" she shouted.

Then Howard was back. "They had two of everything. Place mats. Heating pads. Barcaloungers."

"You were his favorite!" his mother cried, currying false favor for the dead.

Of course it wasn't true. If such things can be measured, I may well have been Howard's father's *least* favorite. I remembered how he tried to buy me off before the wedding. Bygones.

"What can I say?" I said.

Then Howard spoke. "I'm trying to straighten things out. It could take a few extra days. It's really sad here." He kept his voice low, but it sounded sun-nourished, tropical.

Later the phone rang again and this time it was a breather. I figure it had to be that love-locked man in 16J. The woman he was married to would never bend to ecstasy. Instead she was the prison matron of his lust, the keys to everything hanging just out of reach below her waist. Did he know Howard was away? News travels fast in these big buildings.

"Who is this?" I demanded, but he chose to remain silent, to contain his longings for other days, better times.

One day the children and I went to visit my mother and father. Everything in their apartment was covered in plastic: lampshades, sofas, chairs. Photographs ticked away in mirror frames and on tables. The phantom of death was there and I embraced my father in a wrestler's hold.

"How *are* you!" I cried.

"Don't worry about him," my mother said. "*He's* not going anyplace."

"I'm in the pink, Sis," my father admitted.

Back home again, Howard called and I tried to keep things light. "We all miss you terribly," I said. "We've had colds. Jason wanted to know if your plane crashed."

"The kid said that?" Howard asked. He spoke soothing words to Jason. I held the receiver to the baby's ear too.

"It snowed again," I told him.

He said it was murderously hot in Florida and there were

jellyfish in the water. He had to wear his father's swim trunks. "This business could break your heart," he said.

16J's wife came to collect money to combat a terrible disease.

"Come right in," I said. "Why don't you sit down?"

I went to get my purse, leaving her, stonefaced, alone with the children. Did she suspect anything? Had she come to give fair warning? What would she say, that gauleiter of dreams?

But she said nothing. After she left the apartment I looked for messages, for words printed in furniture dust. But there was only my receipt for the donation and a pamphlet telling why I should have given more.

"It *is* lonely here," I thought. Quiet as an aftermath. Howard's presence was fading. Only the Gouda cheese, unspeakable now. His mother had never liked me either. She used to send him to the store for Kotex to remind him of her powers. She bought him a meerschaum pipe and a spaniel puppy to divert his course. But I was triumphant anyway.

Now I imagined a thousand and one Floridian nights, the air conditioner humming in orchestral collusion with her voice, her voice buying time. She had an armory of ammunition, steamer trunks stuffed with childhood. In my head I scratched the air conditioner for the sake of authenticity. She fanned him with a palm leaf instead, a cool maternal breath on his burnished head. "So, where was I?" she asked.

Howard's hair lifted lightly in the breeze. His eyes shut. Her voice shuffled into his sleep, into mine.

In the middle of the night I heard footsteps in the hallway outside the apartment. Then an eloquent silence. I tiptoed to the door, pressed my ear against it. "Who's there?" I whispered. "Is it you?"

But no one answered. Deferred passion could drive a man crazy, I knew. He would probably want bright lights on to match the intensity of his craving, and a million weird variations on the usual stuff. His sheets in the washing machine were green, I remembered. Small scattered flowers on a limitless green field.

I went back to bed and let my blood settle. Maybe it was my motherhood he coveted. There are men like that, childless themselves, who long for the affirmation of new life around them. Mother. Food. Ecstasy. Love. Between a woman's thighs they can either be coming or going, just delivered into the world or willing to leave it in one exquisite leap of desire.

My mother said, "He's taking his sweet time about coming home."

"Things are bad there," I said. "You know Florida."

"I know one thing," she said darkly.

I called Howard but no one answered. I let the phone ring fifty times. They were walking together under palm trees, their faces painted with sunlight and shadow. Later, they would go marketing, just enough for the two of them. Then they would rest on the Barcaloungers.

The man in 16J paced restlessly in his apartment, a junior four with a bad exposure. The couple next door threw crockery and curses, like Maggie and Jiggs. The incinerator door clanged. Children's voices rose from the playground.

The next day I called Howard again. His mother answered the phone. They were just going to have lunch. I could hear dishes clatter, water running.

"What's up?" Howard asked. He wondered why I was calling before the rates changed.

"There's this man," I said.

"Who? What? I can't hear you, wait a minute." The background noises subsided.

"A *madman*!" I screamed at a splintering pitch. Then, softly, "I think he's fallen in love."

"What!" Howard shouted. "Has he touched you? My God, did you *let* him?"

"It hasn't come to that," I said. "Not yet."

The plane circled for two hours before it came down. Howard looked like a movie star, tanned and radiant. The children wriggled to get to him. He carried a cardboard box under his arm. Souvenirs, I thought. Presents. A miniature crate of marzipan oranges. A baby alligator for Jason.

When we were in the car, Howard opened the box. There were no presents. There were just some things of his father's that his mother wanted him to have. Shoe trees. An old street map of Chinatown and the Bowery. A golf cap with a green celluloid visor. It was a grab bag of history, her final weapon.

Oh, it had seemed so easy. The car was stuck in an endless ribbon of traffic. My hand rested on Howard's knee, and the children were asleep in the back seat. I would have settled for just this, all of us stopped in time.

But Howard sighed. "A man has to live," he said.

14

RENEE WOULDN'T REALLY LET HOWARD GO EITHER. Her hold on him wasn't even sexual. I knew I could have dealt with that. It would have been an all-out war and I would have won, because there is something final about me—and steadying.

She started calling up more often. She left cryptic messages for Howard. She even left messages with Jason who was only three or four at the time and loved to answer the telephone. Jason called her Weeny, insinuating her further into our lives with that nickname. "Weeny needs ten," he would tell me.

It seemed to me we gave her plenty of money, although she had given up all legal rights to alimony. They were married only seven months and she decided she didn't deserve alimony after such a short alliance, that you can't even collect unemployment insurance until you've been on the job for a while. But we were always giving her money, anyway—ten here, five there. Ostensibly they were loans, but Renee was hard-pressed to pay them back.

I suggested to Howard that we adopt her, that it would be cheaper, tax-wise and all, but Howard seemed to consider the idea seriously, getting that contemplative look in his eye, chewing his dinner in that slow, even rhythm. I imagined Renee living with us, another bed in that crowded converted dinette where the children slept.

I knew intuitively when she was calling. The telephone had a certain insistence to its ring, as if she were willing me to answer it. She wanted to know if Howard remembered a book she used to have, something she was very sentimental about. Could he possibly have taken it by mistake when they split up? Would I just look on the shelf while she held on?— it had a blue cover.

She called to say she had swollen glands, that she had been very tired lately, and in fluorescent light she could see right through to her bones.

We sent her ten dollars for the doctor. We sent her five for a new book. The annulment had been legitimate and final, but Renee hung in, a dubious inheritance.

One morning Jason answered the phone. "Weeny," he said, narrowing his eyes, waiting for my reaction.

But I wouldn't give him the satisfaction. "Oh?" I said it coolly, raising my eyebrows. "What does *she* want?"

She wanted to stay with us for a few days. Some madman she'd met at the unemployment office was after her, a real psycho. Renee thought everyone she met was a real psycho.

"I'll have to speak to Howard about it," I told her, and I hung up.

I watched a kids' television program with Jason. We tried to make a Japanese lantern, following easy directions, but it fell apart. I decided to speak to Jason instead. "Renee wants to stay here for a few days."

"In my bed?" He looked hopeful.

"Of course not. On the sofa, in the living room. What do you think?"

"I hate this stupid lantern!" he cried, ripping it to pieces.

The baby was standing in her crib, toes splayed, rattling the bars. "Guess what? Renee is coming," I told her, despising my own precocity.

That night I gave the news to Howard carefully, as if I believed it might be fatal. He sighed, but I could tell that he was secretly pleased. He wanted to know how long she would stay, what time she would need the bathroom in the morning, and if I could possibly make some butterscotch pudding, her favorite.

"Jesus!" I slammed pots and pans around, and Howard shivered with fear and happiness.

After dinner I called Renee and told her yes. "Only for a couple of days," I said severely.

"Oh, you're a pal!" she cried.

Later, she exclaimed over the pudding and threw Howard a knowing look. Was I a fool? But her bones pushed their way through her clothing. Her nostrils were red and crusty from a lingering cold. Even Howard's famous benevolence wouldn't be enough. Under the table I found the substantial truth of my own thigh, and I grew calm again.

Of course the living room was closed to us for our nightly consultation. Renee was there with a stack of magazines, a dish of trembly pudding, and the radio tuned to some distant and static-shot program.

I drew Howard into the bedroom and shut the door. It was my turn and I settled into 1942 with a minimum of effort. It was a memorable year, because my parents were discussing a possible divorce on the other side of the bedroom wall. How was that for trauma? I was Gloria Vanderbilt, a subject of custody, an object of sympathy. I imagined myself little again, diminished in bedclothes, and I reinvented their conversation.

"What about the kid?" my mother asked.

"Oh, you're the one who always wanted a kid," my father answered.

Next to me, Howard moved restlessly. "It's a good thing Renee and I didn't have any children," he said.

"That's true," I said and then I tried to continue my story. But Renee coughed in the other room, two throat-clearing blasts that pinned us to the pillows.

"What's *that*?" Howard said.

"Oh, for heaven's sake! You broke my train of thought again!"

"I'm sorry. I only asked."

"Forget the whole thing. It's no use telling you anything lately anyway."

"Go ahead, love," he said, rubbing my back in conciliation. "Come on Paulie, start from 'Oh, you're the one who always wanted a kid.' "

I felt glum. "Forget it," I said.

"Jesus!" Howard said. "I'm going to have to stop smoking. Just feel this. My pulse is slow, my blood must be like clay."

In the morning Renee was watching the playground, from the shelter of the curtains, like a gangster holed up in a hide-out.

"I'm a wreck," she said. "I keep thinking that nut is going to come here."

"Why should he come here? How could he even know where you are? Renee?"

She didn't answer. She moved to the sink, where she squeezed fresh orange juice into a glass with her bare hands. I wished Howard could have seen that. The untapped strength of that girl!

Jason was a traitor. He ran kisses up her freckled arms. "Weeny! My Weeny!" They drank the unstrained juice in sips from the same glass.

Later, I went downstairs and called Howard at the studio from a pay phone. "She has to go."

"I know that. Don't you think I know that?"

"I mean forever."

"Paulie, what do you want me to do?"

"Nominate her for Miss Subways. Get her deported. Howard, I don't know. Why don't you find her a husband?"

"Ha, ha. Very funny. Should I look in the Yellow Pages?"

"Well, *you* married her."

"That's another story," he said, but I refused to listen. "Ask around," I said, and I hung up.

At home again, I tried my own hand. "Stand up straight," I told Renee. "Give them both barrels." When she did, the narrow points of her breasts thrust out like drill bits. "No, no *relax*." I let her try on some of my clothes, but they enveloped her like tents. Instead, we worked on makeup and her psychological approach to men. But it all seemed useless. In ten minutes there were smudges under her eyes from the mascara, and lipstick on her teeth.

"Relax," I told her. "That's the whole secret," and she collapsed in a heap as if her spinal cord had been severed.

That night Howard came home with a man, a trumpet player who sometimes sat in with the Fantasy Five. I had never met him before. He wore dark glasses and a bitter smile. He was divorced too, and spoke about getting burned once and never playing with fire again.

"Oh, *terrific*," I said to Howard, without moving my lips.

But he shrugged. He had done his share. Now it was up to me. I did the best I could, flaunting my domestic joy at this hostile stranger, like a bullfighter's cape. But everything must have seemed bleak to him, through those dark glasses. My dinner was loaded with cholesterol killers, the apartment was overheated and confining. Someone was deflating the tires on his car parked three city blocks away.

Of course Renee didn't help at all. She pretended to be our eldest child, and ate her french fries with her fingers. There was a huge pink stain on the front of her blouse.

"I'll call you," the man said to her when he left, a phrase torn from memory. We were all surprised that he even bothered.

"You didn't have to, Howard," Renee said later, as if he had brought her a frivolous but thoughtful gift.

From our bed, Howard and I lay listening for night sounds from the living room and we were rewarded. In her sleep, Renee called out and I could feel Howard next to me, poised for flight on the edge of the mattress.

Dear Abby/Ann Landers/Rose Franzblau,
What should I do?
Signed,
Miserable

Dear Mis,
Do you keep up with the national scene? Can you discuss things intelligently with your husband; i.e., name all the cabinet members, the National Book Award

nominees, the discoverer of the oral polio vaccine? Have you looked in a mirror lately? Do you make the most of your natural good looks? Go to an art gallery, prepare an exciting salad for dinner, reline your kitchen shelves with wild floral paper. And good luck!

The days went by and somehow we began to settle in as if things were fine, as if Renee *belonged* on our couch every night, leaving those shallow depressions in the pillows.

My mother called to offer some advice. "Get rid of her," she said.

My father picked up the bedroom extension and listened. I could hear the rasp of his breath.

"Hello, Dad," I said.

"Are you on, Herm?" my mother asked. "Is that you?"

My father cleared his throat right into the mouthpiece. *He* was going to offer advice as well, and his style was based on Judge Hardy in the old Mickey Rooney movies. Kindly. Dignified. Judiciously stern. All his days he sat for imaginary Bachrach portraits, in the subways, in the movies. "What I would do . . ." he said, and then he paused.

My mother waited. I waited. I tapped my foot on the kitchen tile.

"What should she do?" my mother insisted. "Should she throw her out the window? Should she stuff her into the incinerator?"

"I believe I was speaking," Judge Hardy said.

"Oh, pardon me," my mother said. "For living."

"What I would do," he began again, "is seek professional advice."

"Thanks, Dad."

"Yes," he said, admiring the echo of his words. "Professional advice." He paced in his chambers.

"It's not normal," my mother said. "It's not nice." Her opinion about other things as well: homosexuality, artificial insemination, and the hybridization of plants.

* * *

The next day I lent Renee twenty dollars from the household money and I looked through the classified ads for a new apartment for her. "Change your luck," I advised, like a dark gypsy.

When the children were napping, the doorbell rang. An eye loomed back at mine, magnified through the peephole.

"Who?"

"Renee there?"

My heart gave tentative leaps, like the first thrusts of life in a pregnancy. I opened the chains and bolts with trembling hands and ran inside. "It's a man!" I hissed, rebuttoning Renee's housecoat, combing her hair with my fingers. But it was no use. She still looked terrible, abused and ruined.

The man burst into the room.

"Oh, for God's sake, it's *you*!" Renee said.

"I told you," he said. "When I want something, I go after it."

"Well, just piss off, Raymond. You make me sick."

"It's you and me, baby," he said. "All the way."

I watched from the doorway. He was a big ox of a man, the kind who invites you to punch him in the belly and then laughs at your broken hand. There was a cartoon character tattooed on his forearm—Yogi Bear, or maybe Smokey.

"Call the police," Renee said wearily.

"The *police*?"

"Why fight nature, Renee?" he asked.

"That's right," I said with a conspiratorial wink.

"He's a maniac," she explained. "He's the one I told you about. From the unemployment."

My hope began to ebb. "Well, you could just give him a *chance*."

Jason came in from the bedroom then, squinting in the assault of light. "Stop hollering," he said.

"My intentions are honorable," the maniac said, crossing his heart. "Cute kid," he offered, referring to Jason.

I reached for that slender thread. "Do you like children?" I asked.

He leaned on his wit. "Say, I used to be one myself!" He laughed and laughed, wiping tears from his eyes.

"Renee Renee," I said. "Introduce me."

"He-has-a-prison-record," she sang in falsetto behind her hand.

They might have been political arrests for all I knew, or something else that was fashionable. "*Honi soit*," I said.

"Bad checks," Renee answered. She was relentless.

I always try to find the good in people and he had nice eyes, gray with gorgeous yellow flecks. I offered him coffee and he accepted. Renee sat down finally, giving in.

They were married two weeks later. Howard gave the bride away, which may not be traditional, but it meant a lot to me, for the symbolism. I gave them a silver-plated bread tray and sincere wishes for the future. Raymond had a lead on a job in Chicago and they left in a hailstorm of rice for the airport.

"That's that," I said, never believing it for a moment.

15

In the zoo
the animals are stunned by night
and dream their jungle dream.
They move with restless joy
in herds, away from city life
where mating is arranged.

April 15, 1961

IT WAS ONLY SUNDAY. IT WAS ONLY MY OWN FLESH, PALE
and sleep-creased and smelling like bread near my rooting
nose. Nothing special had happened, for which I was grateful. Anything might happen, for which I was expectant and
tremblingly ready.

On the other hand, Howard was depressed, hiding in the
bedclothes, moaning in his dream. Even without opening my
eyes, I could feel the shape of his mood beside me. Then my
eyes opened. Ta-da! Another gorgeous day. Just what I expected. The clock hummed, electric, containing its impulse
to tick, the wallpaper repeated itself around the room, and
Howard pushed into the pillows, refusing to come to terms
with consciousness.

My hand was as warm and as heavy as a baby's head, and
I laid it against his neck, palm up. If I let him sleep, he would
do it for hours and hours. That's depression.

Years ago, my mother woke me with a song about a bird
on a windowsill and about sunshine and flowers and the glo-

rious feeling of being alive that had nothing in the world to do with the sad still-life of a school lunch and the reluctant walk in brown oxfords, one foot and then the other, for six blocks. It had nothing to do with that waxed ballroom of a gymnasium, and the terrible voice of the whistle that demanded agility and grace where there were only clumsy confusion and an enormous desire to be the other girl on the other team, the one leaping toward baskets and dangling ropes.

I didn't want to get up either, at least until I had grown out of it, grown away from teachers, grown out of that baby-plump body in an undershirt and lisle stockings. I would get up when I was good and ready, when it was all over and I could have large breasts and easy friendships.

Howard always blamed his depression on real things in his current life because he didn't believe in the unconscious. At parties where all the believers talked about the interpretation of dreams, about wish-fulfillment and symbiotic relationships, Howard covered his mouth with one hand and muttered, "Bullshit."

Was he depressed because his parents didn't want him to be born, because his mother actually hoisted his father in her arms every morning for a month, hoping to bring on that elusive period? Not a chance!

Was he sad because his sister was smarter in school, or at least more successful, or because she seduced him to the point of action and then squealed? Never!

He was depressed, he said, because it started to rain when he was at a ballgame and the men pulling tarpaulin over the infield seemed to be covering a common grave. He was sad, he said, because the landlord is a prick, and the kid living upstairs roller-skates in the kitchen.

Ah, Howard. My hand was awake now, buzzing with blood, and it kneaded the flesh of his neck and then his back; worked down through the warm tunnel of bedclothes until it found his hand and squeezed hard. "It's a gorgeous day, lover! Hey, kiddo, wake up and I'll tell you something."

Howard opened his eyes, but they were glazed and without focus. "Huhnn?"

"Do you know what?" I searched my head for restorative news. His vision found the room, the morning light, his whole life. His eyes closed again.

"Howard, it's Sunday, the day of rest. The paper is outside, thick and juicy, hot off the press. I'll make waffles and sausages for breakfast. Do you want to go for a ride in the country?"

"Oh, for Christ's sake, Paulie, will you leave me alone? I want to sleep."

"Sleep? Sweetheart, you'll sleep enough when you're dead."

I saw that idea roll past his eyelids. Death. What next?

The children made waking sounds in the other room.

"Come on, sleepyhead, get up. We'll visit model homes. We'll look in the paper for some new ones." I patted him on the ass, a loving but fraternal gesture, a manager sending his favorite man into the game.

Why was I so happy? I decided it was the triumph of the human spirit over genetics and environment. I knew the same bad things Howard knew. I had my ups and downs, traumas, ecstasies. Maybe my happiness was only a dirty trick, another of life's big come-ons. Maybe I'd end up the kind who weeps into the dishwater and always keeps the window shades drawn.

But in the meantime I whipped up waffle batter, poured golden juice into golden glasses, while Howard sat in a chair dropping pages of the *Times* like leaves from a deciduous tree.

I sang songs from the forties, thinking there's nothing like the comfort of your own nostalgia. I sang "Ferryboat Serenade," I sang "Hutsut Rallson on the Rillerah." The waffles stuck to the iron. "Don't sit under the apple tree with anyone else but me," I warned Howard, willing coffee and waffle smells into the living room where he sat like an inmate in the wintry garden of a small sanitorium.

"Breakfast is ready!" I had the healthy bellow of a short-order cook.

He shuffled in, still convalescing from his childhood. The children came in too, his jewels, his treasures. They climbed his legs to reach the table, to scratch themselves on his morning beard. Daddy, my Daddy, and he ran his hands over them, a blind man trying to memorize their bones. The teakettle sang, the sun crashed in through the window, and my heart would not be swindled.

"What's the matter, Howie? If something is bothering you, *talk* about it."

He smiled, that calculated, ironic smile, and it occurred to me that we hardly talked about anything that mattered anymore. I had waited all my life to become a woman, damn it, to sit in a kitchen and say grown-up things to the man facing me, words that would float like vapor over the heads of my children. Don't I remember that language from my own green days; code words in Yiddish and pig latin, and a secret but clearly sexual jargon that made my mother laugh and filled me with a dark and trembling longing and rage?

Ixnay, the idkay.

Now I wanted to talk over the heads of my own children, in the modern language of the cinema. There were thousands of words they wouldn't understand and would never remember, except for the rhythm and mystery. *Fellatio*, Howard. *Cunnilingus.*

He rattled the real estate section and slowly turned the pages.

"Well, did you find a development for us? Find one with a really inspired name this time." On other days, we'd gone to Crestwood Estates, Seaside Manor (miles from any sea), to Tall Oaks and Sweet Pines, to Chateaux Printemps and Chalets-on-the-Sound.

All the worthwhile land was being gobbled up by speculators and those tall oaks and sweet pines fallen to bulldozers. The newer developments were farther and farther from the city. Someday there wouldn't be any model homes left for our therapeutic Sundays. Maybe later, when we were old, we'd visit the Happy Haven and the Golden Years Retreat, to purge whatever comes with mortality and the final vision.

But now Howard was trying. "Here's one," he said. "Doncastle Greens. 'Only fifty minutes from the heart of Manhattan. Live like a king on a commoner's budget.' "

"Let me see!" I rushed to his side, ready for conspiracy. "Hey, listen to this. 'Come on down today and choose either a twenty-one-inch color TV or a deluxe dishwasher, as a bonus, absolutely free!' Howie, what do you choose?"

But Howard chose silence, would not be cajoled so easily, so early in his depression.

I hid the dishes in a veil of suds and we all got dressed. The children were too young to care where we were going, as long as they could ride in the car, the baby steering crazily in her car seat and Jason contemplating the landscape and the faces of other small boys poised at the windows of other cars.

The car radio sputtered news and music and frantic advice. *Buy Duz! Drive carefully! Have a nice day!* It was understood that Howard would drive there and I would drive back.

He sat forward, bent over the wheel, as if visibility were poor and the traffic hazardous. In fact, it was a marvelous, clear day and the traffic was moving without hesitation past all the exits, past the green signs and the abandoned wrecks like modern sculpture at roadside, past dead dogs, their brilliant innards squeezed out onto the divider.

Jason pointed, always astounded at the first corpse, but we were past it before he could speak. It occurred to me that there were families everywhere holding dangling leashes and collars, walking through the yards of their neighborhoods, calling, Lucky! Lucky! and then listening for that answering bark that would not come. Poor Lucky, deader than a doornail, flatter than a bathmat.

I watched Howard, that gorgeous nose so often seen in profile, that crisp gangster's hair, and his ear, unspeakably vulnerable, waxen and convoluted.

And then we were there. Doncastle Greens was a new one for us. The builder obviously dreamed of moats and grazing sheep. Model No. 1, the Shropshire, recalled at once gloomy castles and thatched cottages; Richard III and Miss Marple. Other cars were already parked under the colored banners when we pulled in.

The first step was always the brochure, wonderfully new and smelly with printer's ink. The motif was British, of course, and there were taprooms and libraries as opposed to the dens and funrooms of Crestwood Estates, *les salons et les chambres des Chateaux Printemps*. Quelle savvy!

The builder's agent was young and balding, busy sticking little flags into promised lots on a huge map behind his desk. He called us folks. "Good to see you, folks!" Every once in a while he rubbed his hands together as if selling houses made him cold. During his spiel I tried to catch Howard's eye, but Howard pretended to be listening. What an actor!

We moved in a slow line through Model 1, behind an elderly couple. I knew we'd seen them before, at Tall Oaks perhaps, but there were no greetings exchanged. They'd never buy, of course, and I wondered about their motives, which were probably more devious than our own.

Some of the people, I could see, were really buyers. One wife held her husband's hand as if they were entering consecrated premises.

I poked Howard, just below the heart. I could talk without moving my lips. "White brocade couch on bowlegs," I muttered. "Definitely velvet carpeting." I waited, but Howard was grudging.

"Plastic-covered lampshades," he offered finally.

I urged him on. "Crossed rifles over the fireplace. Thriving plastic dracaena in the entrance," I snickered, rolled my eyes, did a little soft-shoe.

But Howard wasn't playing. He was leaning against the braided ropes that kept us from muddying the floor of the drawing room, and he looked like a man at the prow of a ship.

"Howard?" Tentative. Nervous.

"You know, kiddo, it's not really that bad," he said.

"Do you mean the *house*?"

Howard didn't answer. The older man took a tape measure from his pocket and laid it against the dark molding. Then he wrote something into a little black notebook.

The buyers breathed on our necks, staring at their future. "Oh, *Ronnie*," she said, an exhalation like the first chords of a hymn. I would not have been surprised if she had knelt then or made some other mysterious or religious gesture.

"One of these days," Howard said. "Pow! One of us will be knocked on the head in that crazy city. Raped. Strangled."

"Howie . . ."

"And do we have adequate bookshelves? You know you have no room for your books."

The oak bookshelves before us held all the volumes, A through Z, of the *American Household Encyclopedia*.

The old man measured the door frame and wrote again in his book. Perhaps he would turn around soon and measure us, recording his findings in a feathery hand.

Jason and another boy discovered one another and stared like mirrors. What would happen, I wondered, if we took the wrong one home, bathed him and gave him Frosted Flakes, kissed him and left the night-light on until he forgot everything else and adjusted? The baby drew on her pacifier and dreamily patted my hair.

Everyone else had passed us and Howard was still in the same doorway. I pulled on his sleeve. "The baby is getting heavy."

He took her from me and she nuzzled his cheek with her perfect head.

We proceeded slowly to the master bathroom, the one with the dual vanities and a magazine rack embossed with a Colonial eagle.

"Howie, will you look at this, His and *hers*."

He didn't answer.

We went into the bedroom itself, where ghosts of dead queens rested on the carved bed. "Mortgages. Cesspools. Community living." I faced him across the bed and hissed the words at him, but he didn't even wince. He looked sleepy and relaxed. I walked around the bed and put my arm through his. "Maybe we look in the wrong place for our happiness, Howard."

He patted my hand, distracted but solicitous. I walked behind him then, a tourist following a guide. At the olde breakfast nooke, I wanted to sit him down and explain that I was terrified of change, that the city was my hideout and my freedom, that one of us might take a lover, or worse.

But I was silent in the pantry, in the wine cellar and the vestibule, and we were finished with the tour of the house. We stood under the fluttering banners and watched the serious buyers reenter the builder's trailer. Howard shifted the baby from arm to arm as if she interfered with his concentration. Finally, he passed her to me without speaking. He put his hands into his pockets and he had that dreamy look on his face.

"I'll drive back," I said, as if this wasn't preordained.

There was more traffic now, and halfway home we slowed to observe the remains of an accident. Some car had jumped the guardrail and there was a fine icing of shattered glass on the road.

"Do you see?" I said, not sure of my moral.

But Howard was asleep, his head tilted back against the headrest. At home, I could see he was coming out of it. He was interested in dinner, in the children's bath. He stood behind me at the sink and he had an erection.

Later, in bed again, I got on top for the artificial respiration I had to give. His mouth opened to receive my tongue, a communion wafer. I rose above him, astounded at the luminosity of my skin in the half-light.

Howard smiled, handsome, damp with pleasure, yes, with *happiness*, his ghosts mugged and banished from the room.

"Are you happy?" I had to know, restorer of faith, giver of life. "Are you happy?"

And even as I waited for his answer, my own ghosts entered, stood solemn at the foot of the bed, young girls in undershirts, jealous and watchful, whispering in a grown-up language I could never understand.

16

*I*T DIDN'T HAVE TO MEAN ANYTHING. IT COULD HAVE been fatigue, nerves. The magazines had a lot of articles about situations like ours. "Things Couples Don't Talk About." When Your Husband Needs Help." Crammed between the Jell-O molds and the hip-slimnastics, serious-looking guest doctors, photographed wearing their stethoscopes, gave cheering advice to wives of listless men. What to do. What to do.

But it had been a long, asexual winter. The steam heat seemed to dry all of the body's moistures and shrivel the fantasies of the mind. From the nineteenth floor of Building A, I watched snow fall on the deserted geometry of the playground. The colors of the world were lustless, forbidding. White fell on gray. Gray shadows drew over white.

For all I knew it was an epidemic of some kind—regional, even national. It wasn't something you could ask your neighbors. But didn't the whole building seem silent, encased in an icy slumber like a fairy-tale curse?

There were rumors of a sex maniac in the complex. It's about time, I thought. Had he known that we needed him, that winter had frozen us in our hearts and our beds? Was his to be the kiss of awakening?

But even he didn't do much of anything. He was seen twice by elderly widows whose thin shrieks seemed to pierce the brain. There had been an invasion of those widows lately, as if old men were dying off in job lots. The widows marched behind the moving men, fluttering, birdlike. Their sons and daughters were there to supervise, looking sleek and modern next to the belongings: chairs with curved legs, massive headboards of marriage beds trembling on the backs of the movers. The widows smiled shyly as if survival embarrassed them.

Now two of them had encountered a sex maniac. Help, they had shrilled. Help and help, and he had been frightened off by their cries before he could effect the renaissance we needed. I wondered where he waited now in ambush and if I would ever meet him on a loveless December night—that is, if he even existed. Who could trust the word of those distracted women?

But then the sex maniac was seen by a more reliable source. The superintendent's wife came from a mining area in Pennsylvania, a place not noted for frivolity. She had gazed at a constant landscape and she had known men who had suffocated in sealed mines. Her word was to be honored; she had no more imagination that the grocer's boy. After the police were finished, the women of the building fell on her with questions. Did he just—you know—show himself? Did he touch her? What did he say?

She answered with humorless patience. Contrary to rumor, he was merely a white man, not very tall, and young, like her own son. But not really like her own son, she was quick to add. He had said terrible, filthy things to her in a funny quiet way, as if he were praying, and I saw him in my mind's eye, reedy and pale, saying his string of obscenities like a litany in a reverent and quaking voice.

The superintendent's wife said he hadn't touched at all, only longed to touch, promised, threatened to touch.

Ahhhhhhhhh, cried the women. Ahhhhhhh. The old widows ran to the locksmith for new bolts and chains. The men in the building began to do the laundry for their wives. They went in groups with their friends. Did the sound of their voices diminishing in the elevators remind the superintendent's wife of men going down to the mines?

Howard ruined our wash, mixing the light with the dark,

using too much bleach. "Did you see anything?" I asked. But it seemed that he hardly even saw me.

In the meantime there were other men in my life. The children developed coughs that made them sound like seals barking, and the health plan sent Dr. Pearlman. He was thin, mustachioed, bowed by the burden of house calls. Bad boys in bad neighborhoods stole his hubcaps and snapped off his aerial. Angry children bit his fingers as he pried open the hinges of their jaws. I clasped a flower pin to my best housedress, the children jumped on the beds intoning nursery rhymes, but the doctor snapped his bag shut with the finality of the last word. His mustache thin and mean, he looked like the doctors of my childhood. We trailed after him to the door, but he didn't turn around. Never mind. There were policemen to ask us leading questions and to write our fiction down in their notebooks. There was the super with his cruel and burning eyes, the usual parade of repairmen and plumbers.

There was the delivery boy from the market. His name was Earl. I coaxed him into the apartment. Just put it there, Earl. Just a minute while I get my purse, Earl. Is it still as cold out there? Is it going to snow again? Will the price-level index rise? Is my true love true to me? But he was a boy without vision or imagination. He counted out the change and he hurried to leave.

That night I said to Howard, "Love has left this land." When Jason and the baby were tucked in behind veils of steam from the vaporizer, we tried to disprove it. We turned to one another in that chorus of coughing children and whispering radiators. The smell of Vicks was there, eaten into my hand, into the bedclothes, and the lovemaking was only ritual.

There were rumors that the sex maniac had moved on, to fresher territory or a better climate. I had never seen him. Not once crouched in the corner of the laundry room, not once moaning his demands on the basement ramp, not once cutting his footprints across fresh snow in the courtyard.

But Howard had been a sex maniac himself, mumbling his own tender obscenities against my skin, telling me that I drove him crazy. He had been a mugger waiting to turn me upside down and shake out all my sexual loose change. Didn't he remember? Was I being unfair?

It's really no one's fault, I told myself. I huddled against Howard's back. It was the fault of the atmosphere, the barometric pressure, the wind velocity. It didn't mean anything at all.

17

HOWARD'S BASS PLAYER WAS LEAVING THE GROUP FOR a long engagement with a blues singer in Las Vegas. Louis came to the apartment to drop off some music and to say good-bye before he left for the airport. He came in dragging his cased fiddle, his black hair shining with melted snow. "Can't leave this in the car, man," he said. "I'd be out of work in a minute." He was excited, almost manic. You could tell by the way he moved and by the smile he couldn't dim, even when he spoke his regrets about splitting with the group. But *Vegas*, man!

I had never been there myself, yet I saw a kaleidoscopic picture of neon lights, whirling roulette wheels, and over-dressed people killing themselves to have a good time.

Louis was Howard's age, but he was single. He'd had lots of women and one or two common-law arrangements, broken by mutual consent. And he had lived everywhere, even in France for a while, before we knew him. Howard looked pale in the radiant glow of Louis's enthusiasm.

Later, the apartment seemed very quiet, and even the street noises were muffled by a fresh fall of snow. Howard was writing into a ledger at the kitchen table. I watched him from the sink where I was washing the supper dishes. Once in a while Jason coughed lightly in his sleep.

It should have been cozy, just us insulated against the night, with no need for conversation or even music. And yet I felt uneasy, as if sound, *any* sound, would hold back something as yet unknown but surely dreadful. What could be dreadful

in that kitchen? I squeezed suds through a nylon sponge;
Howard wrote into his book. He looked especially sweet to
me then, and boyish in his concentration. "Hey," I said.
"Do you know what you look like?"

Howard held one hand up and scribbled into the ledger.
"Wait a minute, wait a minute," he said. And then, "What
did you say?"

"I said, do you know what you look like?"

He tapped his pencap on the table and he didn't seem very
interested.

I went ahead anyway. "You look just like a little kid doing
his homework."

"Ha!" Howard said. "That's a laugh." But he wasn't
laughing, or even smiling, for that matter. His expression
was more like an ironic smirk, and I felt sorry that I had
broken the safety barrier of our silence.

"I don't see anything funny," I said.

"It's not funny," Howard agreed. "It's actually sad, your
telling me I look like a kid. I was just thinking that I feel like
an old man."

"You?" I said.

"I feel about a thousand years old."

"You don't look a day over nine hundred to me," I said.

But Howard still didn't smile. He didn't even look up.

"What's the matter?" I asked. "You're not sick or anything, Howie, are you?"

Howard closed the ledger and rubbed his eyes. When he
opened them again, he seemed slightly dazed, unfocused.
"No, it's nothing like that," he said. "I just feel . . . I don't
know . . ."

I dried my hands and sat down on another chair, pulling
it close to his. "Give me a little hint. I really want to know.
Does it have anything to do with me?"

"It's nothing, I told you. Only a feeling. I'm probably just
tired."

"Sure," I said, eager to believe him. "Winter can do that.
It gets into your bones and saps all your energy. And you

haven't been sleeping that well, anyway. Tossing all night, talking in your sleep."

Howard's eyes cleared. "I do?" he said. "What do I say?"

"Oh, I don't know. Mumbles, moans. You're probably only dreaming. Have you been having bad dreams lately?"

Howard nodded.

"Do you want to tell me about them?"

"Paulie, you know I don't believe in that stuff. Dreams don't have anything to do with anything else."

"Oh, Howie, you can't mean that! Dreams are an important part of your unconscious life. They're like wonderful mysteries you can unravel. Come on, *tell* me. You'll probably feel better if you talk about it. Is it always the same dream?"

"Yes."

"Who's in it?"

"You are. You and the kids."

"We are? Well, go ahead. What happens?"

"It's a lousy dream," he said. "I can't help what I dream. The house is on fire. You're all inside."

My heart tripped. "Where are you?" I asked.

"Downstairs, in the street."

"But you're trying to get inside, aren't you, to save us?" Howard didn't answer, and he looked stricken with sorrow.

In dreams begin responsibilities, I thought. But I said, "Well, that happens," forcing cheer into my tone. "Everyone has dreams like that, where you're paralyzed, helpless, in the worst situations. But what's *really* bothering you? In real life, I mean. Is business okay?" He hadn't talked that much recently about the studio, or about the weekend jobs.

"Yeah, business is okay," he said. "But that's just it, I'm in *business*. Me, a guy who used to play gigs, who sat in and jammed for the hell of it. Now I'm keeping books."

"Well," I said, not sure of what to say next. "Maybe I could help you with the bookkeeping. I wasn't exactly a whiz in math, but I'd try."

Howard lit a cigarette. "No, it's okay," he said. "The

books aren't that bad. They're only a symbol, anyway. It's the other things. Keeping a businessman's hours. Trying to teach those poor squeaking kids the sax and clarinet.''

''You could cut down on the lessons, Howard, couldn't you? We'd still get by.''

''I suppose . . .'' he said, but his voice was flat with despair. And he looked round-shouldered, defeated. He certainly didn't look like a kid anymore.

It's only Louis, I thought, bursting in here and spoiling everything with his jazzed-up happiness. Louis strumming and thumping new girls with a careless joy, as if they were bass fiddles, or moving free on that late flight to Las Vegas, his plane setting down in a dazzle of lights.

Of course Howard saw only what he wanted to see. He would never picture Louis waking lonely in a motel room or, years later, dissipated and disappointed, and wondering why he had chosen to live that way.

I tried to imagine Howard's old life. I remembered, with a pitching sensation, the first time I saw him in that haze of sweet music. And I remembered Sherry's warning about the special sensuality of musicians. Was it dependent on a whole life-style or only on the particular sounds they made together in dark, evening places?

''And you'd still have your club dates,'' I said.

''Ah, even the club dates are a drag now. I'm hustling for a buck all the time, and there's hardly any excitement, any fun in it.''

Fun! Who had fun at his job? Did he think my job was fun? Let him try to find romance in the kitchen, hilarity in the laundry room.

Even kings and queens probably hated their jobs from time to time, and wished they could climb down from their thrones and be freewheeling and without responsibility. That was the key to the whole thing of course: responsibility, *maturity*. But I knew intuitively that it wouldn't be a wise thing to say to Howard then. Reasonable, realistic talk was the last thing he wanted to hear when he was dreaming of freedom, of earlier times. It would only be taken as a lecture by his leading millstone.

"When the kids are a little older," I said, "I'll get a job too. This isn't a life sentence, Sweetheart."

And finally Howard smiled, but indulgently, the way he sometimes smiled at Jason or the baby. "Forget it," he said. "It's nothing. I'll get over it. I'm practically over it already."

But I wasn't convinced. I still felt uneasy, even threatened, and I searched my head for new ideas. "Say, did you ever think of writing songs?" I asked. "All you'd need is one big hit."

"I'm not a songwriter," Howard said.

"You could write the music. I'd do the words," I said. "Who knows? Maybe that's where I have to go with my poetry."

"Will you cut it out, Paulie?" Howard said. "I'm not a songwriter. I'm a musician." He pushed his chair back from the table, as if he were going to stand up.

I moved quickly from my chair to his lap.

"Jesus! *Easy*," he said.

"Rhyming can't be harder than free verse. June, moon, tune. See?" I snapped my fingers and moved my feet in a fast, desperate shuffle. "We'll be a team, like Rodgers and Hammerstein, like Lerner and Lowe. There must be a fortune in songwriting. Then you'd never have to do anything you didn't want to again."

I spoke rapidly, not letting him answer, blocking all his defenses and the ultimate, fearful truth.

Why hadn't he rushed into that burning building, anyway? It was *his* dream, damn it. Why didn't he smash windows and doors, even scale walls to save us? And who had set the fire in the first place?

But I didn't say anything. Instead I put my arms around Howard, adding love to my argument, and trying to assess his mood. "Do you feel better?" I asked, and I began to place strategic kisses on his ears, along his neck.

"Uh huh," Howard said, but his voice was low and sad, and his arms around me were passive.

I freed one of my hands and I pushed the ledger away from us, across the table. But even when he began to kiss me back, it was still there, just on the edge of my vision.

18

I STOOD AT THE WINDOW BEHIND THE FRILLY CURTAINS in our kitchen and I watched my family take their places in the playground allotted to our building. There was the boy Jason, a tiny nucleus in the sandbox. There were Howard and baby Ann, moving in serene rhythm as he pushed her in a swing. They looked like three brave flags in bright sweaters I'd knitted for them and I became excited with pride as if I'd knitted *them* and not just their sweaters. Deep in the pocket of my apron was the letter from my anonymous friend.

> *My Dear,*
> Watch out for Howard and Mrs. X of C Building. I am not what you would refer to as a devout person, but I will pray for you anyway.
> *Your Anonymous Friend*

The city was full of cranks—lonely, deranged people who couldn't bear anyone else's happiness. I should have thrown that letter right down the incinerator. And yet I'd kept it for days. It rested now in pocket lint and was wrinkled from handling.

Oh, thanks a lot, my loyal anonymous friend. Wasn't everything perfect before? (Or almost?) Now there was the ache of uneasiness, and I'd have to be guarded, breathe softly so as not to miss the innuendos. Why did Howard *really* volunteer to help with the laundry? Did he compare my

bleach with hers near the double-duty dryers? Never fear.
The management had installed klieg lights at the request of
terrified tenants. There was nothing clandestine doing in the
laundry room. And anyway, I was too big to lurk in doorways
and narrow passageways to catch them out.

But what if I didn't wait and watch, but simply lifted the
window and jumped, spiraling slowly toward him, nineteen
stories, eighteen neighbors to wave to in descent. My mother
would have shouted to me in comfort, Everyone is dying
nowadays!

There he was, my Howard, the best and most loving father
I knew. Protective as a mother hen. (Jason sat on his lap at
the dentist's so the father could absorb the pain of the child.)

I opened the window and looked down, feeling as lonely
and as vigilant as a forest ranger. Howard in the green sweater
was standing alone. Both children were together in the sandbox. Cutting across the playground, as if on choreographic
cue, came a woman in a red coat. She was wearing boots,
of course, and they zigzagged in neat steps until she was near
him. Her hair was long, that much I could see, nothing more
without tumbling out.

"Wait!" I shouted. "Don't do anything!" I ran to the
children's room and looked through the chaos of the toybox
until I found them, the binoculars that his other grandfather,
that cheap voyeur, had once bought for Jason. "Wait, wait,"
I called again, and when I went to the window and brought
them into focus, they were standing there and her foot was
pointing outward as if she were threatening to go. Howard's
hands were in his pockets where they belonged. They were
haloed together in the rainbow nimbus of those rotten binoculars. Her hand touched his arm, but I couldn't see her
face.

"Mrs. X," I said. "Go away. Leave town. Everything
was gorgeous. What can you know about someone else's
marriage? The sloppy intimacy of it. Could you pit 'fashionable' and 'lean' against ample and familiar? Could a fall and
boots win out over natural curls and this apron? Purple lilies
on a blue field. You wouldn't have a chance. We only need

an extra bedroom, and we're on the management's list for a five, with terrace.

"Don't complicate my life!" I shouted, and the woman on the twentieth floor shook out her dust mop, and dust-curl stars fell on my head.

Howard gestured and the woman in the red coat turned away from him.

"Run, run!" I called. "He isn't worth it. I'm going to kill him anyway in that place you both go, if I only knew where it is."

Looking through the binoculars again, I saw him follow her and then they disappeared at the concrete corner of Building D.

"Murderer!" I yelled. "Help, police!" and my voice went up like a helium balloon. The children were left alone in that mad city, two unarmed Arabs in that sandbox, the Sinai Desert.

It wasn't fair. It shouldn't have been me so big and wounded on the receiving end. Listen, I made compromises too when I saw him that first time, so handsome with all that dark hair like a gangster. And I let it pass when he saw me and said all those needless things about white valleys and Rubens.

A moment later I looked again and there he came, my Howard, like a victor from battle, and I had to give him credit, he went right to the children.

So that's how it was, and I let the elevator make its deliberate climb, nineteen stories, while I rubbed my hands together and made plans. I thought: Here is the evidence around my neck like a heavy chain, as if the binoculars had captured forever that action, that blurred vision, and I could have *shown* him what I had seen.

But what had I really seen, after all? Only a woman speaking briefly to my husband in a public place. Asking the time perhaps, or for a match. Stepping out of the wind for a moment to light a cigarette or give directions. It's a free country, isn't it?

And then Howard came through the doorway with his

beautiful and powerful weapons: the baby Ann collapsed on his shoulder, her overall leg pulled up over a chapped knee, Jason with a blood-freezing hold on his father's leg. And himself with rosy cheeks from the outdoors, in a green sweater, in trousers. The idiot eyes on the binoculars banged against my breast.

Howard tapped his finger on the Formica counter. "I have to quit smoking. There's no kidding myself. It's killing me. I can't blow my horn. I can't run one block . . ."

"Why don't you just cut down?"

"Because that's horseshit. But the minute I think about it, I change my mind. I don't want to do it."

"You can do it, Howard."

"Ah, who wants to? You have to die from something anyway."

"Listen, you can do it, Howard. I'll buy you lots of stuff you haven't had in years, like Blackjack gum and jujubes."

"Yeah?" He was dreamy, but interested.

Jason pulled away from his father and came to me. "Mommy," he said. "My Mommy," He patted my knee.

"Howard, you can give up smoking!" I think I was shouting. Like a fool, I felt so happy.

"Well, maybe," he conceded. "With God's help," he added, to be cautious.

"*I'll* help you," I cried. "I'll even go on a diet."

Howard looked at me for the first time. He smiled. "You don't have to do that."

"No no, I *want* to. It's the least I can do."

I was thrilled with the idea of a joint effort. It was like the camaraderie at a block party in Brooklyn on V-J day. The war was over and we were going to live forever.

I wondered, did I know anyone with a mimeograph machine? I would make a thousand copies of a letter to my anonymous friend.

Dear Friend,
What my husband does is his business and I'll kill you if you tell lies about him and spread rumors.

I was going to stick a copy in every mail slot in every building.

Howard stood and leaned against the refrigerator. I lifted the binoculars to my eyes thinking I was due for a miracle, a vision, but I only saw him, his edges soft pink, yellow, and orange, and the words Frost Free near his left ear.

19

"*L*ISTEN," HOWARD SAID. "*I DON'T WANT YOU TO* do anything you don't want to do. If it makes you uncomfortable . . ."

"Lover, it was *my* idea, wasn't it? Anyway, I don't feel uncomfortable. I feel excited." I sat on the edge of the bed and pulled the second boot on. There was no zipper, just a long wrinkled stretch of softness. The boots were a delicate fawn-colored suede, and had a new, leathery smell. "Look," I said, "they almost come up over my knees."

It *had* been my own idea. Every relationship needs a change now and then, I reasoned, a charming innovation to regenerate excitement. I had seen the boots in a Madison Avenue boutique window, looking buttery and seductive. Of course I knew that I couldn't keep them. They were only borrowed, so to speak, and the importance of the cause eased any guilt about that. They cost one hundred and twenty dollars, almost my food budget for a month. And they were a little tight on me besides. The salesman was imperious, the way they are in those places. He grunted exaggerating the effort of pulling the boot over my calf. "These are made for *French* feet," he said crossly, pretending a loss of wind. I stood and walked across the pale carpet. My toes were pinched and my legs felt terribly confined, but I tried to walk with confidence. "Are they returnable?" I asked the salesman, confirming his worst fears about me. But he admitted that they were. "Just keep the soles clean," he advised, smirking, and I was sure I could do that.

Howard stood in the doorway now, watching. "Hey, kiddo, this isn't a peepshow," I said. "Come over here." And he came in slowly and knelt at the bedside. At my instruction he kissed one sueded knee and then the other.

"Shall I sit on your lap?" I asked.

"I don't know. Sure. Why not? God, those boots smell."

"Well, it's an *animal* smell." I put my face against his head, listening, waiting, measuring every response with the attention of a scientist. His hair tickled my nostrils and entered my mouth. My buttocks swelled over his thigh and I worried that my weight was too much for him, that his leg might fall asleep. I shifted slightly, making myself lighter.

Howard was passive, would not take the initiative, so I guided his hand until it found one breast and began to explore it. His mouth followed, his breath vibrating like harp strings against my skin.

Now we're getting somewhere, I thought. It wasn't going to be like those other recent nights when we retired to distant corners of the bed like dispirited boxers after a round of clinches. I felt a rush of hopefulness and joy at the first faint stirrings beneath me. It wasn't going to be difficult at all. Even the dead weight of my body wouldn't keep him down. God, I would be *impaled*.

He pushed me gently back onto the bed, and I smiled up at him with encouragement. See, it was so easy, just like old times.

We kissed and I felt him tremble. His tongue thrust into my mouth like a messenger bearing urgent news. Then it idled farther down to my breasts, to my midriff, studied my navel. I moaned and reached for him, cupping him lightly. His hands moved down and touched the boots, seemed startled, moved up and found me. Who needed boots? My thighs spilled open; I was his good, bad girl. I felt like laughing. And I felt aroused too, but not urgent. We had all night if we needed it.

But he burst immediately, a warm abrupt surprise that stopped my blood and forced my eyes open to lamplight. "Jesus," he said. "I'm sorry."

"It's all right," I said, finding my response automatically as if I had said it a thousand times before. Had those magazine doctors advised me to say it? But of course it wasn't all right. The shriveling had already begun inside me, leaving me bereft and aching. All the other disappointments and suspicions rose now and filed silently across the room.

Howard lifted himself carefully, a thin string of semen still joining us, and there was that sucking sound, like a rude remark, when our bellies parted. He leaned over and kissed my throat, making me swallow hard over the sadness there. I was willing to try again, to start from the beginning if necessary, but I knew instinctively not to hold him, not to do anything. The very air seemed to contain the tension of crisis.

"Paulie," he whispered again. "I'm sorry."

"I *said* it's all right."

"No, not that," he said. "I mean about the boot."

What was he talking about? I raised myself on one elbow.

"The boot," Howard repeated. "I got some on the boot."

"What?"

"I got it on your boot. I'll wipe it off."

"Where?" I was sitting up by then, leaning forward.

"Here. It's not a big spot. Wait a minute." He went to the bathroom and came back with a dripping washcloth.

I jumped quickly out of reach. "No, *don't*! Wait! I don't think you should use water. Maybe we can just let it dry and brush it off later."

"All right," Howard said, getting back into bed.

I lifted my booted leg closer to the lamp and examined it. Ruined.

"The stain isn't that bad," Howard said. "They'll get darker with wear—you won't even notice it." And when I didn't answer, "I *said* I was sorry, didn't I? About everything, I mean. I told you I've been tired, that I have things on my mind."

"I'll get the box," I said. "Maybe there are cleaning instructions." I was close to tears.

"Will you forget it?" Howard said. "Will you stop talking about it! You can always buy another pair."

"There are special suede cleaners," I continued, almost to myself, rubbing gently at the spot with a corner of the sheet.

"Are you going to stop it!" Howard demanded. "I don't really give a damn about those boots!" He picked up a magazine from his night table, snapped it open at random and pretended to read.

"Well, I do!" I shouted, jumping up, startled by my own encountered reflection in the dresser mirror; a wild-eyed naked cowgirl. I ran out of the bedroom, down the hallway, ruining the soles too, for good measure.

20

I love things,
their silent waiting grace.
Unbreathing, faithful things
that keep the dark
and hold.
At night,
I take a favorite to bed
and in the phosphorescent light
of dreams, I see
it stays.
Forget men,
turbulent with heat and pulse,
now full of want,
then done.

September 18, 1961

My Dear,
    Fore-warned is fore-armed. While you dally, they are
making plans. I can only wish you the best.
                    Your Anonymous Friend

AFTER THE SECOND LETTER, I BEGAN TO HAVE TROUBLE
sleeping. Staring out through the bedroom window in the
middle of the night, I wished that everyone else in the complex would wake too, that lights would go on with the easy
magic of stars in a Disney sky. I looked at Howard, who was

asleep, and I could see his eyes moving under those thin lids as he followed his dreams. It seemed that he was sleeping more as I slept less. His breathing had the droning resonance of summer insects. I leaned toward him and saw his nostrils flare with each breath. "Howard? Howard, I can't sleep."

He sighed deeply and his hands opened at his sides, as if in supplication, but he continued to sleep.

Across the city, my mother and father slept on high twin beds like sister and brother. There is always a night-light, as decorous as a firefly, burning in their hallway, so that my father can find the way to the bathroom. There is a picture of me on the dresser in their bedroom, and another of the children. My father sleeps with his socks on, even in summer. My mother keeps a handkerchief tied to the strap of her nightgown. Do they dream of each other? Was Howard dreaming of Mrs. X? I knew that if I ever fell asleep, I would have baroque dreams that would have challenged Freud, dreams that could be sold to the movies. But terror and faint stubborn hope warred for occupation of my senses and I couldn't sleep.

Nothing in my life so far prepared me for this. Maybe I had lived the wrong way, in a kind of willful innocence. Maybe I even read the wrong books. In bed again, I opened the Oscar Williams anthology and turned the pages quickly, but now even the once reliable comfort of poetry was diminished. And in all that beauty of language and cadence there were no instructions for marital emergencies.

I felt there was no one I could talk to. My mother would have said, "I told you so!" instantly turning mere suspicion into state's evidence. Judy seemed to have no experience of discord or doubt, and Sherry wasn't even married.

Howard pulled himself awake for a moment, stared at the clock, at my bedside light, at the pile of books and magazines, suitable for an invalid, balanced on my chest. "For God's sake, Paulie, go to sleep," he said, as if he believed it were a matter of choice.

This would have been the perfect time to speak to him, to pull the letters from their hiding place and present them as

documented proof. Is it true, Howard? Is it true? But what
if it wasn't true, after all? If I spoke to Howard about it, even
gently, implying disbelief, something would be forever
spoiled between us. And *I* would be the spoiler. Wasn't that
what really drove men away—the violation of loving trust?

And if it *was* true? My heart worked furiously.

Howard was *there*, beside me in our bed. That meant
something, didn't it? I lay down beside him again, rejecting
all the terrible risks, thinking it was easier in a way to be
uncertain and sleepless.

Once I complained to my mother about my insomnia. She
is old-fashioned and believes in remedies. "Drink milk,"
she urged. "Do calisthenics. Open the window."

My father, who likes to get a word in edgewise, said,
"Protein. Calcium."

But now there I was, alone in that stillness in which I had
a dog's sense of hearing, could hear beds creak, distant tele-
phones, letters whispering down mail slots on every floor. I
wondered, who wrote letters at that hour? Who was calling?
Was it true?

The dead eye of the television set faced me. If I turned it
on, perhaps I would find old movie stars carrying on business
as usual, stranded forever in time with their dated hairstyles
and clothes. There would be a comedy to distract me, and I
would laugh, taking deep breaths. I would grow sleepy, child-
sleepy, milk-warm and drifting. Maybe there would be news,
even at this hour. Wasn't it daytime in China, midnight in
California? Surely there would be bad news and the com-
mentator to intone it. Ladies and gentlemen, here is some
bad news that has just come in . . . Howard would wake, the
children would cry out in their sleep, and the old lady downstairs would bang on her ceiling with a broom.

I walked to the window again and there were other lights
on in the complex, but not many. At a party Howard and I
went to, everyone complained of being an insomniac. I had
never believed them before this. Women confessed they
hadn't slept in years. One man walked the room, repeating,
"Three hours, *three hours*," to anyone who would listen.

He had a built-in alarm system that never allowed him to sleep a minute longer. That's too bad, said the women who never sleep, but they were insincere. Another man suggested it was guilt that wouldn't let him sleep, but the insomniacs united against him. Guilty? The truly guilty sleep to escape their guilt. Ask the ones with old mothers in nursing homes. Ask the ones whose children wet their beds. Ask Howard.

Howard's breath was even and untroubled. He was sprawled in wonderful sleep.

I sat on the floor and placed myself in the half-lotus position and clasped my hands behind my head. I drew my breath in deeply and then slowly let it out, lowering my right elbow to the floor. Then the left elbow. There was a carpet smell as I lowered my head, but it wasn't unpleasant. I looked under the bed and saw one of the baby's shoes lying on its side. I crawled there to get it, and then I lay on my back, watching the changes in the box spring as Howard shifted his weight. From my position under the bed, I could see beneath the dresser and the night tables, where there were glints of paper clips and hairpins and other lost and silvery things. There was a photograph that had fallen from the frame of the large mirror, and I crawled across the floor and reached for it. It was a picture of a group of friends at a party. We were all holding cocktail glasses and cigarettes. The women were sitting upright to make their breasts seem larger and one of the men had his hand across his wife's behind. Oh, fools in photographs! We are all going to grow old. The men will have heart attacks, the women will lose the loyalty of tissue in breasts and chins.

I went to the mirror and raised my nightgown for reassurance. It was such a familiar body, the skin white and smooth, a mole under the left breast just where I remembered it. Childbirth had softened me in places, and the flesh near the waist came away too easily in my grasp. But it looked like a knowledgeable body, memories hidden away behind every curve, in every opening. Didn't that count? Was novelty everything?

I lowered my nightgown and walked into the children's

room. Jason was asleep on his youth bed, and he slept well, but I was filled with sorrow at the sight of him. The baby was in her crib, legs and arms opened, as if sleep were a lover she welcomed. The Japanese mobile over her crib trembled a warning of my invasion, and I tiptoed out and went into the kitchen.

I chose soft, quiet foods that wouldn't disturb the silence: raisins, cheese, marshmallows. I put the last marshmallow on the end of a fork and toasted it over the gas jet. I told myself I would be able to sleep better with a full stomach. I took my mother's advice and drank a glass of milk.

I thought—if we had a dog, if Jason wasn't allergic to animal dander, the dog might have been a companion when I couldn't sleep. I had a dog when I was a child. When it was a few years old, I realized with horror I had established an irrevocable relationship with it which could only end in death. From this grew the knowledge that it was true of all relationships, friendships, marriage. I began to treat the dog more casually, even cruelly sometimes, pushing him away when he jumped up to greet me. But it didn't matter. The dog died and I mourned him anyway. For a long time I kept his dish and a gnawed rubber bone.

We had a bowl of goldfish in the kitchen. There were two, one with beautiful silver overtones to his scales. There was a plant in their bowl and colored pebbles at the bottom. The fish swam as if they had a destination, around and around and around.

I shut the kitchen light and went back to the bedroom. I yawned twice, thinking, well, that's a good sign. Sleep can't be very far away and the main thing is not to panic. I climbed into bed and Howard rolled away to his side.

God, it was the silence, the large silence and the small, distant sounds. If I could speak, even shout, I knew I'd feel better. "I can't sleep and life stinks on ice," I whispered. Silence. I raised my voice slightly. "I can't sleep, and to-morrow, *today*, I won't be able to stand anything." Silence. "Howard, my mother and father didn't want me to marry you. My mother said you have bedroom eyes. My father said you were not ambitious.''

A song I hadn't heard in years came into my head. I mouthed the words soundlessly. I tried to whisper the tune, but my voice was throaty and full.

"Shh," Howard warned in his sleep.

Oh, think, think. Come up with something else. But the song was stuck there, a stupid song, one I had never really liked. I tried to exorcise it with memories of other music. So this is what I've come to, I thought, and the song left my head like a bird from a tree. Instantly other things rushed in: shopping lists, the twenty-twenty line on the eye chart, a chain letter to which I had never responded. (Do not break this chain or evil will befall your house. Continue it and long life and good health will be yours to enjoy and cherish. In eight weeks you will receive one thousand, one hundred and twenty picture postcards from all over the world.) Would I?

Learned men wear copper bracelets to ward off evil. My mother weeps over cracked mirrors while Sherry looks upward to the heavens. Hearts are still broken. They shatter in the silence of the night.

Mrs. X wandered in a one-hundred-years' sleep in Building C. If I had a lover, he would probably be asleep somewhere too. He would sleep in a Hollywood-style bed. He would talk in his sleep and his wife would wake immediately, thin-lipped, alert. In a careful whisper she would question him. "Who?" she would ask. "When? Where?"

My lover would mumble something she couldn't make out.

She would pluck gently at the hairs on his chest, in shrewd imitation of my style. "Who?" she would ask again.

In Howard's dream he was in the war again. His eyes rolled frantically and his legs braced against the sheets.

I whispered, "We're pulling out now, men."

His head swiveled.

"For Christ's sake, keep down."

His hand groped at his sides, slung a rifle.

"Aaargh," I said. "They got me. Die, you yellow bastards!"

The bed shook with his terror.

"Shhh," I said. "It's only a dream. Only a dream."

But he'll die anyway. See if he won't. In this bed perhaps, or in hers. Howard in a coffin. Howard in the earth. Goodbye.

He sighed, resigned.

I walked to the foot of the bed and stood in a narrow block of moonlight. My white nightgown was silver and my arms glowed as if they were wet. No tap-dancing moppet now, Howard. Look at this. And I grasped the hem of my gown and twirled it around my body. Then I lifted myself onto the balls of my feet and turned slowly, catching my reflection in the mirror, spectral, lovely, incredibly seductive. I dipped, arched, moved across the floor in a silent ballet. "Hey, get a load of this," and I did something marvelously intricate, unlearned. My feet moved instinctively, like small animals. Wow, I thought, and Howard flung himself onto his stomach in despair.

I was breathing hard by then and I sat in the rocking chair and thought of my lover again. His wife had given up the inquisition, but now she couldn't sleep either. She went to the window and looked bitterly at her property, at her pin oaks and hemlock, at the children's swings hung in moonlight, at telephone wire that seemed to stretch into infinity. She patted the curlers on her head and went into the next room to look at her children.

Across town, my father walked to the bathroom.

"What's the matter?" my mother asked.

"Nothing. What do you think?"

Before he came back to bed, she was plunged into sleep again.

Howard, Howard. Prices are going up. The house is on fire. My lover is dying of cancer.

My lover was dying, his wife at his side. She was wearing a hat and a coat with a fox collar. She leaned over him.

"Who?" she whispered and her fierce breath made the oxygen tent rattle like dried leaves.

"Howard, my lover is dying. No one cares, Howard." Real tears filled my eyes and rolled down my cheeks.

I climbed into bed again. Not to think, not to think. I yawned, lowering myself carefully to the pillow. Ah, almost there, I told myself in encouragement. I could tell. One minute you're awake and the next thing you're in dreamland.

I shut my eyes, thinking here comes Sandman. Here comes dreamdust. My eyes were shut tight. My hands were clenched. I heard something. There was a noise somewhere in the apartment. Maybe I was half-asleep already and only dreaming noise. Maybe I heard the goldfish splashing in their bowl. My eyes opened. What was that? What was that? Oh God.

The whole damn world slept like a baby—Howard and Mrs. X, my Anonymous Friend, the superintendent of the building, the new people on the tenth floor, old boyfriends and their wives, their mothers and fathers, their babies and dogs. All the bastards at that party were liars. They slept too, secretly, cunningly, maybe with their eyes wide open, for all I knew. They slept, gave in, went under, into the blue and perfect wonder of sleep.

21

I COULDN'T HELP THINKING, IF OUR SITUATIONS HAD been reversed, Howard would have been doing something about it, instead of mooning around, speculating, and hoping for the best. He had always been a jealous and possessive man. Sometimes he even pretended there were rivals for my love, to justify his jealousy.

But aside from inconclusive adolescent groping, there had been only one other man in my life, and that was before Howard. I tried to talk about this predecessor in one of our earlier night sessions, but Howard became gruffly non-directive, grunting out those little Rogerian "Mmmm's" and "So?'s" that I couldn't stand.

"It isn't fair," I protested finally. "After all, you were *married* before."

"Men are different," Howard said.

"What? *What?* How can you say that? I mean, even if you believe it, how can you say it?"

"Because I'm basically honest. Because this relationship is based on that honesty. I've told you absolutely everything about Renee and me, haven't I?"

Oh God, yes, indeed he had. Everything. So realistically, with such allegiance to accuracy and detail, that I began to hear it in her voice too. That insidious whine. Her voice and then his voice, and then both of them together in a rising aria of complaint and misery. The sympathy and the interest I had once felt began to wane. It was no longer an education in the tragic history of marriage. I hated the whole opera by then, the dated theme of falling out of love, those sad stage sets of furnished rooms, and the sound effects of their lives together: toilets flushing, cigarette ash falling softly, blurred radio music behind everything.

"That's the whole point," I said. "Now I'm trying to tell you about *me*."

"Men are different," Howard repeated, his voice a threatening bass accompaniment to the reasonable expression on his face.

Men are different. What was that supposed to mean? That he wasn't interested, that the subject bored him? Or that his interest was so enormous that it couldn't be controlled within the strictures of sane behavior? I opted for the latter. So be it. Nobody says that analysis, either classical or original, has to be chronological. Right? I dropped the subject and skipped back to childhood, the place that Howard liked best for me to be. With a couple of sentences I won him over again, softened that gruffness, soothed his fear. I even lied a little, inventing passages from another life, threw in scenes from books he hadn't read: a little Jane Eyre, Mrs. Wiggs, Rima. Howard moved closer and closer on the couch, hugging me, giving physical support to the lie.

Now, in the heat of my own torturous suspicions, I was ready to use that earlier man again, happy that he had been stored away unused, for a while, and could reappear—presto!—like fresh news.

But Howard didn't want to talk at all, not even about himself. For a couple of days he even had to be coaxed into the living room after dinner. He feigned fatigue, indigestion, nerves, even pretended once to be asleep. But I know his breathing. It's my private science, my specialty, so to speak.

"What's going on?" I asked. "Hey, are you terminating?" Professional jargon was always good, at least, for a laugh.

But Howard barely smiled. He seemed sorrowful and terribly remote.

The anonymous notes crackled in memory. Who was this

anonymous enemy who pretended to be my friend? If the notes were true, if there *was* a Mrs. X, why didn't Howard charmingly cover it all up the way the magazine articles say that erring husbands do? Where were the little extravagant gifts of atonement, the too-hearty demonstration of his affection, and that willingness to please?

He stood just outside the room, framed in light.

"Lie down next to me," I said.

Silence.

"Lover," I said. "Come on."

Slowly, slowly, he moved into the room and finally he heaved his sighing bulk next to mine.

I opened his shirt and stroked his chest hair. "There, isn't that better?" But it was only a rhetorical question, and no real comfort to either of us. "Well, my turn, isn't it?" I said brightly, and then began, expecting an immediate interruption. "It was a chance meeting," I said. "One of those things that happen." I paused, giving him every opportunity to protest, but he was silent.

Feeling desperate, I decided to plunge right in, giving up the romantic notion of a prelude. I had sorted things out first in my head. The man's name was Chester and I had met him in an all-night cafeteria after a big fight with my parents.

Thinking that over, it didn't sound very impressive, or even interesting. The name Chester, for instance, or the all-night cafeteria. The place had been full of loners and rejects, each one staring down at the unaesthetic arrangement of his supper. The lighting was as subtle and romantic as that in an operating room.

"His name was Steve," I said. "We met in a bookstore." I paused again, feeling very pleased with myself. Steve was a terrific name, masculine and casual. Chester sounded too much like an anti-hero.

Howard still didn't say anything.

"We went back to his place." I waited, giving him time to digest that. *His place.* It sounded wonderful, and the comparison with the back seat of a Chevy was inevitable. My own creative power under stress surprised me.

Of course Chester had really lived with his parents, a religious elderly couple who were out that particular evening at a fund-raising dinner.

But who needed them in my story? Out they went for good, taking their third-floor walk-through, their gargantuan wedding bed, their doilies, their gallery of framed sepia photographs.

Instead it was Steve and me, sprawled recklessly in his pad on a tatami mat.

But oh, that aged bed had shuddered, its springs twanging with buried memories, aroused. It *had* to be on their bed, even though Chester had a hi-riser of his own in the living room. More room, more comfort, more privacy. He sang out the reasons with every piece of conquered clothing. But I knew anyway, saw that thin spot on the crown of his head as he bent in lamplight to begin at the bottom, knew that he was really too old to live with his parents, even in those more filial days. Like a bad and vengeful dog, he would leave them our scent, the sheet creases, and the disarray. Take that and that. He was getting even with them for scenes that had happened way before my time.

And I, giving in, adding my small portion of blood, was getting even with *my* parents. Two for the price of one. And it was all so appropriate. The thing we had quarreled about that very night was my so-called wildness, that incipient sexuality they couldn't keep tied to my narrow and virginal bed. So here I was, fulfilling their lousy dreams for spite, without fulfilling any of my own. In a dry rot of agony and regret. "Hey, you're *killing* me, you bastard!" I hollered, but he kept humming or something, some tuneless murmuring sound in rhythm with his relentless motor.

"I was only a kid," I told Howard. "He was much older, more experienced." Let him use his imagination. Let him think of Cary Grant, of Jean-Pierre Aumont.

Were those Chester's baby pictures on the wall overhead? That brown-tinted baby in an ancient pram, that styleless, anxious mother, that slouch-hatted father looking like a hit man for Murder, Incorporated. And were those their footsteps and their voices coming up the stairway of the six-family Brooklyn building? Only sounds of other lives in progress, as it turned out, but they seemed to cheer Chester on in his mad, heartbanging race to finish.

"He was a schoolteacher," I told Howard, because he respected education and because it was the truth.

Howard shifted on the couch then and rubbed his leg, as if it had fallen to pins and needles under the weight of mine. Still, he didn't respond to my story. It was almost as if he hadn't heard anything I'd said. What if all my suspicions were untrue, if Howard was only having a little private crisis that he'd simply snap out of after a while? Would all this confessional stuff spring from his memory later and cause trouble between us?

"I didn't enjoy it very much," I said, covering all possibilities. "First time and everything. Fear, pain, guilt, all that jazz."

Howard scratched his leg.

"We had a little midnight supper afterward. A post-coital buffet, ha ha. We ate with our fingers, as I remember," I said, hoping to evoke an erotic vision where sex and food become interchangeable.

Actually, Chester had jumped up, restored and starving. "Hey, don't just lie there. Come on, I have to fix the bed." He gave me something; a rag, his mother's dish towel, for all I knew, and he helped me to my rocky legs.

In the kitchen he opened the refrigerator, releasing a blast of its stale icy breath, and handed things out to me. In addition to her other, maternal failings, his mother was obviously a careless housekeeper. Some of the stuff in there was petrified with age: collapsing circles of cold cuts, cream cheese crusted yellow, white bread even the Parkway pigeons would have rejected. But I ate anyway, the eating a part of the whole terrible ritual.

And Chester was manic now, a behind-patting playmate with one eye on the clock. He had done his job and had bagged a virgin in the bargain. "Wasn't that nice?" he wanted to know. I let him walk me within two blocks of my home, giving him all false information, an invented phone number and address. I called myself Molly Bloom, once my private fantasy and now a gorgeous nom de plume for his memory book.

It was very late, and the bathrobed sentries, their hysteria rehearsed, were waiting to grill me. But I stopped them dead with the cold concentration of my gaze. If *this* was what they were always so worried about, they could rest easy. Never, *ever* again. I silently pledged myself to a life of celibacy, not knowing about Howard, of course, who was still six months away in my future.

"Go to bed," I commanded, and scared and chastened, they did.

And I went to mine, feeling nauseous and sad, unable to either throw up or go to sleep. The whole terrible experience, sex and spoiled food, passed through me undigested.

Tears came to my eyes in recollection. "It was awful," I confessed to Howard, dropping my guard completely.

But Howard was like a stone, and for once I was sick of my beautiful control, my deference, the whole stupid burden of love. "What's the matter with you?" I cried. "Don't you care about me? Don't you even give a damn about my rotten, fucked-up history?"

But worse even than that, he had fallen asleep.

22

Dear Jackie Kennedy, do you ever imagine being me?
Here, aproned in America
Shutting windows after friends go home
Sifting crumbs and ashes in search of meaning.
Do you imagine childhood in a stucco house
on a Brooklyn street
and uncles in fluorescent light standing guard
on summer's nights?
Do you sleep in vaulted rooms or lie sleepless
and pretend my life?
Without horses, without a word of French or wafers
melting on your tongue?
Why should it always be you
who flies with Alice Faye to Argentina
who loves Charlotte Greenwood as a friend
who gets Don Ameche in the end?
                              November 8, 1961

My dear 19K,
    Are you blind? Deaf? They're getting away with *murder*. My heart aches for you
                              Your Anonymous Friend

THE FIRST TIME I SAW HER UP CLOSE, I FELT A TREMOR OF
recognition. You! I thought. It was a wonder I didn't say it
out loud. All the little clues I had seen through the lens of
those cheap binoculars zoomed into focus. The long hair was

dark and straight, the kind of hair that corny novelists always have fanned out across the pillows. She moved like a dancer, with a confident, but seemingly unconscious grace. And oh, I was right, she *was* slender, with a hand-spanning waist and adolescent breasts. So much, I thought, for the importance of being statuesque.

I had ridden that elevator for days, thinking that I would have to see her eventually, and that I'd know her as soon as I saw her. Even mystical illusions seem reasonable when you're feeling desperate.

Sometimes the kids were with me, riding up and down in that little box, listening to maddening elevator music, while I wondered which floor she lived on, what footsteps would be hers, and if it could possibly be true. The baby usually fell asleep. Any constant motion would do that for her; I had rocked her into unconsciousness enough times. But Jason tended to be cranky. There was nothing in this for him. I made up little games where he was the captain of the ship or the engineer of the train, and I let him push all the buttons when no one else was on. But after a while he became restless and he would whine, "I don't want to play this anymore. Why don't we get *off*?" If he was loud enough, he'd wake the baby, who added her screams to his in that tiny place, where my body seemed to absorb most of the sound.

One day we held the elevator three times for different women who had yelled from the echoing corridors, "Hold it!" But none of them was her. I knew they wouldn't be. They were too harried, too flushed with the hectic pace of their uneventful lives, to exude mystery or excite desire. They looked something like *me*. I was hoping that Mrs. X would appear ordinary too, mortal, even inferior, a testimony to Howard's temporary dementia. But I really expected her to be some kind of Superwoman, as dazzling as a movie star, as regal as a newsreel queen.

In fiction, in films, The Other Woman is an eventual loser, despite her cool beauty and her father's millions. In the end, the true heroine (me) proves she can ice-skate, or swim, or tap-dance better, and the hero is easily re-won. Done. The

Other Woman has to settle for a supporting actor or get lost. Whatever her original attraction, it has nothing to do with the true foundation of lasting relationships. It seemed to me that people who have memories of bitter, locked-bedroom quarrels, who stay up with croupy, teething babies, who accumulate dreary or ecstatic calendar days together, *stay* together. Of course statistics knock the hell out of that theory; hardly *anyone* stays together anymore. All over the city, the country, the *world*, newer, fresher, second wives share duplicate door keys with men, while those first wives, burdened with domestic experience and stretchmarks, have lonely nights, and days spent in collecting child support.

But not me. Not Howard. Whatever it was that held him, it was only ephemeral, as glancing as an attack of petit mal. It had only to do with the life of fantasy, and no one can come up to the invention of our dreams.

Mrs. X didn't look that exciting. She was very pretty, of course, if you liked that fragile, pale, dark-haired type. But the truly exotic thing about her was her newness. The thrill of the stranger: new textures, odors, tastes. I stood close enough so that the scent of her skin and clothing was discernible without effort. But I sniffed the air anyway, like a badger hound. It was a fruity, powdery smell that I knew from dressing rooms in department stores, from the insides of other women's pocketbooks.

In those movies, The Wife usually managed to be smart-looking, even if she was a madcap. I tried to remember who— Greer Garson, Deborah Kerr, all the way back to Irene Dunne. She was always full of the confidence that comes with terrific breeding. Too late for that certainly, too late to go back and adjust speech patterns, carriage, a whole life-style from which you emerge the adult everyone knows. I thought ruefully that I might have changed my slacks at least—a small stain had developed over the right thigh. And my sweater was stretched and faded. But I came quickly to my own defense. What else could I wear in the middle of my daily life, a woman with two small, stain-inflicting children? And I thought bitterly that Edith Head hadn't designed the costumes for this encounter, that there was no appropriate dress for what I was doing.

It didn't matter anyway. She never looked at me, even as I memorized her, the geography of her hairline, the circumference of her throat. Either she didn't sense my interest and my curiosity, or she didn't care. Ah, that would have been even more important to Howard than her newness—that calm, splendid indifference!

What a relief from my own unflagging concern, my too-muchness that he swore he loved and falsely claimed he needed to survive. But she never looked at the children either, not a glance at their faces, radiant with good will, at their little bodies teeming with Howard's chromosomes and mine.

Ah, Mrs. X. I wanted to say a thousand things to you. If only I had, maybe things would have turned out differently. "The jig's up," I might have said, or even a warning quote from Auden: ". . . games that call for patience, foresight, maneuver, like war, like marriage." But Andrew Marvell would probably be more her style.

Had she sent those letters to me in her own behalf, to begin unsettling things in my marriage? I could have asked for a handwriting sample or at least dusted her for Howard's fingerprints. But I kept my silence and let the violins and vibraphones of that insipid music take over, until we came to the lobby. Click click, she was walking across the floor, almost out the door, on those delicate shoes, and I hadn't said anything to her, hadn't even heard her voice.

"Miss," I said finally, rushing so fast that the stroller nearly clipped her in the heels. "Oh, miss!"

She stopped and I braked, breathless with fear and from my sudden nerve. In the end I couldn't look at her eyes, as if I believed whole carnal scenes would be reproduced there for my edification. But she was waiting and I had to say *something*. "The time?" I managed at last, squeaking the words through the rusted hinges of my jaw.

She pushed back her sleeve from a flawless wrist, and looked with a charming myopic squint at her watch. "Three o'clock,'' she said. Or maybe she said, ''Four o'clock.'' I don't know. I don't remember. She said something in that voice that was hers, and I nodded mute acknowledgment with my foolish smiling face, and then she was gone.

My powers and my blood flooded back at once. ''Oh, you dumb stupid bitch,'' I told myself. ''Oh, you imbecile, you fat *moron*!'' I knocked my head against the bell system panel over and over again. Several trusting people buzzed back to let me in. Others called suspiciously over the intercom: ''Who? Who is it? Who's there?''

Jason blinked.

I didn't even know her name.

23

"*H*OWARD," I SAID. "WE HAVE TO TALK." I HAD called him at the studio and in the background I could hear the bebopping sounds of a singing group.

"I can hardly hear you, Paulie," he said. "We're making a tape here. I shouldn't even be answering the phone. Is there anything the matter at home?"

"*Nothing!*" I shouted. Plenty. "*But we have to talk!*" Why hadn't I said it to his face at breakfast that morning, or even to his back earlier, as he lay hunched, but not sleeping, on the farthest edge of the bed. "What are you doing way over there?" I could have said. "What's going to happen?"

"I'll have to see you later," Howard said. "I can't hear a thing." In the background the singers said, "Woo, woo, woo!"

I was supposed to visit my parents that day. In the morning Howard had said, "What are you doing today?" and I had answered, "I'm having lunch with my folks. Will you be home in time for dinner?" Who had written this idiot script for us, and why were we so obediently playing it out?

He had promised to be home in time for dinner that evening. So, that's when it will be, I thought, and I was furious and I was terrified. Recently he was often late for dinner, or had it somewhere else. Oh, I didn't need Ann Landers to tell me what was happening. I didn't have to have all those lies and the notes and that sad distance between us in bed before I wised up.

I was shivering. My hands were so cold, I finally had to

128

wear gloves while I dressed the children. I looked out the window. If only it were spring. If only it were over.

I tried to play it out in my head, a little dress rehearsal in preparation for the real thing. I would tell him that I knew, that I'd known for a while. He would try to deny it at first, but I would show him the notes, recite the evidence until he confessed. He would be relieved to talk about it finally, although he hadn't wanted me to find out, to be injured in this way. It was all over anyway. It had only been a sort of fling, a madness. I knew him, didn't I? His history sometimes led him into weak moments, into bad judgment. He had been suffering too, scared to death of losing everything. But he could come out of this stronger than he had been before, wiser, more faithful, if I would only let him.

Let him!

My mother would have advised revenge, some swordplay, at least a little suspense. But I only wanted it to be done with, to be over. Reprisals were not my style.

Howard would swear on the heads of our children that there had been no real substance to their relationship, that even the *other* part had played itself out quickly, like those sparklers we used to light as children on the Fourth of July. All dazzle and then darkness. There were no mysteries. But he had to find it out the hard way. There was only *this*, the perpetual thing between us that could not be properly defined. He would make a confetti of the notes and sprinkle them over our heads like a blessing. And could I believe him?

But it would not be the simple confession and empty contrition of a man caught in the act. I would know that from his eyes, from the quality of our embrace. She had never meant anything to him and I was his great love, his one and only, and the mother of his children.

We would both weep a little in relief, and then I would decide to forgive him completely, without strings, without those little tugs of resentment and jealousy. If it was done, it was done. That was the way I was.

Oh, I wished I had said, "Come home right now, Howard. It won't hurt more than a minute, Sweetheart, and then it will be all over.'' I was really crying a little by then, wiping my tears with the leather palms of my gloves, and the baby was peering curiously into the blurred glitter of my eyes.

24

"*O*H, MY GOD," HOWARD SAID, WHEN THE CHIL-
dren and I came through the bedroom door with the uncanny
timing of a vice squad. He was throwing things into a suitcase on the bed: shirts, ties, socks, everything in a desperate,
strangled mass. The bureau drawers hung open and even
some of my own clothing was flung over the corners of furniture, or lay in small nylon puddles on the floor.

Howard had said he would be home in time for dinner.
But it was only the middle of the day and he was still supposed to be downtown at the studio. Finding him there, then,
I felt as shocked as if I had encountered a robber rummaging
through our belongings. And Howard looked just as shocked
and alarmed to be discovered.

"What?" I managed to croak, meaning of course, why?
The children, taking their miracles where they could find
them, ran to hug him. Their main love, their great tamed
beast. "Daddy!" they cried, and I felt a swell of envy for
their innocence. A father home in the middle of a weekday,
a workday, was worth far more than two on the job. How
much easier it was to be the children, I thought, who were
only at thigh level to the soap opera of adult lives. Yet everywhere, at that very moment across the city, people lay on
their therapists' couches and remembered; dragged out dusty
dramas of childhood from the attics of memory. Remembered mothers and fathers, those major villains, in ecstasy
and bitterness, in screaming battle and more ominous silence; the stuff that made them the inadequate quivering

131

grown-ups they are today. Children aren't innocent, I knew, only defenseless. And here we were, traumatizing our own, maybe ruining forever their future relationships with other fucked-up people.

Stop! I wanted to shout, but Howard might have taken it on the simplest level, thinking I meant stop packing, stop messing up the bedroom, or stop going away with Mrs. X, when I meant stop in a larger sense, as if I were talking to a projectionist showing a screening of our lives. It was time to rewind, to go back a few reels and discover all the bad places, the mistakes, and make them right before it was too late. But I was crazy—it was already too late when your husband was packing, and another woman waited in a private place and in all her private places for him. Look! Howard was kissing the children, clutching them to his chest like a soldier leaving for the front or a murderer off to the chair, as if he were being taken from them against his will. "Oh, my God," he said again, but it had the unholy ring of blasphemy.

"I thought you were going to your mother's today," he managed finally, confusing me. Somehow, *I* was in the wrong now for not being where he expected me to be.

"Wait a minute," I said. "Just wait a minute! You're the one. What do you mean, *I'm* supposed . . . Howie, you were going away like *this*?"

He looked at the children, then lowered his eyes. "I was going to call," he whispered. "Tonight. Easier for everyone."

"Easier for Benedict Arnold," I said. It was so terrible to be absolutely in the right. The sound of my own heart seemed to fill the room, a drumroll for all the action yet to come.

"Shhh," he said, but I hadn't raised my voice. I was too out of breath to shout, as if I had been running, or as if I were an invalid who couldn't afford that sudden expenditure of passion and still expect to ever get well.

"Don't think you're dealing with a fool," I said. "Oh, I've known. I've known all along!" I went to the dresser drawer in search of the evidence, those warning notes from my anonymous friend. There was so much junk in there:

bills, canceled checks, cleaning tickets, the very literature of our domestic lives, and I threw them across the bed at him, while I searched for the letters.

Howard let the papers settle in silent snow around his feet, more bad weather from his marriage. "My God," he began again in that irreverent litany. "Paulie, don't, please," he said, and by then my head ached and my vision was fuzzy from all the vying pressures of rage and sorrow, and the tears waiting just behind my eyes for the dam to be lowered.

How was it that he was begging me? And despite his agony, he was still packing. I saw one of my own brassieres caught in the tangle of his underwear, going in with the rest. How would he explain *that* to Mrs. X in their love nest? As a silly but necessary souvenir of his marriage? As a secret fetish not yet revealed to her? He seemed to be taking everything. Would he throw the children in next? But at last, the suitcase was slammed shut, and he leaned over it, palms pressing down, eyes shut, and took great labored breaths.

"Don't go," I said, recognizing with horror the words I had said so often on lazy mornings when he first drew his body heat away.

"I can't help it," Howard said. What did that mean? That wasn't what he was supposed to say. It was so difficult to concentrate. Everything interfered: the pattern of the wallpaper, the voices of the children, street noises.

"Why?" I asked then, Jason's favorite question, to which he often didn't want the answer either.

"How should I know?" Howard cried, distracted, as if he were only an innocent bystander to this mad scene, instead of the romantic lead.

"What do you mean? Howard, what are you *saying*?"

"Oh, Jesus, I don't know. I don't even know what I'm doing. I didn't plan on this, Paulie, believe me. It only happened. But I *have* to. I have to go away."

"Why? It's only in bed, isn't it? That isn't going to last. What does she do, anyway? Tell me what she *does*, what you do together."

"Paulie, what kind of a bastard do you think I am? Do

you want me to give you the details? *All right! Okay!* I can only tell you that it's wonderful, special, that I can't do without it, without her, that I can't even think about anything else, that I'm screwing up on my music, on everything.'' His voice was hoarse and broken with anguish.

The effect was worse than a physical blow. Graphic details would have been far better: words from a sex manual, the things that were done on page 48 or 49, meaning it was all only something that could be learned. And I was such a fast study, and willing.

But this meant he had an obsession, didn't it? My very own disease that had begun in the back seat of a car, with wings stretched open, in a symphony of cries, a disease that had spread and become our whole lives.

''Is it this?'' I said, gesturing toward myself. ''I tried. Mayo. Weight Watchers. The Diet of the Month. *You* can't even stop smoking for a day. I saw her, you know, with her hips, with that hair . . .'' The words bubbled out.

He rushed across the room and embraced me. ''Oh, Paulie, love, it has nothing to do . . .'' He groaned and pressed me to his shirt front with its beating heart. Then he began kissing me and tried to prop my listing body against the bedroom wall.

But I pulled away and ran to the other side of the room, to the children. ''He's going!'' I said. ''Say good-bye to your father. He's leaving us!'' I grabbed Jason's shoulder.

''Ouch!'' he complained, wrenching free.

''Stop it!'' Howard commanded. ''What are you doing?''

But I couldn't, I wouldn't. Who was he to give orders? ''Time for lunch!'' I barked, with the authority of a drill sergeant. I picked the baby up so abruptly that she screamed and then held her breath. Jason and Howard ran behind us into the kitchen.

''It's impossible,'' Howard gasped. ''Don't you know I don't want to hurt you or the children? But all of a sudden . . . everything . . . Listen, I feel as if I'm living someone else's life.''

''Hey,'' I said. ''Do you think it's a bed of roses around

here? Do you know that I haven't finished a poem in ages? Do you even care? All my energy, all my poems go into the oven, into the washing machine!"

"I care," Howard said, "I care. But this is what you wanted, isn't it?" He swept his arm at the whole familial burden: Jason, the baby rigid in her high chair, curtains, linoleum, kitchen cabinets jammed with the stuff of survival.

I was stunned. What was he talking about? We were surrounded by his mother's discards, the junk she didn't take to Florida. I hated it all. I hated her. Who had wanted any of this? Did I want that high chair, that butter smear on the wall, that little boy blinking nervously at his reflection in the toaster? Maybe I could have been an astronaut, a movie star, the prime minister of Israel.

And then I understood. He meant that I had chosen this life when I decided to keep that first pregnancy. The onus was on me then, for disappointments, for damaged dreams, for all the ugly furniture we had known and might know in the future.

"Not fair!" I shouted. "Two! It takes *two*!"

"Don't yell!" Jason said, and he put his hands over his eyes.

"I can't help myself," Howard said. "Try and understand." I thought he was going to come close again, to try and rescue himself in the crush of an embrace, and I felt all the muscles of my body tightening in union, bracing themselves against the insult of such a cruel seduction.

But he just stood there. "We have to talk," he said. "We have to make some arrangements. Paulie, be *sensible*."

The baby had roused, was banging her spoon for service on the high chair tray and I raised my voice over the din.

"We're all going to die, Howard! You're not the only one!"

He knew what I meant and he looked at me in acknowledgment. But knowing isn't everything. He went back into the bedroom for the suitcase anyway. He put on his jacket in the doorway of the kitchen and I watched him, dumb now and slack with misery. Ends of clothing hung from between the hinges of the suitcase.

"Byebye," the baby crooned, and even Jason waved, the small limp flag of a paper napkin in his hand.

"If you go, don't ever come back!" I hissed, but he was already down the hallway, hustling off to his new life, and the urgency of his footsteps broke my heart.

25

*E*VERYWHERE I LOOKED, PEOPLE WALKED ARM IN ARM, two by two. The whole awful world was a tilting ark of couples. It was something I hadn't really noticed until Howard was gone. Teenagers walked by, entangled like jungle vines. Movie stars changed partners, but managed to be paired with somebody by press time. Even my mother and father, survivors of a hundred-year marital war, were still together. Sometimes they hardly spoke to one another. As a child I was sent back and forth between them bearing secondhand questions and answers. "Daddy, Mom says do you want pot roast or chicken? Baked potatoes or mashed?" Dragging my feet, a grounded carrier pigeon for the code words of their anger.

But at night they always lay down side by side, their weight balancing the mattress, their shoes scattered in the shadows under the bed.

I thought that there ought to be an annual parade honoring the veterans of bad marriages. Battered wives and castrated husbands could ride bleeding on flower-decked floats, their spirits buoyed by ticker tape and the cheers of the crowd. There could be a marching band banging out the love songs of each generation. We celebrate everything else in this country. Why not couples, the miraculous endurance of legal coupling?

My own children had become a couple, of sorts. Before, they had often been enemies, quarreling over toys, competing for my attention, or for Howard's. But now he had left

and I had become an unreliable stranger, subject to dangerous mood changes. I was a wallflower, an outcast, a one-
legged bird staggering for balance. I certainly didn't act like
Mommy anymore, that grown-up who was to be trusted.

Sometimes I hugged them in a smothering and painful
embrace that belied mother-love, and other times I crept under the bedclothes and hid there, talking to myself and waiting for solutions in the darkness. Was I crazy? Who was to
say?

I did other suspect things: ate weird combinations of food,
stuffing myself with sweets, snacks, the junk meant to lure
the kiddies on television commercials. I even laughed at some
of the shows, when Popeye gave Bluto his comeuppance,
when cartoon cats were flattened by cartoon mice. Take that,
and that, I thought, thinking, of course, of Howard and that
woman, but reduced to infantile symbols.

"Who wants to give Mommy a big juicy kiss?" I asked,
holding my arms open.

The children stared ahead of them at the television set.

"Come on," I said. "First come, first served."

This time Jason looked up warily and he blinked, that new
habit of his. Primed by fairy tales, he knew a witch when he
saw one. He sidled closer to his baby sister on the floor.

Go ahead, Sweetheart. Drop your eyes. Get into practice
for when you grow up and screw around.

I got up, whistling courage, and went into the bedroom to
look at myself in the big mirror. Maybe I could let my hair
grow. And I could have it straightened. As soon as things
settled down around here, I was really going to go on a diet,
a sensible one this time, with eggs and fish and stuff like that
in it. I could exercise too, and set definite goals for myself;
a certain weight, certain measurements before the first signs
of spring. I began to jog in place right then, my reflected
image blurring in front of me. But my breasts bounced and
I felt a touch of vertigo.

"Whew!" I sat down on the edge of the bed, suddenly
enervated. A huge yawn rose in my throat. God, I could

hardly stay awake. But if I fell asleep then, right in the middle of the day, I'd be up all night again in that lousy silence.

The main thing was to keep myself busy until I could make plans. I picked up a magazine from the night table on my side of the bed, but there were only money-saving recipes and stories with poignant, but happy endings. Those liars.

It had been a long time coming. It was something I knew as well as my own mortality, and was just as unwilling to accept. Of course it wasn't fair. I had *children* for him, that family man. Never mind how it all began. I gave up college to become the cheerleader for a losing team. And somewhere in the confusion my own poetry had been lost.

I yawned again. Move, I told myself. Get moving before the blood freezes going upstream.

I went into the living room and switched off the television set. The children continued to look at the gray screen, following the pinpoint of light to its diminished flicker.

"Hey!" Jason said.

"Guess what?" I shouted. "We're going out!"

Annie frowned, a signal that I was too loud.

"We're going to Grandma's," I announced in a softer voice. "Hurry up and get your jackets. Jason, don't do that with your eyes, lover, okay?"

My mother said, "Well, do you hear from *h-i-m*?"

"Mother," I said, "why are you spelling? Yes, of course I've heard. You know Howard. He speaks to the children on the hour, so he won't miss a single nuance in their development. He's with *h-e-r*."

"Don't be wise, Sis," my father said. "You always were a headstrong girl. You always knew everything. Someday you'll slow down and listen to an older person."

"Yes, Dad. Thanks."

"It's not thanks we want," he said. "It's respect." He went into the bathroom and closed the door.

"Nerves," my mother said. "It goes to his prostate. We didn't need all this."

The children climbed on the plastic-covered sofa and it crackled and wheezed like Saran Wrap.

"I'll pick them up before supper," I said.

"I hope you won't let him get away with this," my mother said. "When he comes back."

"When he comes back? How do you know he'll come back?"

"Leave them alone and they'll come home, wagging their tails behind them," she sang.

My father flushed the toilet and opened the bathroom door. "Do you have a joint savings account?" he asked.

"What?"

"Do you have a joint account with him? Either/or signature cards?"

"Yes. Why?"

"She asks *why*," he said, in an aside to my mother, who only rolled her eyes heavenward.

"Because," my father said, "if you'll take my advice *this* time, you'll go down to the bank and take out your share, which, considering you've got the children, should be way more than fifty percent."

"Why should I do that?" I asked.

"Because if *you* don't, *he* will. It's a question of whoever gets down there first! He'll clean you out, finish you off."

"Howard would never do that," I said.

"Listen to her! Oh, you're a babe in the woods. Still wet behind the ears. Women like *her* aren't in it for the fun of it. It's dough they want. Gifts. Furs. The night life."

Howard and I had about twelve hundred dollars in that account. What was he talking about?

My mother shuffled up to me. "Lincoln Savings on Queens Boulevard is giving out premiums this month. Get yourself a four-slice toaster by the by or a nice electric blanket."

I edged toward the door.

"Where are you going *now*?" my father asked.

"Nowhere. I don't know. I just need time to think."

My father prepared his face to tell me what he thought about thinking, but my mother saved me. "Don't get started,

Herm,'' she said to him. ''Take it easy and you'll last longer. Put the set on for the children.''

They were already gazing dutifully at the blank screen, Jason's lids fluttering, baby Ann loving her thumb. They'll probably be blind before they're teenagers, I thought. But I took the opportunity to make my escape.

Thinking didn't really appeal that much to me, either. Hadn't I always acted best on impulse? Ask anyone. Ask Howard. Ah, back again, full circle.

I walked without destination in my parents' neighborhood. There are ways to get men back, I thought. I had just passed a newsstand, its racks loaded with women's magazines. Any one of them probably had an article listing ten surefire methods.

I had a few of my own: seduction, threats, complacent waiting. And there were the children, of course, my little aces in the hole. Howard was the most devoted father in the world and he suffered the historical guilt of all fathers since Abraham.

There was one other alternative. I could just let him go. That idea left me so breathless that I had to stop and lean against the window of a pizzeria. I shaded my eyes and looked inside. The pizzaman stared back at me, his floured hands at rest on a circle of dough. There was a telephone booth in the rear of the store. I had the number where Howard could be reached in case of an emergency. All his life he had been readied for emergencies.

I turned and looked down the street. A young couple embraced in a green car that was parked just a few feet away. That's how it all begins, I could have told them—in cars, in the mystery of the flesh.

Jason had been begun in the back seat of a Chevy. If he ever happened to ask about it though, I would lie. I would tell him it was in an oversized downy bed, canopied and draped, with gilded cupids and swans looking on. It might as well have been for the way I had felt.

I went into the pizzeria and called the number Howard had

given me. What was I going to say? Come back, nothing is forgiven? Or, good riddance to bad rubbish?

The telephone rang three times and then Howard answered. "Hello? Hello?"

Improvise, I told myself, but instead I breathed, huh, huh, huh, like an asthmatic dog. This is an obscene phone call, I thought.

"Say something," Howard commanded. "I know it's you. Is there something wrong, Paulie? Will you *answer* me?" Then, "This won't get us anywhere, you know." He sounded as kind and righteous as Perry Mason.

I hung up.

The pizzaman was still looking as I came out of the phone booth. How many women and men came there for desperate phone calls, the steam of their passion and discontent fogging the glass door? He looked disapproving, as if he knew about Howard and me and the disorder of our lives. I slipped out and went next door to a novelty shop. I'd bring something home for the children, a souvenir of this new phase of our existence. But the atmosphere was unsettling, and I chose quickly: a rubber bath toy for Annie and a wooden back-scratcher for Jason, in the shape of a hand.

Back home again, we were bravely three. The rubber fish eluded them in the tub, was defective and took water and sank. I toweled them dry before the soap could be completely rinsed off. "Bed, bed, beddy-bye," I sang. The telephone rang, and as if we had an unspoken agreement, no one answered it. Jason raked the backscratcher across the velveteen of the sofa, leaving a furrowed trail. Then he moved it against his legs, giving himself pleasure. The baby played for extra time too. She called for water and for kisses. But, finally they went off, sleep overtaking them like a highwayman.

I went into my bedroom, *our* bedroom, and stood in the quiet, in the pink bedstand light, waiting for something to happen. The telephone didn't ring again. Even the heat had been turned off for the night. All the noises of the world were remote and muted.

I walked back to the children's room and replaced covers

that had been flung off. The backscratcher was in Jason's shoe on the floor near his bed. I took it with me, idly scratching one arm and then the other. Then I took off my clothes and climbed into bed. I pulled the wooden fingers of the backscratcher over my body. Slowly, slowly, in the same gentle rhythm. I felt lulled, sleepy. If Howard was there in the room with me, I could probably seduce him, I thought. How could he resist, in that same room, in that same bed, seeing those familiar blurred images through his eyelashes as he turned to me? With the backscratcher I satisfied one place and aroused another. How could he do without me? How could this happen?

I sat up and pulled the backscratcher across my chest, and I saw the pink line of the scratch fade and then rise in the pallor of a welt. It was as if I had pierced through to the heart itself.

26

*M*R. X CAME TO THE DOOR WEARING AN APRON sprigged with violets; he held a wooden spoon in his hand. What was this? I wondered.

I was expecting a rage and anguish to match my own, some senseless, unshaven man surrounded by overturned chairs, cigarette butts, and the wreckage of his feelings. But the place was as neat as a model home. Maybe I had the wrong apartment. *He* was certainly all wrong, not just the apron or the absurd domestic symbolism of the spoon. It was *everything*. He was too slight, too short, too shy and too eager at once.

But it was Apartment 10J in Building C, the original love nest, the very scene of the crime. He probably thought I was collecting money for something. The spoonless hand was reaching toward his pocket even before I spoke.

"No, wait," I said. "I'm Howard's wife."

He just stood there. The spoon dripped something pale between us onto the carpet, but he didn't seem to notice.

Was he deaf? A moron? *"How-ard,"* I said again, slowly, with exaggerated lip movement.

"I know," he said sadly. "Yes. Won't you come in? I'm just making something." He waved the spoon and I passed down the hallway to the kitchen of the apartment where something was burning on top of the stove.

"Soup," he said, raising the flame for a moment and then shutting it. The soup frothed and sizzled over the sides of

144

the pot, and then subsided. "Would you like some?" he asked.

"Look," I said, and I sighed. "This isn't a social call. You must know that." I looked around, snooping for clues. Did they have children? Had Mrs. X left something of herself there, a sign of intended return? Why was this idiot eating soup?

"I'm hungry," he said, as if he had read my thoughts. "I haven't eaten much for a few days." The hand pouring soup into the bowl trembled. His knuckles were white.

"Well, go ahead," I said grudgingly. "I guess you'll need your strength." And even then, despairing, feeling wildly restless, I noticed that the burnt canned soup smelled *good*, that under other circumstances I would have had a bowlful myself.

If only Mr. X had been handsome, or at least *craggy*, a possible contender for his wife's affections. But he was awful, those thin defeated shoulders and the neat little paunch of cartoon husbands. Thin hair, bad teeth. He smiled at me and blew on the soup, causing a small temporary tide.

"Has she ever done this before?" I asked. "Gone off with anyone?"

He shook his head, slurped and swallowed.

I drummed my fingers on the tabletop and I was glad to see it made him nervous. "Well, are you going to *do* anything about it?"

In another room a bird began cheeping and trilling. Mr. X smiled. "I don't know what *to* do," he said. "I thought I'd just wait it out."

He was even crazier than my mother. Leave them alone and they'll come home. "You mean see if she'll lose interest and come back to *you*?" It was all I could do to keep from hooting, from pulling him up from his chair by his shirt collar. I felt like beating him up. All that misplaced anger was turning me into a bully. Who was this passive freak? If he had been different, assertive, attractive, maybe his wife wouldn't have left him in the first place. But my anger settled when I realized he could counter with similar conjectures about me. There was obviously some great shared deficiency or we wouldn't be sitting there together, deserted, would we?

It was hard to tell, sitting in the kitchen, just what she might have taken with her. Not pots and pans, I imagined. "Do you have any children?" I asked, without much hope. It was usually harder for women to make the break from kids in a situation like this.

"No," he said. "We tried for a while. There doesn't seem to be any real reason. Not medically. We've both been tested. Bunny's okay. My little fellows were sluggish under the lens, but far from dead. Sometimes these things are psychological, sometimes . . ."

"Okay, *okay*!" I said. "I don't want to know about it."

He seemed both offended and close to tears.

"Did she take her clothes with her?" I asked, in a more reasonable voice. I was the cool detective now, questioning the skittish but important witness.

"Take a look," he invited. I followed him into the bedroom. This room, I thought, this place, that *bed*. Now its surface was smooth and innocent, but it was easy to imagine the tangle of bedclothes, the haste, the heat. How could Mr. X be so calm?

He opened a closet door. There were dresses inside and my hope quickened, but he said, "She took a lot of stuff with her. I guess these are discards, more or less. Bunny is a great dresser." He said it with such obvious pride, he might have been her love-blinded father rather than her cuckolded husband.

From the corner of the room, the bird, a parakeet, eyed us nervously from his perch in a gilded cage.

Childless, I thought. A keeper of caged birds. A vain, selfish woman with clothes to spare. Spike-heeled shoes like weapons on the floor of the closet, atomizers still containing her man-trapping scent on the dresser top.

"What's her real name?" I asked.

"Bernice," he said, and for some reason I felt a small flash of happiness. Howard would find out that *nothing* is as it seems.

"Listen," I said. "Mr.—er—"

"Clark," he said, with that helpful, eager expression he'd had at the door. "Call me Clark."

He'd always be Mr. X to me. "This is going to sound terribly personal, but I think you and I can dispense with all that formality, considering our situation. I don't want to know what you do for a living. I mean, you're not rich or you wouldn't be living here. I don't want to know your life history, your sperm count, or any of that junk, okay?"

He nodded.

"The thing is, I'd like to know what kind of marriage you had. Have. It's really important."

"Average," he said promptly.

Average! What kind of marriage was that? People with average marriages were statistics, were silhouettes in insurance ads, were bloodless, passionless shadows. I wanted to know what kind of *marriage* they had. I was breathless with impatience and with the knowledge that I had to control myself.

"Mr. X," I said, through my shark's smile. "Nobody has an average marriage. You can't say that about marriage. It's a complicated relationship. Fire and ice. Passion, camaraderie, bonds of sin, love, ecstasy. It's a dangerous, even a death-defying act." I grabbed his shirt-sleeve and held it.

"Why did you call me that?" he asked.

"What? What did I call you?"

"Mr. X. That's a strange thing to call me. I told you my name is Clark."

"Okay," I roared. "*Clark. Clark Gable, Clark Kent, Superman, Mr. X.* Who cares? Tell me about your fucking marriage."

"For one thing," he said, pulling my fingers one by one from his sleeve, "we never used language like that."

"Maybe that was your problem," I said.

"Chacun à son goût," he answered.

I stamped my foot and the parakeet flapped and fluttered, scattering seed. Mr. X looked alarmed.

"All right. Forgive me," I said. "Look, I'm a little distraught right now. I love Howard, despite everything. We really have a wonderful marriage.''

He snorted.

"No, really," I said, pinching my fingers bloodless for self-control. "This is a kind of insanity and I'm hoping it will pass. Like an existential crisis? God, don't you ever read a book or go to the movies? Men *go* through things like this sometimes for no apparent reason.''

"I could imagine reasons."

"Don't be bitchy now. Please. I can't stand it. Clark?"

"What?"

"Did you write the notes?"

"What notes?" His answer was fast, seemed genuine.

"The letters I got from someone who claims to be my friend, telling about Howard and your wife."

"Why would I do that? It wouldn't have changed anything," he said. "I tend to be a fatalist," he added, smiling.

And I tended to be a murderer. But I had to control myself. "Clark?"

"What?" He was clearly growing intolerant, a parent being harried by an endlessly questioning child.

I gathered my face into an expression that might have conveyed friendship, or at least neutrality. "Maybe we could get together on this?" I said.

He decided to be coy, feeling his sudden advantage. I could tell by the artful pause, by the way he took off the apron and hung it carefully in her closet, next to the abandoned dresses. "I don't see what you mean."

"Don't you want to win her back?"

He seemed to think about it. "I guess so. Sure."

"Then maybe we could cooperate, work out some strategy between us." I wasn't exactly certain of what I had in mind. I just wanted an ally at that point, someone on my side.

A slow, sly expression crossed his features. First the eyes, opening a little wider, blinking knowledge; then the muscles of his cheeks passing the message to his mouth, which curled at the news.

I hated him then. No wonder Mrs. X had gone. She probably would have gone with anyone, with the scissors grinder if her tolerance had exhausted itself on a Tuesday when he came around, or with the superintendent of the building if he had had the imagination to match his lust, or with any of those faceless, faithless husbands who opened and closed doors in the complex a thousand times a day. Of *course* she would be willing to go off with Howard—there wasn't any mystery in that!

"Two can play the same game, you know," Mr. X said, and he winked at me.

I stared at him. It took a few minutes for his meaning to take hold. Jesus! "Thanks," I said. "Really, but my heart wouldn't be in it."

"Large women are not exactly my favorite either," he said obviously wounded.

There was a dark, brooding silence between us. "How's your health?" I asked, after a while.

"My health?"

"Yes, heart, lungs, stomach, that sort of thing."

"Why, do you want me to fake a heart attack or something?" He was incredulous.

"Of course not," I said irritably. As a matter of fact, it was exactly what I had intended.

"I'm in great shape," Mr. X said. "And I'd never pull anything like that anyway. What kind of lousy victory would it be?"

"Of course," I said. "That's not what I meant. Say, have you spoken to her since they—she—went away?"

"Yeah. On Wednesday. No, Thursday. She called to have me mail dry cleaning tickets to her, and to let me know where I'd find certain things."

"So you know where they *are*?" I moved toward him.

He stepped backward, just out of reach. "Don't get excited. Of course I know where they are. Don't you? What good does that do?"

"In a hotel? A motel? In another apartment? Where?"

"Take it easy, for Christ's sake. You really come on strong. Say, did you ever think—"

"Don't!" I screamed. "Don't you dare tell me what I did wrong! I don't want to hear it from you. We had a gorgeous marriage! The best!"

"I'll bet."

"Give me the address."

"Please go," he said. "I believe you've overstayed your welcome."

"Oh, come off it. We're in this thing together."

"I prefer to keep my silence. *Hey*, you're hurting my arm."

"I'm sorry. Listen, I blow up, but it doesn't mean anything. Ha ha. I'm just a volatile person."

"We don't have anything in common," he said.

"How can you say that?" I cried.

"If you don't leave . . ." he began.

I was desperate, but still willing to try something else: wile, even seduction, if necessary, a step-by-backward-step to our original cautious but friendlier relationship.

But he did something then, some silly, vain gesture. He passed the dresser mirror and he looked at himself, tucked in that little paunch and smiled a yellow, satisfied smile. He was humoring a madwoman, a lumbering lunatic who dared to think *she* had a chance in hell against his Bunny, that debutante, that famous great dresser. It was too much. I lunged at him, aiming for vital parts.

He yelled, "Help! Police! Help!" He yelled with operatic courage and surprising volume for such a little man.

Of course nothing happened. That was the thing about living in the city. You could act out the drama of your life without interference from strangers. No one hammered on the wall promising aid, no sirens sounded in the distance. I could have murdered him, or at least done him serious harm, and nobody would have cared. But it was too easy, and pointless, besides. My own eyes filled with tears. "Oh, be quiet," I said. "I'm not going to hurt you. I'm *heartbroken*. Can't you see? Won't you give me their address?"

He shook his head and maneuvered quickly ahead of me,

back down the hallway. "Go," he said. "Just go before I . . ."

"Before what?" I shouted. He had opened the door and my voice bounced around the walls of the corridor. Finally, there was a little action. Chains clinked at other doors. Eyes peered through the prisms of peepholes. Invisible dogs growled.

"Before what?" I bellowed, playing to the unseen but listening crowd. "Before you sic that bird on me? Oh, you little prick! What do you know about anything? With your apron and your soup and your little fellows and your average marriage!" Even empty-handed, without the address or an ally, I felt buoyed by the glory of having the last word.

But he had the last wordless gesture, the slam of that heavy door, and its resounding echo still in my pounding head and heart when I found myself back in my own apartment.

27

I DIDN'T NEED MR. X AFTER ALL; MY FAITHFUL ANONymous friend supplied the address I was looking for, only a few days later. Howard and Mrs. X were still in Queens, in a residential hotel just a bus ride away. Howard had taken the car. He needed it to get to work, especially at night, and I hardly used it myself. In one phone call he had instructed me to take taxis whenever necessary; he was going out of his way to be generous and fair.

I decided to do my dirty work on a Saturday, a time when Howard usually didn't go to the studio. When I woke that morning I felt nervous, and my nervousness took the form of fatigue. I yawned and stretched. "I can't stop yawning," I told Jason, and even as I spoke my mouth pulled wide again, and my eyes closed over weary tears. I went back to bed with my clothes on, pulling the covers up over my head. I'm too tired to go, I thought, letting one arm move slowly out. It looked thinner than it had a few hours before. I was struck by its whiteness, its frailty. I yawned again. Where was I going to find the energy to get out of bed, to walk to the bus stop, to board the bus?

Yet later I combed my hair. I took the children to the baby-sitter's apartment and I left on my mission. When I got to the street where they lived, I saw that I'd have a choice of places to wait and watch. At the corner near the bus stop there was a pharmacy, modern and lined with cosmetics and boutique items and school supplies. Somewhere behind the depths of merchandise a white-coated pharmacist peered out, hands poised on the cash register.

Then there was a luncheonette and from the street I could see the long line of the counter with its squat row of stools, the gaudy chrome of the fountain and the mammoth signs that tell you that Pepsi-Cola hits the spot. At any hour there would be at least one slouched figure on one stool, bent over inhaling the steam of coffee, and the fountain man would be slowly moving down the length of the counter with a rag. All the necessary sustenance of life was in these two places. If I became hungry or thirsty while I waited, I would have something to eat or drink at the luncheonette, and there were magazines and books to read for amusement. If I felt wounded or unbearably sad, the pharmacist would fortify me with patent drugs, and if a cinder blew into my eye, he would roll back the lid and pluck out the pain. At both places there were telephone booths and if I became lonely I could call a friend.

Next to the luncheonette there was a laundromat and then a storefront dancing school and then a beauty parlor. The corner building was an apartment hotel, a fraternal twin to the one I'd be watching across the street.

I hesitated, not sure where to begin, and I thought of the dangers involved. There was, of course, the danger of being seen, of being recognized. Don't look now, but you-know-who is spying on us from the drugstore. No, *there*, behind the Modess, don't look.

But they *wouldn't* see me. I had an omnipotent sureness of that. I had come to see, not to be seen. I had come to seek final and absolute information, to *know* what was happening. That was the real danger, that the knowledge would be intolerable, that the reality of seeing them together would be worse than all my fantasies and dreams of it. A huge yawn broke loose inside me and opened like a parachute. God, would I be able to stay awake?

Then I saw the blue car with the license number I knew by heart, with the red ribbon Howard had once tied to the antenna to help me find my way back in large parking lots. Is it possible to love a car? I hadn't missed it, yet I was stunned by the sight of it. It was parked on their side of the street, directly opposite the laundromat. I remembered that I still had the key to that car on my keyring and that I was able, if impulse inspired me, to open the door and drive away.

Sitting in that blue interior (would it still smell the same?), taking it somewhere private and then tearing at it for clues, for clues to them: ticket stubs, candy wrappers, a comb. But would there be clues to me as well, to Howard and me together? I always loved sitting beside him in that car, enclosed, cozy. Everything went by—cars, houses, streets—but we were constant in the cool blueness of our car, listening to the whoosh of landscape.

If I saw them, if they came out of the building, I would watch them enter the car and I would have to imagine the rest. For a moment I wondered why I had come at all; no one had forced me to. That cold and empty place in my bed, that absence from every room meant that he was somewhere else, in a warm place, and with her. But I had to see for myself.

I began my vigil in the pharmacy, and I listened while other women bought bath powder and decongestant and mineral oil. When it was my turn I bought a roll of film, remembering too late that Howard had taken the camera.

"Anything else?" the pharmacist asked, and I glanced around for ideas.

"Do you mind if I browse?" I asked. I wandered up and down, restlessly bringing my eyes to the window where I could see the car, at least the trunk end of it. My fingers glided over gilded clocks, over boxed soaps, and cradle gyms. And then I came to the little glass case that held the accoutrements of sex: the jellies and salves, the powders and douches. I began to tremble and I thought, perhaps I am going mad. The pharmacist was watching like a ferret from behind the fort of his apothecary jars. Did he think I'd take something?

The blue car was immobile. People walked past it: a boy carrying a sack of laundry, two girls holding hands, a man who turned suddenly and looked directly at me. My heart thumped in response, but he kept walking. When I came outside again, I held my hand palm-upward, testing for rain. The early morning had been cloudy and I had hoped for rain. Rain would have been a natural screen and an excuse to linger in doorways and in stores. But maybe they wouldn't come out at all if it was raining. And I remembered the languorous joy of rainy days in bed, leaving the warmth occasionally to bring something back: a book, a cigarette, something to eat.

I went into the luncheonette and noticed that it was lunch-time. Several people were sitting at the counter and two men behind it were making sandwiches and pouring drinks. Was I hungry? For once I wasn't sure, but I sat down and ordered a hamburger and a glass of milk. I had taken the stool closest to the door and I turned and saw that almost the whole car was visible from my seat. This was where Howard probably bought his cigarettes.

The man brought the hamburger and he smiled at me. Did I look nice to him? Did I seem like a reasonable woman, a non-spy, a victim of the circumstances? I ate the hamburger and watched the street. I thought of ordering coffee to stall for time, but I couldn't even drink the milk. I slid off the stool and walked to the magazine rack. Next to *Good House-keeping* and *Esquire*, there was a stack of those newspapers with stories about cows giving birth to human babies and of children being kept for years in closets and birdcages.

The headlines said: MAN WAKES AFTER FORTY-YEAR COMA. A photograph showed the man kissing his corsaged and smil-ing wife on the cheek at the end of her long vigil. Talk about just rewards. Talk about tenacity and devotion. Well, I cer-tainly wasn't going to stand in that place watching the seasons change, waiting forever. Would I get my just rewards anyway?

Across the street the door of their building opened, but only a man with a dachshund on a lead emerged. The man looked skyward and the dog squatted on the sidewalk. Then they went back inside. I decided it was time to move on.

The laundromat had an air of abandonment. There was a round area of lighter paint on one wall where a clock had probably been ripped off. A machine for the dispensing of detergent and bleach was plastered with out-of-order notices. Over the washers there was a sign reminding customers that this was their laundromat, to keep it clean and not to overload the machines. *Absolutely no dyeing in these machines*, it ordered. And underneath someone had written, *Drop dead, drink Clorox, eat shit*. There were year-old copies of *Time* on a splintered bench. They were filled with ancient news. All of the washers were dancing with action. Soap rose up like the foam of the tide. Pink things came to the fore, then blue, then green. In the rear of the store, four dryers were spinning furiously. Were *their* things in there? There was a cork bulletin board next to the dryers and I went over to read the notices. There was an ad for the dancing school next door, an inevitable offer of free kittens, a reward proffered for the return of a man's diamond pinky ring, and an election flyer from last November for a defeated candidate. Did I expect a notice for me from Howard? Help, I am being kept captive by desire. Was Howard himself my anonymous friend? I thought of those mad killers who leave frantic messages scrawled in blood or lipstick across their victims' walls. *Somebody! Please stop me before it's too late.* I could rush into their building and crash into their room like Wonder Woman. Maybe I'd find Howard tied to the bed, bound by stockings, writhing while she did to him the things he loved best. I looked across the street. "Come *on*," I said. "I can't stay here forever."

Next door at the dancing school, I shaded my eyes and looked through the window. It was a reception room filled with waiting parents. Some carried babies and there were children's shoes and clothing jammed into the cubbies on the walls. I almost expected to see my own mother there the way I remembered her at Miss Peel's, my private wardrobe mistress, her arms loaded with costume changes.

I went inside where I could hear the bum-diddy-bum of the piano. A baby in the reception room began to cry and his mother waved a ring of keys in his face and he cried louder. From the other room a voice said, "And *again*, and *again*," and there was a thunderburst of tapping feet.

"Is yours with Madame Dorothy?" a woman asked. I realized she was talking to me.

"Yes," I said.

She hunched forward and cupped her hand to her mouth. "What do you think of her?"

"Well, *you* know," I said.

"Yeah," she agreed, and we exchanged conspiratorial smiles.

Then a door behind us opened and a herd of leotarded little girls rushed into the room. I thought: any one of them *might* have been mine, any one of them might have been *me*, for that matter, pushed back in time. What is this urgent connection between parents and children, between husbands and wives? The little girls seemed interchangeable, with their plump buttocks, their hair straying from ribbons and clips, that chorus of high-pitched excitement. And yet each belonged to *someone*, homed to one waiting mother. I left in the chaos of reunion.

It was getting colder now, the winter sun pale and cloud-wrapped. I put my hands in my pockets and stared across the street. I was almost finished with my stations of the cross and nothing had happened. And what if it did? If I saw them would I become paralyzed, would I faint, scream for a cop, for an ambulance, for the National Guard?

I looked through the window into the beauty shop. There were several women in different stages of becoming more beautiful. They all seemed happy. The hairdresser slapped his thigh with a brush and leaned intimately over the woman in his chair. A pretty girl in a white dress swept curls of hair into a tidy hill. I wanted to go inside. I wanted to lie back and have someone wash my hair. I wanted to be happy too.

And then I looked across the street and Howard and Mrs. X came out of the building holding hands and my eyes were caught where they were joined and I forgot to look for clues, at their faces or the way they walked. They climbed into the blue car and the doors closed bang bang and the motor roared and they were gone. It was true.

28

Dear Howard,

Here's what's happened to me. I've turned into the kind of person who writes letters she doesn't intend to mail. Do you remember I told you my mother used to do that? She called it getting it off her chest. She wrote plenty of them to my father, of course, digging up ancient grievances like arrowheads, reminding him of sacrifices made and promises not kept. *Her* sacrifices, *his* promises. She wrote to cousins who had insulted her at a wedding twenty years before, and to her dead mother-in-law, who left everything of value to my father's sisters, even though he had contributed the most to her support.

So here I am writing to you, but I'm not going to bring up old injuries if I can help it. This is going to be more like those mimeographed newsletters out-of-town friends send at Christmastime to help you keep up with their lives.

Here's what's been happening to me. Everyone is offering advice. Judy and Lenny want me to start something legal against you or go into therapy. With luck I might find a therapist who practices law on the side. Lenny says my passivity only encourages your behavior.

Sherry says I got out just in time, before I lost my youth and looks. Who wants to be tied down to household drudgery when I could be having fun? She wants me to try marijuana and a comprehensive horoscope reading. She's encouraging us to move in with her. I could save on rent money and be where all the action is.

I guess you can imagine what my mother and father are saying.

The kids have been pretty good, considering the situation. Judy says it will all come out twenty years from now, with Annie jumping into bed with men old enough to be her father, and Jason having big problems with sexual identity.

I figured maybe that prophecy of asthma would come true now. Jason would start wheezing and you'd come running. But tragedy doesn't always happen when you need it the most. Instead, Jason blinks a lot, a terrific new habit, especially when he looks at me. I know you're supposed to ignore it, and I do, for a long, long time, and then I can't help myself; I say, "Stop doing that, you're driving me crazy," and of course that makes it worse.

Annie won't use the potty anymore. I guess she'll be wetting the beds of all those old guys who will symbolize you. Do you think I should go to a real shrink? Would he really be able to *shrink* me, ha ha? The truth is, I'm not losing weight, even now. I feel fragile and starved, in a way, but the mirror doesn't lie. If food is lovely when you're happy, it's pretty good when you're sad, too. I eat in bed a lot. You don't need Freud to figure *that* out.

I think word has gotten out about my new status, whatever it is. Is there an underground newspaper for flashers? Headline: PAULETTE F. HAS BEEN LEFT FLAT BY HER HUSBAND. GIVE HER A COUPLE OF QUICK LOOKS TO CHEER HER UP. Two on the subway in one week. One in the *library* the other day, I swear it. He laid himself on the shelf, a poor little bookworm between Dostoevsky and Dreiser, probably hoping someone would reach in without looking.

The super finally sent his oldest son up to fix that faucet I told him about two months ago. When the kid left he pressed my left nipple as if he was ringing a doorbell. Earl, from the market, was here too, and I think he was willing to give me a tumble, even before I could check out the order. Would he still have expected his tip?

I took the children to Pearlman for their checkup, and the old devil seemed interested too. But he's not what I need, Howard. He has nothing to do with old longings and that adolescent rise and plunge of the heart. He has no remedies for the madness of dreams or the wistful sanity of what was familiar and dear. Oh, Howard.

So. What have you been doing with yourself? *Don't answer that question.*

I just wanted you to know that I'm not sitting around waiting. I'm looking for a part-time job. I'm thinking of going back to school. And there are plenty of men in this world. *Così fan tutte*, kiddo.

Confession: When you came for the children last Sunday, I looked through the window. When I saw you cutting across 108th just like old times, I wanted to drop a water bomb on your head. On Valentine's Day, I wanted to send you a dripping calf's heart.

What do you want me to do with all that junk you've left here? This isn't a warehouse.

                                                            Paulie

29

*M*OST OF THE ADS SAID, *N*O SKILLS NEEDED, BUT when I'd get there it was a different story. Even the ones who admitted to looking for *Lite typing, good personality*, really wanted a smiling bellringer, Liberace at the keyboard of an Underwood.

I hadn't been prepared for any of this. Instead, I had been passed from my parents' arms to Howard's like the baton in a relay race, and I had given up all sorts of possible lives in the transition.

After the first day of job-hunting, I swore that I wouldn't make the same mistake with my own daughter. Girls raised on fairy tales find out fast enough that spinning straw into gold is only seasonal work. As soon as Annie was old enough to walk without holding on, I was going to send her to a trade school and get her ready for the real world.

At Alexander's there were at least thirty other applicants. Each of us held a newspaper opened to the circled ad. *On-the-job training. All departments. No experience necessary.* The woman waiting next to me told me she was a night-student at a school for beauticians, and was hoping now for an opening in cosmetics or wigs. "What about you?" she asked.

"Oh, anything," I said. But I was secretly hoping for the best, for someone to spot my latent executive or artistic abil-ity. On-the-job training, I thought. Buying might be nice. Or window design. Even a job in personnel would be better than selling. Walking through the main floor of the store that morning, I had felt depressed. People surrounded sales tables, looking like farm animals at feeding troughs. Blouses and skirts flew from hand to hand. "Watch the merchandise!" a saleswoman screamed. One woman was making her way slowly across the floor in mincing little steps, the shoes she was trying on still joined together by nylon thread. Would she make it to the mirrors before closing time? A voice on the loudspeakers announced action on the second floor, and a small herd broke loose and stampeded to the escalators.

Upstairs, in the fur department, the coats were chained to the racks. A large woman, trying on a bushy raccoon, looked like King Kong, struggling against captivity.

The beautician and I wished one another luck and went to separate cubicles to be interviewed. "Experience?" I was asked by the personnel clerk.

"None," I said cheerfully, and when she frowned, I pointed to the line in the ad that declared experience unnecessary.

"Well, it's *preferred*," she said.

Why didn't they say that? I wondered. But I only said, "I learn very fast."

"Stand up," she commanded.

I stood, and she walked around me, clucking her tongue. She was a little bowlegged thing in a polyester pants suit. "Just a minute," she said. She picked up her phone and dialed three numerals. "Mr. G. ? I think I've got one for you. Yes, now. Can you come by?"

Mr. G. seemed overjoyed to see me. He walked around me too, and I began to feel pleased and expectant. "Perfect!" he said. "Terrific!" He patted the personnel clerk's shoulder and asked me to come with him. I followed down a long corridor to a door marked *Harold Granick, Security*.

"Oh, wait a minute. Listen," I said. "I don't think . . ."

But Granick wasn't listening. "Have a seat," he said, and he began to whistle and rummage through the papers on his desk. He looked up finally, clasping his hands in front of him. "Do you have any idea of the amount of money lost each year by retailers because of shoplifting?"

I was trying to come up with a reasonable guess, but the question must have been rhetorical because he went right on.

"Do you know that important scientists are working around the clock trying to come up with a foolproof detection system?"

This time I didn't even bother trying to answer. I just sighed.

"Do you want to spend the rest of your life behind a counter in housewares? In men's underwear? Do you think there's a real future in selling?"

"Would I have to carry a gun?" I asked.

That broke him up. "A sense of humor, too!" he said. "Oh, lady, you are wonderful! Well, we don't shoot our shoplifters here at Alexander's, although that might be the ultimate solution. In fact, we don't always have them arrested either. Mostly we try to deter criminals, to intimidate them by letting them know they're being watched at all times. For instance. Say you spot someone stashing merchandise under his coat. He's still in the store so you can't accuse him of anything, right? All apprehension must take place outside the store. Your job wouldn't be accusatory or punitive, mind you. In fact, you're the *good* guy. Like Pat O'Brien, you give him one more chance to go straight. What you would do is go up and ask if he'd like a salesperson to help him with that blanket or ski jacket or whatever. Do you get it? You're perfectly pleasant, but he knows you're on to him. You give him a chance to get out of it, to say, no thanks, I've changed my mind, and to drop the goods. Let him go to Korvettes or Mays if he still wants to steal. Let him go to Bloomingdale's if he's got class.

"You look nice, you have a nice sweet face. No uniform, no walkie-talkie, no gun, ha ha. But you look, well . . . *formidable*. And there'll be a real guard within yelling distance all the time."

"I don't know," I said.

"Are you worried about the discount?" he asked. "This is a democracy, Sweetheart. The same as for sales personnel: twenty percent on personal purchases, ten on everything else. And variety! You'll be in shoes, in jewelry, in appliances, in haberdashery! Just give it a try. I think you're going to love it."

* * *

Granick started me out in the basement. He said I could work my way up, and then he laughed and punched me on the arm. He introduced me to a couple of saleswomen and to the security men in the area who demonstrated some simple hand signals that would bring them running. "Keep your eyes open," Granick said. "That's the main thing."

It was interesting for a while, from a sociological point of view. There were the men and women who seemed very poor, sifting through tables and racks for real bargains. And the rich ones, with Gucci bags and shoes, who had gone underground to satisfy the hunting instinct. Teenage girls in dressing rooms struggled with their mothers for power, and small children lay scattered on the floor, felled by boredom.

Which ones are the real crooks? I wondered. The rich women, who spend almost all their time shopping and become easily prone to that occupational disease—kleptomania? Or the truly deprived, who reason that they must take what will never come to them legally in this life? I could have been Margaret Mead out in the bush, observing the rituals of survival. I saw all the little imperfections of physicality and dress: bald spots and birthmarks, errant slipstraps and run-down shoes. *Everyone* looked innocent to me, made vulnerable by close observation. Maybe the real crooks were in inventory, I decided, juggling the books.

But according to Granick, there were shoplifters everywhere. They were walking out right under our very noses, with jewelry stuffed into special interior pockets, with small appliances plugged into every orifice. I wandered through the aisles, watching.

Finally I saw my first one. I gasped. He certainly didn't look very professional. He took a radio and jammed it right into the front of his coat. It wasn't even done surreptitiously; he just shoved it in until it was out of sight. His chest bulged a little and I wondered why he hadn't settled for a smaller, less conspicuous model. Maybe this was only a setup, devised by Granick, to test me.

I walked toward the man at a casual pace, but my heart was knocking. "Hi!" I said. "Do you need any help?"

He looked me over coolly. "No," he said.

"Well, I thought you might like a salesman to help you with that radio."

"What radio?" he said, staring me down.

Had I really seen a radio? Now I wasn't sure. There were so many people, so much noise. Even if I had heard the one o'clock news coming through his coat buttons then, I would still have been in doubt. "I thought you needed help," I said. "I must have made a mistake." I smiled and backed away.

Later I saw a woman go into the dressing rooms. She wore a loose coat and she carried several dresses on hangers. In a while she came out and the coat wasn't loose anymore. In fact she appeared to be pregnant, at least eight months gone, and her hands were under her belly, securing it. I walked behind her, trying to come up with the right opening. Are you hoping for a boy or girl? I might have said. Or maybe I could have offered myself as a midwife to deliver her of those dresses. This was my big chance, I knew that. I had let the man get away with the radio, but I could redeem myself this time. I followed her up to the main floor. She kept going, with a determined waddle, toward the doors. When she was twenty feet from freedom, I cleared my throat and extended my arm. *Hold it!* I thought, but I didn't say anything. Maybe she *needed* those dresses. And who was *I* to question the convenience of a sudden pregnancy? Let them sic security guards on the *real* thieves, the ones who steal other women's husbands.

She went out through the doors and I watched her go, watched her disappear into the anonymous safety of the crowded street.

"I'm turning in my badge," I told Granick later, back in his office. "I just don't have the heart for it."

"I hate to see you go," he said sadly. "You looked like a natural."

We shook hands and I was unemployed again.

30

*A*DVICE CAME ON WINGS. *IT SEEMED THAT EVERYONE* wanted to get in on this act. In other circumstances I would have spurned them all and continued as I was, a confident self-starter. But things hadn't gone well for me, to say the least, and I began looking to my advisers for guidance.

Judy and Lenny had suggested a lawyer or a psychotherapist for marriage counseling. I knew I wasn't ready for legal action yet; I was still too involved in affairs of the heart. And a marriage counselor didn't seem like such a brilliant idea either. I was only half a marriage myself. The partner who had behaved so erratically, the one who needed treatment, would be absent. How would that look? And what good would it do me anyway?

But Judy insisted that it would do me a great deal of good, that she and Lenny had been helped once through a crisis of their own. I was surprised to hear her admit to having problems requiring outside assistance. The Millers had always seemed so smug as they went smoothly along on their pilgrimage through life. This is how (they said) to do things: to have a baby, to raise it right, to read a lease, to get the most for your money.

They had had hard times anyway, had sailed through rough waters, as Judy put it. I didn't find the nautical reference unreasonable. And if they had foundered on that raging sea of matrimony, Howard and I had definitely capsized. Help! I wanted to shout. Woman overboard!

But Lenny, in that way he has of switching metaphors,

said that counseling had proved *educational*, that it had given them *tenure* in their marriage. And of course they knew a good man for me to see.

I resisted at first, worried about money and about my own doubts picked up from those years spent with a nonbeliever. But finally I agreed to go.

During the bus ride there, I rehearsed my defenses along with a list of grievances. I thought that Dr. C. would probably be a sinister non-directive Austrian or a mad Sid Caesar German. I invented snappy rejoinders for his leading remarks. A lip-reader sitting opposite me would have had a treat, but at least the doctor would find me prepared and maybe even challenging.

When I got there, I saw that he looked ordinary and approachable, a man in his late fifties wearing eyeglasses and a wedding band. There was a faint familiar odor of cigarettes and after-shave in the room that stirred unsolicited feelings in my chest. I sat down on the other side of the desk ready to win him over. I smiled a brilliant smile, crossed my legs in a sweeping courtroom gesture, and then burst into a storm of bitter weeping.

This obviously didn't seem so remarkable to him. With a fluid gesture, he moved a box of Kleenex in front of me, the first of its lot popped into position. I pulled it out and continued to weep in big gulping noises and without a word of explanation. I laid my head on the desk and even dampened a corner of the blotter. It may have been put there for that very purpose, for all I knew. Dr. C. sat through it quietly, a patient and blurry reminder that I'd have to get down to business eventually.

As soon as I could stop crying, I told him everything, starting at the beginning with the dance at N.Y.U., with Howard's music and that first sight of him knocking me senseless. I told about my pregnancy and our decision to get married, about how terrific things were between us despite that shaky start, about the deep commitment I believed we'd had; and all those intimate details recalled in my own voice in my own rhetoric, finally brought on another onslaught of tears. Would we both be drowned?

But no, I grew calm again and finished that abridged, but accurate, account of Howard and me. I punctuated it with little anecdotes and funny asides, but Dr. C. hardly smiled. I guessed he didn't have much of a sense of humor. I blew my nose for the finale and then I sat back exhausted but ready for the diagnosis and prescription.

But it seemed I hadn't gone back far enough to suit Dr. C. What about *before* that? he wanted to know.

"Oh, that's all irrelevant," I said. It was *now* that was giving me trouble, it was *Howard.*

"We'll get to that," Dr. C. said, "when we get to that."

"There isn't time," I insisted. "This is an emergency, a crisis."

But Dr. C. wanted to call all the shots himself, and he said that I was being manipulative. *Me!* He took out a notebook and wrote something in it. I tilted my head trying to follow his scrawl. Black marks against me, I thought, just like in school. Behind him the wall of diplomas looked down sternly, announcing his authority.

Was I frequently depressed like this?

Did I know that my tears were really a cover-up for suppressed rage?

Did I often make inappropriate jokes?

Had I always been a little overweight?

"Tell me about your mother and father," he said.

If it was mothers and fathers he wanted, I would tell him about Howard's instead. I could give him enough stuff to fill a *thousand* little spiral notebooks, enough to make him the star of the next Viennese conference.

"But Howard isn't my patient," Dr. C. said in an unbearably gentle voice. "You are."

Patient! How had I become that? Just a few minutes off the street, and only looking for a little professional advice. Howard was the one, I explained, a husband and father running off in the middle of his life, risking everything for the sake of mere sexual impulse. *Howard* was the one, for God's sake, with his Oedipal hangups, with his little depressions, with his hypochondria, his fear of death, his weird history.

"But he's the man you chose, isn't he?" Dr. C. said, and we sat in the silence that followed like two figures in a wax tableau.

I could see that if it was up to Dr. C., he and I would be in for a lifelong relationship. But that wasn't what I needed now. I was *bleeding*, and I wanted tourniquets and splints for my wounded spirits, not that painful interminable probing for splinters.

"We cannot treat the symptoms," Dr. C. said, "without uncovering the causes."

"Thanks anyway," I said, standing up, all the crumpled Kleenex falling like blossoms at my feet.

31

We are all living these lives,
four-generation novels
that are plotless
except for birth and death.
Halfway through we're bored,
we skip pages.
Truth plus fiction
make the best story,
so we lie and invent passion.
Dozing, we dream
a new dream
with tough symbols,
without heroes.
We wake, our breath
drugged with ink,
our heads mobbed
with characters
found in subways
and offices.
The dustcover promised more.

December 30, 1961

WE SAT AROUND LIKE CHILDREN WITH NOTHING TO DO. IT
was raining and the shades were drawn against any available
light. Sherry's boyfriend Spence passed the joint to me after
inhaling so deeply it was a wonder he didn't hyperventilate.

He smiled or did something resembling a smile, his eyes still bugged out from the effort of drawing in smoke.

I smiled back and took the joint between my thumb and forefinger the way the others had done. I inhaled cautiously and was grateful that I didn't choke or sputter on the smoke. I was definitely the new girl in town, but I still didn't have to seem inexperienced or inept. The thing was to swallow it, Sherry had said, and keep it down as long as I could. I wished she wouldn't make such a fuss and give me so many instructions. I wondered why some people automatically become leaders in this world and are constantly indoctrinating others into their way of life. Before this, Howard and I were always just a step behind Judy and Lenny Miller, following them into marriage, into parenthood, into a mass-housing existence, according to easy directions. Now we were a first among our friends, a separated couple, but no one seemed to find us inspirational. As far as I knew, their marriages were all still intact.

And here was Sherry, saying *this* is the life, four individuals, no one subservient to anyone else, each doing his or her own thing on a rainy Sunday afternoon. Only this wasn't actually my thing. It was hers.

Howard had smoked marijuana, had once promised to bring some home for us to try together, and never did. Did he use it now with Mrs. X for heightened pleasure?

I was hoping it would have the promised effect as quickly as possible, so that I could enjoy the camaraderie and the glorious freewheeling mood that Sherry was always raving about. Instead I was so burdened by sadness that I could hardly sit up straight. Of course the furniture had something to do with that too. But where were those terrific flashes of insight, that new intensity of vision? Bring on the fireworks, the dancing girls.

It reminded me of those gloomy Monopoly games we had played as children on inconclusive Sundays, when there was nothing else to do. The thin lopsided cigarette we passed among us might as well have been a pair of dice or that pink and yellow money we once exchanged for hours without ever tipping the balance of power. I knew I wasn't being fair. A few lousy puffs and I was making judgments.

Spence, Sherry's current live-in companion, was a writer. His typewriter stood uncovered on the corner table with a page of typescript still wound in the roller, in mute testimony to what he did. But we didn't need mute or subtle clues. Spence liked to talk about it. Sherry had told him that I was a writer too, and I had made all those silly and nervous disclaimers: "No. *Not really.* Only a few poems," putting him into a position of benevolent superiority. I could send him some of my poems for a critique, if I liked, he said. He had a wonderful facility for editing other people's work. He would *be* an editor, in fact, if it weren't so draining of his own creative powers.

At least I didn't fall all the way into the trap. I didn't ask where I could read his work, or what he was working on now, or any of those leading questions to which I didn't want the answers.

Spence took a letter from his pocket and passed it to me. The others had obviously seen it before. It was from a well-known novelist and critic and it said, yes, Spence was indeed a promising and original writer, and that it certainly wouldn't be easy for someone whose work was so oblique and personal to find a reading audience, but the critic had admired him and remained sorry that he couldn't be of any practical help at this time. The letter was soft with age and handling and was reinforced at the creases with mending tape.

I tried to assess Spence's age, but it was hard to do in the shadowed room. He was older, I suspected, than that boyish haircut and those youthful clothes implied.

The other man was a friend of Spence's from childhood. I think they were cousins or pretended to be. There appeared to be old rivalry between them that had never been resolved. The cousin or friend, Richard, sat cross-legged on the daybed, most of the pillows propped behind him. There wasn't a comfortable seat in the room. The daybed was open and was so deep and wide that we sank in at awkward angles. If I wanted my feet to touch the floor I would have to sit at the very edge, but then my back would have been unsupported. We all sat or slouched or lay there anyway. Even Sherry's cats, two fat, altered males, moved restlessly among us, trying to find comfortable places for themselves. The only chair that looked decent was piled with books and papers that might have been manuscripts. I was afraid to ask that they be moved, certain that merely mentioning them would invite a reading.

It was so dreary and dim. I leaned across Richard to light the lamp, but it was like a flashlight with a weak battery, and its pale halo hardly penetrated the gloom. Sherry probably had nothing larger than a forty-watt bulb in the whole place.

There was a kind of expectant silence in the room and I wondered if everyone else was as conscious of it as I was, and if they were desperately trying to think of things to say too. They didn't seem to be. Richard passed the joint to Sherry and then studied his fingernails. Sherry inhaled and shut her eyes as if to enclose herself in some private ecstasy. Were they feeling it already? Even the cats seemed to be in a dreaming languor that looked enviable.

Howard had once said that there weren't any real hallucinations with marijuana, but there were new revelations in ordinary experience. Colors were purer, for instance. And he was able to hear unexpected things in music, to separate sounds in a wonderful sharpening of the senses.

The colors in Sherry's room were drab and refused to reveal anything. Green. Brown. It could be some deficiency in myself, I knew, some genetic failure that wouldn't allow me to go beyond concrete experience into another dimension of perception. Maybe it was this very lack in me that Howard recognized, that he could no longer endure. Willingness was simply not enough. Yet he had never brought the stuff home to share with me, had never given me a chance to sharpen my senses.

I wished there were two or three joints going around at once. It took so long between turns, another inevitable comparison with Monopoly. Any effect it might have would probably wear off between drags. So far I didn't feel anything.

Was it real, undiluted McCoy? Spence had assured us it was, using all that new street language that made me feel like a foreign tourist: nickel bag and Panama Red and hash. The wisest thing, I decided, was to keep quiet and smile a lot, even though we were equal partners in this, had all chipped in for it.

"How are you doing, Paulie?" Sherry asked, and I just smiled again. Anything I might say would probably be all wrong, would be anachronistic. My head was stuffed with words left over from the forties. Did anyone still say, "I feel groovy," or "I feel copacetic"? I wasn't going to take any chances. And I still didn't feel anything anyway. I looked at the others, trying to detect visible changes.

"Do you remember," Richard said, "when my father took us on that overnight to Lake George?"

"Oh, man," Spence said. "Don't bring that up now. I'm just starting to feel mellow."

Mellow? Wasn't that an oldie too?

"How're *you* making out?" he said to me.

"Fine," I said. "Just fine." I felt thirsty though. Was that the beginning, the first sign? No one else said anything about being thirsty. I wondered if it was only the egg and anchovy sandwich I had had for lunch.

"Yeah, well," Richard said, and then lapsed into silence. I hated the silence with its obvious need to be filled with conversation. And my stomach was starting to make those bubbling and growling noises. Could everyone tell they were coming from me? I wished they'd play the radio or sing to drown out my stomach, and so I could test my sense of hearing for increased sharpness.

"I once went to Lake George," I said.

Richard giggled. "Was that your *stomach*?"

"I don't think so," I said. "Was it yours?" I asked Sherry.

"I am so stoned," she said. Why hadn't *I* thought of saying that? "What I like best . . ." she began.

What? What did she like best? She never finished and no one else seemed to care. Somehow I knew that it would be irregular for me to ask. There are so many unwritten rules that keep changing with every phase of our lives. Once my parents had whispered in their bedroom. Other girls had whispered near the lockers in school. Downtown now, Howard whispered across pillows to Mrs. X. Who made up all the rules anyway?

I guessed that I was supposed to be thinking about what *I* liked best myself. They were all clearly thinking about *something*. Their postures were so relaxed, as if the daybed had grown even softer to accomodate their new suppleness. Richard, a small man, seemed to disappear into the pillows.

Maybe it was my weight. Maybe marijuana was like medicine, and you needed more if you weighed more. Hell, even Monopoly would be better than this, I thought, this lying around with others and still being so miserably alone.

Sherry switched off the lamp. The joint was so tiny I had to hold it between my fingernails. I wondered how you put it out, and I imagined one of us having to swallow it, like evidence. And what if the place really was raided? *Queens mother of two caught in dope raid.* Go directly to jail. Do not pass Go.

Richard stuck a toothpick into the underside of the joint. He sucked out the last of the smoke and then he opened it into an ashtray. So that's how it was done. Spence had lit another one and it was coming to me. Maybe this one would be a little stronger. Or maybe my virginal bloodstream just had to be broken in. I lay full-length on my edge of the daybed, and folded my arms across my chest.

"You look dead, Paulie," Sherry said, and she laughed. I did too.

"Don't bring Lake George up again," Spence said. "I'm finished with all that."

"Boardwalk," I said.

"There's no boardwalk at Lake George," Sherry said. "You must be thinking of Coney Island or Atlantic City." She lay down too, her leg against mine, and she took my hand. "Don't be sad," she said.

"I hate that word," Spence said. "It's a little brown sack of sadness. I never use it in my work. I use sorrowful, dejected, downcast, depressed, melancholy. But I never use sad.''

' "I have to go home,'' I said, without moving. "The children. Supper.''

"This was bad stuff, Spence,'' Richard said. "It didn't do much for me.''

"That's *your* problem,'' Spence said. "I feel good. I feel high.''

Were they going to take a vote? I sat up and moved across the bed. "Excuse me,'' I said to Spence, whose legs were in my way. I climbed over him and found the floor. I went to the bathroom, opened the toilet and sat down. The basin was a mess, all yellow stains and chips. Underneath was a cats' litter box, filled with some pungent green crap. I urinated, listening carefully, expecting some terrific and edifying crescendo of sound, but it was only a modest, uneven trickle. I went back into the other room. "Well, I have to be going now.''

"We were just getting started,'' Sherry said. "But if you have to . . . We'll do it again real soon. Okay?''

"Copacetic,'' I said.

32

"*P*UT YOUR CLOTHES ON THE HOOK BEHIND THE screen, dear," the instructor said, squinting through cigar smoke. "See if the last girl left the hanger in there."

I stepped behind the screen and I wondered about that last girl. I liked the anonymous reference. It seemed best to be unidentified in a situation like this. Then I wondered if my silhouette would show through as I undressed. The screen was made of some flimsy material, and I thought of old movie musicals where Betty Grable would take off her clothes behind the dressing room screen and fling out gorgeous undergarments while she spoke to Cesar Romero on the other side. A kind of innocent sexuality we all fell for.

I didn't fling anything. The other girl had taken the hanger, and the hook was only a crooked nail. Instead I laid my things neatly on a folding chair, the way I did when I went to the doctor.

But there was no clinician waiting on the other side with charts and scale and stethoscope. I could hear the sounds of chairs scraping and easels being moved into position, and the voices of men and women.

The robe I had bought for the occasion looked all wrong now, in this last moment before my debut. Chenille, in a natural beige color, it had seemed practical and workaday in the store, but now I knew it had the air of someone's bedroom about it, an intimacy not to be shared with all those strangers on the other side. I didn't want to come out. What if they all whistled and shouted? Take it off, take it off, cried

177

the boys in the rear. I could hear the stripper's entry music, a drumroll and a screaming trumpet. Oh, if Howard could see me now!

I came out slowly, peering around the screen first, curling my toes against the possibility of splinters from the wooden floor. No one cheered. No one whistled. There was a dusty little platform with a backless stool on it. An electric heater glowed on one side. The students and I looked at one another, me dropping my eyes first. Most of them were young, boys and girls almost neutered by their uniforms of paint-stained jeans and workshirts.

There were a couple of slightly older people, one man and one woman who had positioned themselves on the outer corner of the group, like chaperons. I thought of my own mother and father and felt a thrill of deception. I had told them it was office work, part-time.

Everyone was busy arranging large newsprint pads, making last adjustments to the angle of easels. The instructor's name was Jim. "Okay," he said, with an offhand gesture to me, and I stepped to the platform and disrobed in one continuous movement. Done! It was really me, naked in front of all these strangers. I had done it once as a child too, at a birthday party in a hot, noisy room. Nothing but a party hat and ruffled anklets. My mother had run after me with a throw rug, screaming as if I were on fire. It was a story Howard loved.

The room had grown very quiet. The rustling of papers had stopped. Jim looked me over, narrowing his eyes in what I took to be professional approval. "We'll start with a few standing poses," he said. "We'll do fast ones. Five minutes." He held up a stopwatch. Then he faced the students and said something to them about working with bold, rapid strokes, about trying to capture the action of the pose and not concentrating on anatomical detail.

The heater blazed near my legs, but the rest of me was frozen. Oh God, my nipples would get hard, the way they always did when I was cold. I stood, bending one knee slightly, curving one arm until my hand found my hip and rested there. Was it all right? Did it look like a normal pose? Or did I look like some lunatic waiting for a bus, who had forgotten to wear any clothes? I had prepared myself like a bride for this: shaved my legs with Howard's old razor, scraped the dry skin off my feet with pumice, and clipped my toenails straight across. But I hoped I didn't *look* prepared in that way. I wanted them to think of me casually as they would think of any other model, or not to think of me at all. Sherry had gotten me this job, through an artist friend. I said I had experience, never specifying what kind. It paid well and the hours were flexible.

The charcoal scratched like whispers around the room. I could hear my own breath. Would they be able to detect my runaway heartbeat, that frog-pulse in my throat? I thought of the pictures Jason had begun to draw, those lovely, sexless stick people who dwarfed trees and buildings. I imagined my torso as a child's drawing of a face, a bearded face with a single nostril and the bovine eyes of breasts.

My leg was killing me, it was full of pins and needles. It had to be more than five minutes already. I wished I had worn my watch. But that would have looked strange, like a man wearing just his socks, or the socks and mask combination of those men in blue movies. Why didn't the women wear masks?

"Five minutes. Change!" Jim said, and I shifted position, resting my weight on the other leg, wondering idly what I'd do if I were menstruating. Were you supposed to go out there with that little telltale firecracker string sticking out? And what did male models do about erections? Did they have to think deadly thoughts to control them? I was sure all the wrong thoughts would occur to me. Perversely, I would think of sizzling sex goddesses throwing themselves into wildly erotic positions. Thank God I didn't have to worry about *that*, too.

Jesus, this was hard work, work for the head in assembling distraction against what the body was doing, and work for those poor undisciplined muscles that cramped and ached even in these so-called "easy" poses. And it seemed to go on forever.

"Break!" the instructor said, and I put on my robe, feeling shy, even more conscious of this as a private act than when I removed it. Some eyes still followed me. The man in the back looked pensive and sad, his hand poised on the edge of his pad. I wondered what I was supposed to do now. Were there rules of protocol to be followed? Was I supposed to slip back behind the screen and wait to be summoned? That seemed so lonely. It would be as if I were being punished for naughty behavior, for that birthday party striptease.

Instead I strolled among the easels to see what they had made of me. One or two of the drawings seemed remarkably good. There was a strong sense of life, of movement. The worst of them belonged to the sad-eyed man in the rear. I could see he had no aptitude for this. Despite the instructor's early warning, he had used small careful lines. His drawings didn't look like me at all, they didn't look like anything human. Not those legs stuffed like Christmas stockings, not those bull's-eye breasts. He had tried to cover up by adding details: veins and shadows and creases that appeared only as smudges or strange tattoos. I could see that he was terribly embarrassed, so I moved to the next easel quickly and without comment.

By the end of the session I was exhausted, but I was surprised to realize that my own embarrassment had dissipated. What was a body among bodies? No one had been lewd or suggestive. It was not anything like those awful dreams where you find yourself on a busy street without a stitch, without a voice. It was only a job, like other jobs.

One student, a young girl, came up shyly after I was dressed, and thanked me. I was the most interesting model she had worked with that semester: the others had been stingily endowed, had the fleshless angles of a Giacometti. But I was worthy of Lachaise, she told me, and I had a natural ability to assume affecting poses.

I felt proud. And pleased. Did you hear that, Howard? I had come out again in the world, and so far nothing too bad had happened to me. Jim removed his cigar and nodded. "See you on Friday," he said.

I was going to emerge even further. One of these days I would register at a Poetry Workshop at the New School. I would join a gym and slim down. I could do anything.

Only at home again, among the artifacts of my real life, did that buoyant feeling of success begin to vanish.

33

*T*WO MEN CAME INTO MY LIFE THROUGH MY MODELING job. For a while I thought there might even be three, including the instructor Jim, but his interest in me stayed aesthetic and not sensual. He sucked on his cigar and called me dear, and I could imagine him referring to me as the "last girl" to the model who would follow. I didn't mind, though. There was always Nathan and Douglas.

Nathan was the man in the back row who couldn't draw. He was a physician, an ear, nose, and throat specialist who professed a profound love for the human body. He wanted to express this in ways that were not clinical. He was in love with anatomy outside the books and off the charts.

We went for coffee together after class, and for a while his melancholy eyes intrigued me. I've always been a sucker for eyes like his. He came to class Wednesday, his day off, when all his colleagues were out on the golf courses or home with their families. Didn't he have a family? Yes, of course: a wife, two sons, a housekeeper, a brace of spaniels. Jim gave Nathan special attention, tried to get him to *see* the bone and cartilage and muscle beneath the skin, to understand the perspective of form next to form. Jim played a spotlight on me, moving from one area to another, pointing at, but not quite touching my breasts, which were *tilted*, my neck, which was *columnar*, and my belly with its maternal slope. I thought of "The Anatomy Lesson" by Evan Connell, and I wished they would keep their distance.

Nothing helped. Nathan's drawings continued to be flat

and distorted. Was that how he perceived me? Did he think anyone could walk on those poor boneless legs that could never have supported the gargantuan torso he drew? Poor Nathan. It wasn't that his wife didn't understand him, but that he didn't understand the nature of form. Or that he couldn't interpret it artistically. "I had hoped I could *learn* to do this," he said once. "But I guess there are some things that can't be taught."

"You're getting better, I think," I said, which wasn't true, but Nathan smiled, obviously touched by my attempt.

In a few weeks he began to reveal his intentions. He wanted to go to bed with me, he said, to make love to the body he already loved in his awareness, his sensibility. It was the only other creative idea that had occurred to him. We were sitting in a neighborhood luncheonette drinking coffee. Nathan shredded paper napkins until there was a small snowbank in front of him.

Well, a proposition! Did you hear that, Howard? A perfectly decent man, an educated, sensitive man who knew the mysteries of the eustachian tubes and the semicircular canal, wanted to go to bed with *me*!

But there was no answering rise of passion in my own body. Nathan wasn't a bad-looking man, those nice eyes, and what seemed to be a trim, reasonable body. Would there be an antiseptic smell? Could an ear man do a safe abortion if necessary? Why didn't I feel anything? All this time had passed, in which he had gained courage, had moved his chair and easel closer and closer to the front of the room, until I was afraid he might simply tear off his own clothes, jump on the platform and join me in the embrace of Rodin's "Kiss."

I supposed I could work something up, given better circumstances and more time. This uneasy conversation in a booth, back to back with a group of bumping, squealing teenagers, could hardly pass for foreplay. I had been without sex for a while and I wondered now if something Sherry had once quoted was really true: "Use it or lose it." Would I dry up, become a sealed impenetrable wall? I could have asked Nathan; he *was* a medical man. But it didn't seem appropriate.

Nathan, finished with the napkins, began on a book of matches. "I'd like to go to bed with you, Paulette," he said. "I'm not in a position for courtship, but I respect you, you must know that." Did men still say such things? "And I hope you'll value my candor." The matches were torn out one by one, and laid like accident victims across the table. I remembered that a boy I knew in high school would carefully tear open the bottoms of two paper matches into four strips each, to simulate arms and legs. One match would be placed on top of the other in an ashtray and then set afire. The strips would burn and curl, entwining the two match "people" into carnal position. Well, here was my chance if I wanted it. Here was unlicensed lust.

"Nathan, I'll have to think about it," I said. "It's not you," I added quickly. "You're sweet and I *do* value your candor. It's just that I've been through a bad time recently. It's hard for me to assess my feelings." Whatever that meant. I hardly felt *anything*, only a free-floating anxiety and a desire just to get through each day. But Nathan accepted it, at least for the time being. His nervous fingers found my own and squeezed them.

Douglas never said anything that direct. After a few days in the classroom, he began to stand out among the other young men wearing tight, faded jeans. He was taller for one thing, and he wore cowboy boots, which I found oddly appealing as if he were a small boy in costume. He had actually come from the West, from Montana where his family still lived on a ranch. He had come to New York to make his fortune through his "gift." At least that's what his teachers in Billings had called his facility to reproduce artistically what he saw in life. There was no genuine interpretation, no vision of himself and his own experience brought to his art. Of course he was a thousand times better than Nathan. But that wasn't very difficult. I felt anyone could be better than Nathan. Douglas's drawings *almost* resembled me, except they were idealized in the style of those ads that said, DRAW ME! AND WIN A FREE ART SCHOLARSHIP!

I reasoned that it was only his youth, even though other young people in the class had done serious and exciting work.

Douglas was quite beautiful, with dark golden curls and a wonderful smile. Once, when he laughed, I noticed that there wasn't any silver in his mouth. He didn't even have any cavities! He wore a braided leather wrist band and something on a long silver chain around his neck.

Douglas didn't proposition me. We walked in the park near the school and we held hands like adolescents, swinging them between us. He spoke earnestly about himself, using all the romantic language he had ever heard connected with art. It was mostly anachronistic: he was hoping to rent a *garret*, and he was eager to *suffer* for his work. Douglas had graduated from high school and then spent a year "looking for himself" in the West, and then two more in the Navy, before he came to New York. He confessed that he hardly ever read books, they made his eyes ache, but once he had read somewhere that art was long and life was short and he had been intensely moved. He was crazy about Rembrandt and Michelangelo, he said, but he seldom went to museums. I thought how much he would have liked *La Bohème*. I wondered vaguely if he was a homosexual.

Not so, he had been in love with a girl named Bobbi Lynn since childhood. She had married his best friend while he was in the Navy, although she was still very much in love with Douglas. He believed he could send for her with a night letter, and she would drop everything and come.

Douglas walked like a cowboy, a crooked, long-legged gait that I found amusing. He said, finally, that I had a terrific body. Rembrandt would have loved it too. He said the drawings he did in class were hardly representative of his work, of his true ability. Some day I could come up to his room after class if I wanted to look at his other things, at his paintings. He didn't mention etchings, but I thought I knew his meaning.

34

Dear Howard,

I have gotten laid. It looks really strange written down like this, as if I'm a linoleum rug or a carpet. But it's hard to think of another way of saying it. Making love is something else, and having sex sounds awkward, like something ordered in a restaurant. I'll have the sex, what will you have? What I want to say is, it was not an act of vengeance, no biblical eye for an eye. I did it just to do it, and now it's done. I won't give you the details except to say my mother is wrong, all cats are *not* gray in the dark.

Yesterday I couldn't open a jar of peanut butter. It was one of those you grip and turn to open. There were other things we could have had for lunch, but the sandwich bread was spread on the plates, waiting for the peanut butter; the kids were sitting there like two truck drivers at a road stop, ready to eat and then roll. I tapped the lid with a table knife until it was dented all around, but not even slightly looser. I knocked it on the edge of the sink, chipping the enamel in two more places. The damn thing was sealed shut.

Get some bologna instead, I told myself. There were eggs, cheese, other things. I could have gone downstairs to the super. You know how he opens rusted drainpipes with just a dirty look. If I stepped out into the hallway and waited a few minutes, *somebody's* husband, *some* man, would have shown up by and by. A flip of the fists

186

and then done! But I wanted to do it myself, that was the important thing. I'll show him, I said to myself. I say that a lot lately. What kind of world is this where women have to have secretarial skills and wait for men to open jars of peanut butter?

I ran the jar under hot water, even though it wasn't stuck because of anything congealed. I knew it wouldn't help even as I did it. Mighty Joe Young must be working for Skippy these days, tightening lids. I tried biting it, but there was no place to get a good grip. Teeth marks next to the knife dents. The kids were whining by then. I wedged the jar between my knees, turning myself into a human vise. I imagined all of us found a hundred years later, by anthropologists of the next civilization: Jason, a small resigned skeleton in a striped polo shirt, his skull resting on the plate where the bread had been, and Annie's bones loose in the high chair where she had once fitted so plumply, and myself with teeth clenched from the effort of turning this lid, and the jar itself a receptacle of mysterious dust.

Finally I went to your toolbox in the hall closet and took a wrench, the heavy one that bends my wrist when I lift it. I went for the jar of peanut butter as if it were an enemy, an invader of our unprotected household. The wrench was a murder weapon. I lifted it over my head and brought it down so hard that the glass shattered and fell in a musical rain to the floor. The baby, catching on, banged out a wild tattoo on her high chair tray, and Jason took two plates and crashed them together like cymbals. *Bam! Pow! Smash!* Let everyone be warned!

Later, Judy told me that there is a little gadget for opening tightly closed jars and bottles. I bought one at the five and ten. It is called Un-Screw.

Paulie

35

I DECIDED ON DOUGLAS, ALTHOUGH IT MIGHT HAVE BEEN Nathan almost as easily. But he was a married man, after all. Could I be both homewrecker and wrecked home at the same time? It seemed too complicated. And where would Nathan and I have gone together? My apartment was out and he had a wife waiting at home. To his office, then. I saw it all. It would have to be on a Sunday or a Wednesday when he had no hours, when you couldn't find a doctor in all of New York even if you were dying. But I'd have one all to myself. Could you do it in such a sterile atmosphere? Would the roll-paper on the examining table shred? I imagined my feet conveniently arranged in stirrups while Nathan scrubbed up, but then I remembered that Nathan was an *ear* man; he would never have that kind of equipment. I wondered idly if I'd have performed miracles for his art. If he could have followed with his own hands those shapes he worshiped, would he have become Leonardo? The truth was I could not imagine it at all, even with a man who loved the human body that much.

My cowboy would be easier. He had his own room, no visible attachments. His parents and sisters and ex–girl friend were all far away in mythical Montana, a state I could not even place on the map inside my head. Nathan did seem more sensual than Douglas, but I was willing to settle for the relative simplicity of plain lust. How wise I was becoming, refining the differences between passion and sensuality.

We went directly from class. Creeping up the long staircase to his room in an East Village brownstone, I had an irrational fear of being seen. By whom? This was the way it probably was for Sherry in her chosen life, following fragrant young men up stairways to strange rooms, new events. It might have been less extraordinary for me too, if I had never known Howard.

The place was a mess, which made the seduction seem more spontaneous. Wouldn't a man *prepare* in some way, at least by making the bed in the morning before he left, or by gathering up the clutter of magazines and glasses and ashtrays? Douglas made vague apologies for the disorder, but I thought he had probably never noticed before that he lived this way.

What next? We had had so many long talks about his work, about his family back in Montana, about his ambitions and his dreams. I thought we would start from there, with some sympathetic conversation for starters. Or maybe we could get a little high to ease things. There was bound to be some marijuana in all this rubble. Or he could offer me a drink? Were there clean glasses?

But there was hardly time for cocktails or conjecture. Douglas was on me in an instant. I was still breathless from all those stairs and I couldn't understand his urgency. He had seen my body so many times before. I should have been ripping off *his* clothes instead. But Douglas managed everything himself.

The bed looked as if it had already been loved in. We flung ourselves down on old wrinkles and twisted blankets. He looked even younger now undressed, more innocent, not a shadow of experience on his body. Briefly, shockingly, I thought of *them*, of Howard and Mrs. X. Could she appreciate his body without having witnessed its changes? And then my attention went to Douglas, who clamored for it with his crazy heartbeat, his invading tongue, with his broncobusting thrusts, who was finished before I could think, and then lay winded on my breast. "Whew!" Douglas said. It was only the excitement, he explained, the first time and all. But was it good for me anyway? he wanted to know. We were still fastened like match people. The next time was going to be better, he promised.

I didn't know he had meant it to be so soon. In a little while and with hardly any effort, he was ready again, but I was not. I was determined not to be cheated again. *My* turn, I thought. I pushed aside the medal that hung from Douglas's neck chain. It had dug its impression into my chest the first time around. I embraced him, teeth set for success, eyes shut for fantasy. And I conjured up everything I could possibly use, rummaged through ideas like a madwoman, like a thief looking through jewelry for the real thing. Why wasn't this enough, damn it—this panting little blond god, getting set to thunder inside me again, his kisses so urgent and sweet, his breath as fresh as my children's? I didn't know. Why did I need old erotic images, movie stars, other people's husbands, fantasies of private acts in public places? Oh God, wasn't *anything* going to work? And Douglas was riding now at the head of the posse, banging his way into the underbrush. Wait for me! I wanted to shout. And before it was too late, I let Howard in, lifted my own hips with new energy, holding that kid in a bearhold. It was all confused. Douglas was whimpering and I was holding him, holding Howard, who also watched jealously from the window, from the foot of the bed, who opened his mouth over mine to hold back the cries.

36

Dear Howard,

You always said that you didn't believe in anything but yourself, remember? But I could tell that you were superstitious anyway. You knocked on wood discreetly *under* the table, and you avoided ladders and spilling salt. So I thought you might be interested in the results of my horoscope reading.

I know I was just as much a skeptic, that I used to call them "horrorscopes" behind Sherry's back. But after all these years of resistance, I've finally let her chart mine for me. Maybe sometimes you have to open your mind to other possibilities outside yourself. I'll be honest with you, I was disappointed at first. The lingo sounded absurd, all that rising and all those houses. I was hoping there'd be tall, handsome strangers in the offing, or long voyages and even mysterious letters. (Although you'd think I'd had enough of *those*.)

Sherry said that I was a romantic, that I should have gone to a gypsy tea-leaf reader instead. Astrology was a *science*, for God's sake, not a game. Oh, I said, I thought that was *astronomy*, I always get them mixed up. She was insulted and for a few minutes she was petulant. What was the use of trying to deal with such a pigheaded, know-it-all nonbeliever?

I swore that I was sorry and begged her to give me another chance. I had tried almost everything else already. For weeks I played solitaire, saying to myself, if

191

this one comes out, it means Howard is on his way back. Then, saying, that one didn't count, it was only a warm-up. If I won the next time, you were really coming home. I kept losing so I changed my strategy and I decided if it *didn't* come out, that would be a sign of my changing destiny. But later I found the ten of hearts under the mattress in the baby's crib. How could I help but feel suspicious, sardonic?

The daily horoscope in the newspaper looked like a fake. It was too impersonal, intended for too many people at once. How could it be that all Capricorns were destined for lousy travel conditions on the same day? My father, the super's wife, Mamie Eisenhower, Dr. Pearlman, Beverly in L.A.; if they all decided to get on a jet plane together, would it go down in a minute like a kamikaze Zero?

I weighed myself at the drugstore a few times, just to get those little printed fortunes that come with your weight. But they were as enigmatic as fortune cookies, and didn't seem like reliable predictions at all. Things like: *Success comes from within*, or: *Friendship is the key to many doors*. And the scale is way off, besides.

"I'm ready," I told Sherry. "What's going on?"

But it wasn't to be that fast or that easy. It wasn't enough for Sherry to know just the date and place of my birth. She had to know the exact time too. I couldn't find my birth certificate, so I had to ask my mother, and you can guess what *that* was like. She wanted to know what I needed it for: a passport, a divorce? Well, what-ever it was, it was my funeral. Then her face lit up with revived memories. There I was again, that pushy, over-sized fetus, trying to gain the world through the eye of her cervix. Oh the torture, the blood!

But it was worth it in the end. I mean my listening and waiting for the information. 3:32 A.M. That's when I was born. In the middle of the night, in the middle of a snowstorm, maybe the worst one in the history of New York. They couldn't get a taxi, of course, and the snow came up to their knees. When her water broke, it formed icicles under her dress.

Ma, I wanted to say, forget it, I was *there*, remember? And I *know* that you're born in someone else's agony and die in your own. But finally, I was able to rush off to Sherry with the necessary facts, and she went to work on them. I sat there and watched while she consulted books and charts and drew diagrams. She kept making little sounds like "ummm" and "ahh!"—sounds of discovery and surprise. By that time I was impatient. "What *is* it?" I asked, but she quieted me with a wave of her hand and kept scribbling and mumbling.

I went for a walk and when I came back Sherry was nodding and smiling as if she had the best news in the world for me. Well, I said to myself, if astrology is good enough for kings and horseplayers, it's good enough for me.

It was a very involved report, pages really, dealing with almost every aspect of my life. But I'll give you only the highlights. The main reason things have been so bad for me, and between us, is because my progressed Venus was in direct opposition to Pluto. But things are definitely going to change. What I mean is, this is going to be a propitious time for me, for creative endeavor, for financial investments, for sound health. And yes, Howard, even for love. Definitely for love. It looks as if I'm heading for some wonderful months ahead. My sun is trining Uranus. I know that sounds like mumbo jumbo to you, but you Scorpios are like that, always feeling superior to your environment.

I'll tell you something else, Howard. Sherry says that you and Mrs. X aren't exactly a match made in heaven either. Of course she didn't have specific data to go on, but Sherry would bet anything that Mrs. X is a two-faced Gemini with the sun rising in her second house, and I can go along with that. Gemini and Scorpio—forget it!

So I'm due for some splendid luck and you're heading for a fall. Someone else might be vindictive and overjoyed with the prospect of revenge, but you know how I am. Do you remember how I even used to muster up sympathy for you and Renee?

I went home that night, feeling hopeful and lighthearted. When I got to the nineteenth floor, the couple next door, our warriors, were waiting for the elevator. They were all dressed up. She wore an evening gown and a corsage. He was wearing one of those dinner jackets made of cut-velvet upholstery. He was snapping his fingers and moving his hips in time to a bossa nova playing in the elevator as the doors closed behind them. Good sign, I said to myself. The lion shall lie down with the lamb, or at least they'll go out dancing.

I felt so elated that I sat down in the kitchen with a fresh sheet of paper and a newly sharpened pencil. There's probably a poem in all this, I thought, in that aura of celebration. And all those lovely astrological words—cusp, constellium. But I couldn't write anything. I suppose it was the elation. Elation and depression, they can both burn you up in a flame of feeling. But I don't care. There are good days ahead, Howard, and it's only a matter of time.

If you're still skeptical, go out on some clear night and look up at the skies, at those dizzying galaxies of planets and stars. Or better still, to the Hayden Planetarium and hear that voice like God's in the darkness naming the parts of the universe, and see how superior and sure of yourself you feel then.

Aquarius

37

*J*ASON AND ANN WERE CRAZY ABOUT DOUGLAS, EVEN though he referred to them as "the boy" and "the girl," as if they were kids in a Tarzan movie, two rudimentary creatures, as yet undefined and unnamed. Douglas called me Babe, a strangely pleasing word that combined toughness with innocence, and implied a playful familiarity. We *were* playful together. Douglas's youthfulness was largely responsible for that. Not that I wasn't still young myself. I only had a few years and a few pounds on him. But experience had imposed gravity. I was a householder, a mother, a lapsed wife, while Douglas was only himself, free to be frivolous if he felt like it. He initiated pillow fights, and body assaults with shaving cream and Reddi-Wip that became sexual encounters without even a transitional pause. When he was serious, or tried to be, I felt maternally indulgent, a little condescending, and yet inevitably aroused.

He was so sweet. When he came to our apartment, he often insisted on cooking for us, on making grilled cheese sandwiches, his "specialty," that were weighted with grease and overflowing with the cheese that glued them to the plates. He made up games, the dangerous, thrilling games of an older, fearless child, offering his own body as a playground.

"Watch out! Somebody's going to get hurt!" I'd say, and it was usually him, coming up bruised but flushed with triumph. The children, as easily faithless as I, climbed his back as they had climbed Howard's, pulled Douglas's ears and hair, and rode the snorting and rearing horse he became for them for what seemed like hours. To wall-neighbors, we must have sounded like an ordinary family just having a boisterous good time.

But we weren't like a real family at all. There weren't any of those terrible complexities of mood, of power struggle and ambition that seem built into marriage. We were more like Tarzan and Jane ourselves, intelligent savages in a primitive jungle existence, a day-by-day pursuit of survival and pleasure.

Douglas's disposition was as regular as a pulsebeat; he never seemed restless or bored. What's more, he had terrific physical endurance. In bed he was invariably ready. We limited our lovemaking to his apartment, because I dreaded the complications of his being discovered by the children one morning in their Daddy's "place." Although I day-dreamed often about *Howard* discovering us and becoming wild with jealousy and remorse. He would certainly have envied Douglas's sexual stamina and would have felt threatened. As for me, it was reassuring in that time of crisis. See, I could have said, it's *me* who's responsible for all this activity, *me* who's the inspiration for this animal lust. Still, I wasn't absolutely sure. Douglas could be carrying around erections the way other young men carry wallet condoms, in optimistic anticipation of meeting *someone* to use them on.

I never spent the whole night with him, just fell into short recuperative dozes between rounds, from which I'd be awakened, punch-drunk, but game, by his busy hands, his curious mouth, and by the reckless insistence of his penis, hammering for entry at all my doors. He was always hard *before* foreplay. Foreplay was obviously a concession to me as WOMAN, that awesome being whom God, in His infinite wisdom, had made different.

Douglas hadn't been illuminated by Freud yet, and he didn't appear to be burdened by castration fears or Oedipal guilt, those famous softening agents. He could simply *think* himself erect, or get that way somehow in the ephemeral passage of dreams. "Babe?" He whispered it in a voice that was tentative and belied his desire.

"You're going to burn yourself out," I whispered back once, but that was only good for laughs. He was as reliable as an Eveready battery, as persistent as a drill.

Yet there was a thoughtful and old-fashioned aspect to Douglas, an honorableness that made him gallant. He always took me home, rousing from post-coital stupor to get dressed, buttoning himself up wrong like a thick-fingered, sleepy child. And he'd see me right to the door.

Later he'd send little notes, often written in verse, that congratulated me on my charms and celebrated his own happiness. They had a commercial quality, like those greeting cards that aim for aesthetic distinction by using several dots after each line, Thinking of you ....Loving you .... Keeping warm by the glow of memory ....The notes reminded me of his drawings, and yet I knew he was sincere, and I was touched.

Douglas phoned between visits too, his voice husky with intimacy. At those times he was youthful as well, wanting to gloat, to recount the activities of the day before in a kind of code or double-talk that couldn't be understood by any possible interceptor. Sometimes, I could hardly understand him myself. He'd ask after the "twins," and for a moment I'd be confused, thinking he was referring to the children, when it was really my breasts he meant, those "twin peaks of Paradise" that showed up with such frequency in his poems of praise.

In that melange of nicknames and endearments, Jason called Douglas Doggie. It was more than just an infantile mispronunciation. Jason, like most children, could be surprisingly accurate, and I suppose Douglas was a kind of animal to him and Annie, a labile one that could change with ease from a prancing pony to a cuddly, tail-wagging dog.

When Douglas visited on Saturday, they never confused him with Howard, who would arrive on Sunday. Howard, even in absentia, was still *Daddy*, that title earned through history and permanently installed in memory.

I wished the children would give Howard some of the hints

I was dying to drop myself. Or that *someone* would. Where was *his* anonymous friend?

  My dear,

    Watch out for Paulette and Douglas of Art and Life.

But the neighbors minded their own business for once. And the kids wouldn't confuse the two men, wouldn't call Howard accidentally by Douglas's name, even in the wild excitement of play.

Still, they could squeal on me, couldn't they?—could tell about dear Doggie, our constant new companion. Howard might think I'd decided to overlook Jason's allergies and brought home a pet.

I began to speak more pointedly about Douglas to Jason, in that careful diction usually reserved for teaching birds to talk. I said that Douglas was *Mommy's friend.* Let Jason try *that* on Howard. Mommy's friend makes us grilled cheese. Mommy's friend can draw all the cartoons on TV. Mommy's friend is like Captain Marvel in bed.

I waited for a sign, for some of that unfair, insufferable outrage I knew Howard was capable of. He had a lot of experts behind him and much of literature. Men did it, women only had fantasies about doing it. If women *did* do it though, they paid dearly in the final pages. People ostracized them, they poisoned themselves with torturously slow-working stuff, or they ended up under onrushing trains.

But Howard remained obstinately silent.

Douglas was the one who was jealous. He said it just about killed him to think I'd had a "sacred" relationship with someone else and that the boy and the girl were the products of that relationship. He imagined other men staring at me in luncheonettes, at bus stops. He couldn't blame them, but still it bothered him. It bothered him too that I was posing in the nude, although he knew that there was nothing lascivious on *my* part. Some of the creeps in class might forget themselves though, might forget we were all there for art's sake. His possessiveness annoyed and amused me at the same time. It was silly, but silliness seemed to be a suitable antidote to grief and rage. I needed breathless high-school romance, Archie struggling with Reggie over Veronica.

Nathan had dropped out of class, and I felt relieved about that. His relentless yearning gaze had become as terrible to me as his drawings. Now I imagined him regretting his losses elsewhere, his sighs echoing in the dim, waxy corridors of other people's ears.

One afternoon, when the lesson ended, I felt chilled. It was a damp, miserable day and even when I was dressed, I still felt naked, cold and vulnerable. The studio began to look unfamiliar to me, even alien. What was I doing there, anyway?

Douglas and I went to his apartment where he tried to warm me with his breath, with his own radiant heat. But the feeling persisted, expanded further into thought. What was I doing *here*, with this kid, letting him do these things to me?

I kept shivering, my teeth rattling, hoping I was just coming down with something, while Douglas tried desperately to restore me. He tried in the same ways I used to restore Howard, to warm *his* spirit, to kindle love, and I was moved by his efforts. And I was grateful to be the beneficiary for a change, the one admired, nurtured, resuscitated.

"Oh, Babe," Douglas said, and even when I lay numbly under him, Sleeping Beauty kayoed by spells, no part of his body rejected me, not even for a moment.

"It's all right," I said at last, kissed back to life. "It's all right," I kept saying, knowing that it wasn't, but knowing too that there was no sin in taking what you really needed.

38

In this kitchen
where supper steams,
the broth and bones
breathe heat.
Now the late sun
throws hoops of light
across the tiles.
And you,
waiting for food,
are food yourself.
The bones of
my desire.

February 1, 1962

THEN THE CHILDREN AND I REALLY DID BECOME ILL THE
way pining princesses do in fairy tales. But the sickness in
our case was actually viral, not spiritual. We coughed and
wheezed and ran escalating temperatures. I guessed this was
the moment I had been waiting for; a chance to use the children. It didn't seem terribly unfair or even crafty. Fate itself
was on my side. The kids were really *sick*. Feverish and
listless, they slept in the afternoon and woke with burning
skin and hoarse weeping. They even called for Howard themselves—those croaking cries of "Daddy, Daddy," that would
have swayed the harshest judge, so I called him at the studio
and pleaded their case. Of course he said he would come.

I felt awful myself, but the illness seemed to stimulate the brain, even as it slowed down the body. I couldn't stop thinking, going over past transgressions and triumphs, forcing life into a doubtful future. When I fell into restless dozes, my thoughts conveniently projected themselves into dreams, and twice I woke suddenly, certain that Howard had said my name and that I had answered him.

But it was quiet in the apartment; only the raspy breath of the children and the complaining rattle of rising heat.

Howard was coming and I had everything worked out in my fevered head. I would tell him that we were moving to New Mexico or Arizona. I had picked two places so distant in miles, so alien to our own geography, that he would be stunned. And the children were going with me, that was the main thing. If he didn't like it, he could grieve. It was his turn. Despite that big display of sorrow and regret, he hadn't done any real grieving. Or if he had, he still had Mrs. X for easy, instant comfort.

Now his lamentations would have to come airmail or in long-distance phone calls, diffused and filtered by the remoteness of separation. About how he missed us, about how he couldn't help himself, it was as if he had lost his senses, and how he didn't want to do anything to hurt us.

"Oh, bullshit," I said aloud, and I looked at the clock. It was only three, but it was late winter, and there was already a gloomy foreshadowing of evening. Howard had said he'd get there as quickly as he could, that he would come straight from the studio as soon as he could get away. I was still so sleepy and my hands and feet were terribly cold. They were too far from the hot center of my being to get any natural warmth. I shivered and climbed into bed again, tucking my hands into my armpits, letting my feet search out shelter under the blankets. I squinted and looked at the clock again. Five more minutes, I told myself, and then I'll get up and do something. Open some windows. The whole place stank of illness and confinement. I sniffed my hands undercover and they smelled of Vicks, but so did everything. A little refreshing catnap and then I'd get up and bathe. Feel cooler. Scented powder. And maybe he'd stay for supper. The children would beg him to, I could count on that. I'd make something good. Five minutes more.

Then I was awake and I saw that the clock had moved forward when I wasn't looking. The room was dark. Maybe Howard had been there and left! And where were the kids? "Jason? Annie?"

Silence. And then I heard giggling from another room. At least they were safe for the moment, hadn't gone into aspirin bottles or drunk Lysol the minute my back was turned. I wished they'd come and get into bed with me; a little warmth and I could tell them my plans.

"Jason? Bring Mommy water."

"*Please*. Say please," Jason reminded me, his face rising from the foot of the bed.

"Oh yes, I forgot. Please. And where's your sister?"

But he was gone. Then his voice, shrill and wily, came from the bathroom. "I can't *reach*."

"Use the stool, Jasie. Get a big glass and let the water run for a long time so it's very cold." What an effort! It was as if I had shouted across the Alps. I fell back and waited in the racket of my own breathing.

The baby pulled at my feet and her hands were small fires.

"Hi," I said brightly. "Mommy is sick."

"Sick," she echoed, turning my toe hard between her fingers.

"Oh God, don't do that, Annie. Just stay here and keep me company."

But she waddled away.

Then Jason was next to me, so close that his eyes looking into mine blended into one huge relentless swimming eye. His hand shot up, holding a large brimming glass. Before I could protect myself, some of the water spilled, rode down the neck of my nightgown in an agonizing icy stream. Jesus!

I pulled myself up and took the glass from his trembling grasp into my own. It had been so cold on my neck and chest, but seemed lukewarm and medicinal when I drank it. I wondered if it came from the goldfish bowl and the idea made me laugh.

"Say thank you," Jason warned me, unamused, and he and the glass disappeared at once.

It's all that fucking television, I thought. We wouldn't even have a set in Arizona or New Mexico. We'd live close to nature in some primitive but comfortable way. Howard would be sorry, that was the main thing.

And I remembered again that he was coming. It was after five—he should have been there already. The children were murmuring together in the living room. Battery-operated toys buzzed across the floor. Well, if they were playing, they had to be feeling better. That was something. Though, guiltily, I had hoped they would at least *appear* sick enough to arouse their father's concern. The way they had been only yesterday and during the night. But it was no use. Their voices rose now in high spirit, in that familiar convalescent frenzy. In another hour they'd be jumping on the beds, fighting with one another, full of the ebullience of survival.

Get up, I told myself. I felt dizzy and had to hold on to the bedpost until the room settled. Then over to the mirror in two lumbering steps, and there I was. I looked crazy, that was my first impression. Like those deranged, rag-wrapped women who mutter to themselves in subway passages. Tangled hair, swollen features, and the wild gleam of fever could do that. And the nightgown I had been wearing had been chosen for comfort, not seduction; for its worn, pilled fabric, its billowing shapelessness that wouldn't adhere to tender skin. A comb, I thought. Soap.

But his key was in the door, just like old times. Why didn't he ring, damn him? He didn't live here anymore.

I had no time at all. I was still struggling with the inverted sleeves of my bathrobe when he and the children came into the bedroom together. Howard was out of breath. "Traffic," he said. "Stuck on the bridge. God, you look terrible."

"I'm better," I said severely. It was one thing to play on his sympathy with sick children. It was another to use myself. "I fell asleep, that's all." I pulled a comb as far as it would go through my hair, and then they followed me into the kitchen. "I'll make us some dinner," I said, lurching toward the sink.

"Don't bother . . . I can't stay . . ." Howard began, but I waved my hand and said, "*We* have to eat anyway, don't we?"

The children were going full-force by then, one attached to each of his hands, pulling him in different directions, overflowing with accumulated news, with deferred affection. They showed him everything: the kittens romping on their rumpled and stained pajamas, the junk food I'd been buying just to keep peace, the coloring books we had defiled with red skies and orange clouds. It was "Daddy, Daddy, Daddy," in what seemed like one continuous head-bursting shriek.

I took out silverware and dishes, cans and boxes. I rummaged in the refrigerator and found four large apples I had meant to cut into a pie on one of those fleeting, martyred days. I searched in a drawer now for the corer. I would bake the apples for Howard. It was such an old favorite of his. They would come from the oven, warm and fragrant and rosy. In my fevered dream at the stove, I thought of them as flesh, those perfect apples, that still life with hope.

Of course he protested. He couldn't stay. He wasn't that hungry. I didn't look well. On and on. But I was so busy I only heard fragments of his alibis. I chopped and sliced and pared and mashed, and set things steaming and sizzling on the stove and in the oven. I put up the baked apples and a frozen slab of pork that would take hours and hours to cook. Potatoes. Soup. Thinking, Food is love, and resisting a sudden impulse to sing.

In the other room, the children were still in command, and I could hear the reassuring sounds of old family games, of bear-wrestling and "Mountain," where they climbed their father's legs to reach the peak pleasure of his embrace. He was knocking them out. They wouldn't stay awake long enough for anything. And when they fell asleep he would go.

Howard came back into the kitchen with the children following right behind him. He leaned against the refrigerator and the smoke from his cigarette veiled his eyes. "Do you need anything?" he asked. "Any money?"

"I've been working," I said. "Part-time."

"You don't have to do that. There's enough."

"I *want* to do it. It's a way to get out of here, to meet people."

"What are you doing?" he asked.

I found that I couldn't meet his eyes. "Posing," I said, turning my back as I spoke.

"What? Posing? Do you mean modeling?"

"Yes. For art students. At the Art Students' League."

It took a moment for the idea to register. "Do you mean in the nude?"

I turned to face him, defiant. "Yes." Did he want to make something out of it?

He tried to put his face in order, to return my gaze directly, but he only succeeded in looking bewildered.

"Are you so surprised?" I said.

"In a way. You were always sort of . . . shy."

"Shy?" Now it was my turn to be surprised.

He corrected himself quickly. "I don't mean shy, exactly. Just *private*. You know."

I knew. He was talking about the exclusiveness I had always felt about our bodies, about his and mine. "I *like* it," I said sullenly.

"I didn't mean anything. You have a right to do what you want."

"I know that. You don't have to tell me." And the subject fell between us, all things unfinished, unsaid.

Howard filled two bowls with soup. He sat the children at the table and baby-fed them, first one and then the other, until the soup was gone. Then he took them into their room. I tiptoed after them and stood just outside the ring of lamplight in the doorway and watched while he changed their pajamas and tucked them in. He sat on a straightbacked chair between their beds, and he sang songs to them, one song apiece, so that nothing would be diluted by the act of sharing. While he sang, his fingers made little folded birds from sheets of kraft paper, and his feet tapped out soothing rhythms related to the current song.

Oh, he's a living wonder, I thought, a regular paternal one-man band. The children loved it, of course. Fair-weather friends. Never mind that he'd be gone the minute they dropped their guard and wandered into sleep. The *second*. It occured to me that I should have encouraged them to sleep longer before he came. I could even have drugged them, some harmless, sleep-inducing stuff that would have left them maddeningly awake now. Howard wouldn't be able to just walk out on them under those circumstances. He would be caught interminably in this career of magician-entertainer-father. Let him take out his whole bag of tricks. Let him juggle the three rotten lemons that were in the back of the refrigerator, compose birthday songs months in advance, rock their beds with a fierce concentration and all of his energy. "I'm not tired," they would say. "Daddy, don't *go*," and his heart would be won, and he'd stay.

But instead they slipped into sleep like deserters, and I went back to my post in the kitchen and looked into the oven at the sweating roast and the apples. My final ploy for extra time. At least Mrs. X wasn't waiting downstairs in the lobby now, with her motor idling, the way she was on visiting Sundays.

And I had the magic of this familiar domestic scene on my side. Those sleeping children, the food-steamed kitchen, the clock strategically set at the parents' hour.

He came inside then, embarrassed by his handsome good health, shy and uneasy in the sudden privacy between us. "I'm going now," he said. "Is there anything you want me to do first?"

Did he think I would ask him to catch up on household chores, to change light bulbs or fiddle with the toilet tank? "Stay for supper," I said, and before he could object, "I have to talk to you. It's important. There's something I have to tell you."

"Tell me now, Paulie. But I really can't stay."

I pretended I didn't hear him, folded napkins, set out water tumblers. If only I hadn't slept so late. If only I'd had a chance to change my clothes. Why did I ever think it was possible to win his attention with food? It was all wrong. My head ached. The clatter of dishes and pots jarred me. All wrong, all wrong. The way to a man's heart is through his cock, not his stomach. But he wouldn't come close to me, wouldn't even stand still. He smoked a cigarette for camouflage and to give his hands innocent occupation. He looked restlessly at his watch.

"The kids and I are moving to New Mexico," I said. I hadn't meant to say it so abruptly or in such a threatening voice. I had meant to come on easy like a salesman who knows that if his product can't compete, he can always count on the winning quality of his pitch.

"*What?*"

"New Mexico. We need a change."

"Paulie, what are you talking about?"

"A change of scenery. A good climate. Indians," I added, irrelevantly. "And we'll get fewer colds."

"Paulie, I think you're really sick." He reached out as if to feel my forehead and I jumped back, that motion setting off a resounding chain of aches in my bones.

"*Don't touch me!*" I screamed. Touch me. That's what I meant to say, but I was irrevocably committed to the defense.

"Hey," Howard said. "Please don't be like that."

"Like what? Like *what*?"

"Ah, listen, Paulie. I know how you feel."

"No, you don't," I said. "How could you know how I feel?"

"Because I know you. Because, well, you know—I love you."

"Love? Do you mean l-o-v-e? *Love?*"

"Shhh," Howard said. "Hold it down. The children."

Ah yes, the children, those turncoats. I gripped the edge of the counter for balance. Raising my voice had made me dizzy again. "Well, I'm getting out of this joint," I said. I looked around, as if for new ideas. Inside the oven the pork roast defrosted, sputtering fat. A fine mist drifted about us.

"Look at this place," I said. "Who can even breathe? We're all being poisoned by escaping gas."

"That's only grease," Howard said. "Don't dramatize." Then, "Who are you going with?"

"What?" I had lost track.

"Who are you going with to New Mexico?"

"Oh," I said. "That's a good one. Oh, ha ha ha."

"Why are you laughing? What's so funny?"

"Who am I—ha ha—*going* with? Ha ha ha."

"Paulie, I don't see the joke. What's so funny? Answer me."

But I couldn't answer, and I couldn't stop laughing either. It wasn't funny, I knew, just terribly ironic. But I felt weak against that giddy onset of laughter, and dangerously close to weeping.

"You don't expect me to believe this, do you?" Howard asked. "I know you. You wouldn't leave your precious city unless you had a damn good reason. Stop it, Paulie. You're hysterical."

"Ha ha ha. Oh God, I *can't*. Oh ho. It's killing me." I held my side where it ached, just above my waist.

"But it's not *funny*," Howard shouted. "You're hysterical. It must be the fever."

"Then hit me," I gasped, between bursts of laughter. "Isn't that—oh ha—what you're supposed to do? Go ahead, hit me."

"Will you cut it out, Paulie? Will you just please cut it out?"

The tears were running now. "Don't," I moaned. I laughed and laughed, holding up my hand like a traffic cop to ward off his words.

Howard seemed worried. "Look, I'll talk to you," he said. "Do you want to talk? We'll eat supper, okay?" To prove his good will, he sat down at his place at the table.

But I had started a shuffling dance step and I was making playful little jabs, like a boxer, at Howard's arms, his head, his neck. "Go ahead, why don't you hit me?"

He put one hand up to protect himself and the other reached

out and held my wrist. It was only a restraining gesture, but still the first time he had touched me in such a long while.

"Let go," I said, trying to pull free. I was vaguely aware of something burning in the oven, of distant street noises and footsteps in the apartment overhead. "Let go, you bastard, or I'll kill you!"

By then he had both wrists. He was standing again and he was shaking me, just hard enough to send my fevered head into another spin of vertigo. I used my feet then, kicking at his shins with my soft, weathered slippers, aiming my knee at his groin.

"Oh, Jesus," he said, sidestepping, losing his grip on one of my hands. "Are you crazy?"

But I reasoned that I was relentlessly sane, that craziness seemed like an unattainable luxury, an enviable escape. And I was so *tired*. My knees buckled and I reached behind me for support. My hand landed in a moist tangle of potato peelings and apple cores. *Apples*, I thought bitterly. "Apples!" I shouted. "Oh, damn you, damn you to hell!" My fist closed around something, metal or plastic. Without looking back, I raised it in swimming fury, and, with a feeling close to ecstasy, brought it hard against his chest.

Howard staggered back. He fell against the table, moving it noisily to the far wall, rattling silver, upsetting china. His hand moved across his chest as if he were going to make a declaration or swear his allegiance to the flag. Something— *blood*, was coming out between his fingers.

I looked at my own hand, still clenched. It seemed to be someone else's, or my own still, but disembodied and out of my control. I was holding the apple corer. I had stabbed Howard with the apple corer.

"Oh, my dearest!" I cried, rushing him.

"I'm wounded," he said, in a soft, cautious voice. "I think I'm wounded."

"Oh, my God, let me see." I pulled his hand away, ripped his shirt open where the blood was following the oxford weave in a slow trickle. There, below the nipple, was a crescent-shaped puncture wound with fresh blood just welling up. "Let me, let me," I murmured. "Shhh, shhh," even though he wasn't saying anything at all, just staring down at himself in horror. He was always such a coward about blood, about the frailty of human flesh, and it was me who had brought him now to this mortal recognition.

"Don't look," I told him. "Let me," and I wiped, first with the hem of my nightgown, and finally with some wet paper toweling. After a while my heart slowed and I saw that it wasn't bad, that it wasn't really deep. The blade of the apple corer was bent almost at a right angle to the handle. "It's only a flesh wound," I said. "Howard, it's all right."

By then he was paler than I had ever seen him, and dazed-looking as if he had suffered a blow to the head instead.

"Howard, Sweetheart, are you all right? Oh, I didn't mean it."

"A little light-headed," he said. "The shock . . . the blood . . ." His forehead and lip glistened.

I took his hand and led him into the bedroom and he went with me like a small and trusting child.

"Just lie down," I said. "Here, put your feet up." Strangely, I felt much stronger then myself, as if it were a question of taking turns, one of us powerful and one of us vulnerable at all times. My turn, I thought, and I pulled off his shoes, putting my hands inside them to catch their warmth as I lowered them to the floor. I put the other pillow under his feet.

"Just till I catch my breath," Howard said. "What's that smell? Is it still bleeding?"

"Only Vicks," I said. "No no, don't look at it, it's stopped. But I have to bathe it now. Will you let me bathe it? I won't hurt you." I knelt at the side of the bed with a basin of warm soapy water and the king-sized Band-Aids I kept for the children's scraped knees. I could see his heart leaping under his breastbone. I worried about putting the Band-Aid across the hair of his chest, where it would surely get stuck. I went to the desk drawer and found my manicuring scissors.

He started, as if from a doze. "What are you doing?"

"Nothing. Just rest. Only these hairs." I snipped carefully, Delilah, letting the soft, dark tendrils scatter on the sheet. Power, I thought. Power and love.

And then without thinking at all, I lay down next to him and took his hand in mine. "Howie? I didn't mean it," I said. "Do you know that? It was the fever. I must have been crazy."

He didn't answer and I wondered if he had fallen asleep. Battle-weary and vanquished, it wouldn't have been unreasonable. Violence wasn't that far from sex, just as I'd always suspected, and I could have drifted into a kind of post-coital dream myself. But when I lifted my head to look at Howard, he was staring straight ahead across the room.

"Howard?"

"It was an act of love," he said at last.

"What?"

"Love," he said again, and this time his voice was stronger and full of wonder. "Oh, Paulie, listen, I've come to my senses."

39

I CALLED THE ART STUDENT'S LEAGUE TO SAY I WAS quitting, but I felt I owed Douglas a more personal notice of farewell. He hadn't asked too many questions about Howard and me in the first place. In his gentle way, Douglas never urged me to talk about anything painful. He knew the basic facts of my life, and he recognized the underlying sadness that was there, even in the midst of our fun. I think he was secretly thrilled with what he saw as romantic tragedy.

"Unfinished business," I told Howard brusquely, as I left the apartment to speak to Douglas. I allowed Howard his own conclusions. I felt entitled to a little mystery, and besides, I hardly wanted the details of *his* departure from Mrs. X. My restless imagination had wandered into speculation anyway, and I had visions of frenzied kisses, and of carefully packed, zippered garment bags, fat with the costumes of their affair: boa-trimmed negligees, pom-pommed mules, underwear that would disintegrate in a laundromat.

Howard had come back with the same suitcase, as crazily crammed as it had been the day he left. I gave it one triumphant glance, but I didn't offer to help him unpack.

I called Douglas from the drugstore phone. "I have to tell you something," I said. "I'm coming over."

Douglas was scared. "What? What is it?" he asked, his quavering voice giving him away.

Poor Douglas. Did he think I was calling to say I was pregnant? He should have known I had long outgrown the wanton optimism that allowed mistakes like that. Maybe he'd be relieved to find it was only love's betrayal and the homing instinct of a strayed husband.

But when I saw him and told him about Howard's return, he didn't act relieved at all. He seemed shocked and sad. "Wow," he said, letting himself fall backward into a chair. "I don't know why, but I didn't *expect* this."

Oh God, was he going to cry? "I didn't either," I said. "It just happened."

"No no no," Douglas said. "I'm not blaming you."

That confused me a little. I didn't think I had confessed guilt. But I took it as the cue for my next move. "Howard's the children's father; he's still my husband. He regrets everything."

"Right, right," Douglas agreed, raising one hand and then letting it drop into his lap. "I think you're doing the right thing, the *only* thing. It's just that I didn't expect it just now."

"I didn't either," I said again, and we had come around full circle. I felt more than a little uncomfortable struggling for words in that room where we had attempted so little conversation before. The place was as disordered as the first time I'd seen it, the unmade bed hogging most of the space, looking like an absurd memorial to our relationship.

Douglas himself had come to the door barefoot, wearing only unbelted jeans. His naked chest was as gorgeous as a laborer's, as vulnerable as a child's. I had once loved only Howard's body, praised its beauty and imperfections alike, celebrated its companionship with mine. Now I knew how men feel in their arrow-straight lust for certain women. I, too, had become a connoisseur of flesh.

On the way to Douglas's place, I had played out this scene between us in my head, preparing both parts, directing all the action. After all, I was tougher, older, probably *born* wiser than Douglas.

He was dear, even precious, but still a little comical, a perpetual kid.

Hey kid, put on your pants, my husband's home. And there's more to life than surefire fucking. Even Howard's found that out now.

I gave Douglas terrific lines too—lines that showed a new mature strength, that damned the conventions of marriage and all limits on desire. But he wouldn't say them.

I felt a flutter of disappointment and impatience. I knew that the last thing I needed was resistance, a lover who wasn't going to give me up without drama. And yet, I *wanted* a little drama, a minor performance in which we formally acknowledged the sacrifice we were making.

Howard had given up Mrs. X in the middle of his passion. The possibilities of their farewell scene flashed before me again and I felt mean-spirited with envy, while Douglas sat slumped and defeated, his eyes filling with tears.

Douglas, I wanted to say, don't be so honorable, don't be so sad. Be angry. *Howard* is the interloper here, not you, with your good will and your grilled cheese and your innocent drawings.

Even Jason and the baby put up a courageous fight when they were afraid of losing something they wanted.

This isn't fair, I thought. It hurts too much to be fair. And for one wild moment I wondered if I really *had* to give Douglas up, if I just couldn't keep him somewhere safely on the sidelines, the way Howard had once kept Mrs. X. My backstreet cowboy. But in the next instant I knew it was a crazy notion, crazy and childish. It would never have occurred to Douglas anyway. That wasn't how his mind worked. This was a happy ending, no matter how lousy we both felt. It was the sort of ending he loved best in the movies, too. He would miss me all right, in body and in spirit. He would miss the boy and the girl too, the idyll of all our good times together. Still, Douglas would want to do what he thought of as the right thing. Maybe he believed it was the kind of suffering he needed, the pain that would make him a deeper artist.

He stood. "I'm going to miss you a lot, Babe," he said, that last word almost inhaled in a sob.

How I wished then that he'd straighten the bed or put on a shirt, either gesture final, and appropriate to the end of things between us.

But instead he reached out slowly to me, and I took his hands in mine. "Dearest Douglas. Oh, *good-bye*," I said, and when we embraced, the fierceness of his hug forced out my breath and I was startled by that familiar jolt against my belly.

40

Every day
I move to
a new neighborhood,
making doorkeys
useless.
No one here
speaks English,
or remembers
my mother.
But the slatted
sun still seeks
dust
felled by polish,
those chairs
with the gentle
curves
of seated women,
and the child
who waits
in a worn Persian
bower
for a time
to push off.

April 23, 1962

"WHAT I WOULD DO," MY MOTHER SAID, "IS RIP THEIR
hearts out, both of them, and feed the pieces to the cats and

dogs in the neighborhood." She said it quite calmly while she wrapped an ashtray in a page of the *New York Post* and tucked it into a carton.

"That's your mother for you," my father said in wondering admiration.

She continued. "Plain death would be too good for them. They'd have to suffer a lot first."

Ma, I wanted to say, what about forgive and forget? What ever happened to turn the other cheek, and live and let live? But I didn't say anything, just sighed and looked at the stripped walls of my living room where paintings had left lighter spaces like ghostly shadows of themselves.

"Well, at least you're getting out of this dump," she said. "At least you'll be living in a real house."

It was the worst thing she could have said. I still felt a tearing and unreasonable love for that apartment where Howard and I had begun. I missed everything already: even the indelible sink stains and the crowded cupboards, the poor narrow light and the faulty plumbing. I felt as if I simply *belonged* there, as if it were my natural home.

But there were a thousand good reasons to leave. At the head of the list, of course, was Mrs. X herself, slender and fragrant, and only yards away again in Building C. And Howard and I definitely needed something else, a symbolic change to mark this turn our lives had taken. Our apartment really was terribly small. The children and their belongings were forcing us into corners. I looked around, eager to find fresh fault with it, but my eyes filled with tears.

"You're depressed," my mother said accusingly.

"No no, it's not that. It's just that I got my period this morning. You know I'm always a soft touch on the first day."

My father, who had been packing books, began to whistle tunelessly between his teeth, and he moved to the window. I had forgotten about him, that talk like this always embarrassed him. It was what he called "woman's talk," that dealt with human functions or illness. It occurred to me then that despite all the man-made words for our parts, worshipful or degrading, women still have a closer, more loving and critical sense of our own bodies.

Maybe, in the same way, we have a deeper sense of where and how we live. I looked at the chaos around us. Practically everything Howard and I owned was in cartons and barrels. We were transporting it all from one place to another like exiles.

The supermarket boxes had brought in nests of waterbugs and roaches. In the last nights when one of the children woke and called for water, an insect freeway came to frenzied life in the sudden kitchen light. Thinking that *they* would still be here after we were gone, I went after them with folded newspapers and a misdirected rage.

Howard was wild about moving, kept up a manic monologue about space and light and air. Cancer, heart attacks, even the common cold, were waiting for us like muggers in the dark alleys of the city. He wondered if I realized the inevitable relationship that would develop between our children in that crowded room they shared. Already there were minor seductions and an outbreak of bathroom language.

I didn't remind him of how we used to laugh at model tract houses and ridicule the plastic lives of people in the suburbs. He probably wouldn't have listened anyway, in his new intense state. One night he swore off cigarettes forever and made us all accompany him to the incinerator where he sacrificed an unopened carton to the flames below. He hugged and kissed the children until they shrieked complaint, and it seemed he was always near me, always bumping into me. We collided in the hallway or when we took turns in the bathroom, and even in our sleep like two blind night animals.

"I guess you forgive him," my mother said. "You're such an easy person. Maybe that's your whole trouble."

I wondered what she would say if she knew about Douglas, or about the stabbing, if she could have seen the blackness in my eyes and in my heart. But maybe she would have decided that I had been merciful, or at least just.

I didn't answer and she said, "Oh ho, not me, sister, he'd

have to win back *my* respect, prove himself before I'd look into those bedroom eyes again."

"Ma," I said.

"I'm different," my father said. "If he walked into this room this very minute, I'd shake his hand and wish him all the luck in the world."

"You!" she said, wiping him out with a glance.

"Howard's not walking in, Dad," I said. "*You* know that. I told you he's giving a lesson until six tonight."

"I only said, *if* he did. Listen, Sis. Put the past behind you. It's a brand-new page and everything's going to get better."

"Well, maybe things will be different," my mother conceded. "You'll be living in the country, for one thing. It's a different pace."

"It's not the country, Ma. It's only the suburbs."

"But there's nature there. Who knows?—maybe you'll start writing poetry again like you used to, with the flowers and all that nature around you."

Why did she only acknowledge my poems when it was impossible for me to talk about them? And why did she think I'd write about flowers?

41

*T*HE BUYING OF THE HOUSE WAS A STRANGE EXPERIENCE.
I couldn't help thinking that all legal procedures were the
same in a way: marriage, divorce, even real estate transac-
tions. The language was so formal and humorless and seemed
to have nothing to do with what was really taking place.
Deeds. Lots. Escrow. But how were we going to *feel* in those
new rooms, in that suburban stillness? What was going to
happen?

The lawyer for the other people, the sellers, chewed gum
and ruffled papers for effect.

"I feel nervous," I told him. "Like a bride."

He stared at me. "I don't get it," he said.

"Oh, as if one of you should say, 'Do you take this house
on Lot fifty-three, Block one twenty-five, and promise to
love and honor it, to keep a high wax shine on its floors till
death do you part?' Something like that."

"That's a funny way to look at it," he said, and he went
back to his papers.

But I could see that Howard felt the same way I did, despite all his enthusiasm on the way to the bank. In the car he
could hardly wait to get there, leaning on the horn the instant
lights changed, taking his rampant happiness out on me with
urgent kisses and radiant smiles. But later, seated around the
desk in the mortgage office he looked the way he had at our
wedding; pale and confined. He took a cigarette from the
deeds clerk and his face disappeared in a screen of smoke.

All that signing, all those pages of printed gibberish. I

reached under the table for Howard's hand, but it was cold and damp like my own, and we quickly let go.

Right after we took title to the house, the former owners moved out. We drove there the next day to look the place over and to supervise the painters. Jason was worried and confused for a while. He shadowed me through all the rooms and once, after using the upstairs bathroom he came rocketing down the stairs. "Hey!" he shouted, his eyes blazing with fear and anger. "I almost couldn't find you!"

"That's one thing you don't have to worry about, kiddo," I told him. "I'll be here. I'll probably *always* be here." I was talking to myself as much as to him, but Jason plastered himself to my hip and wept in relief.

I thought I understood his confusion and his alarm. During those weeks of transition, I often had bad dreams. I'd wake suddenly, wondering where I was. If I cried out, Howard, that heavy city-sleeper, would hardly rouse, but he'd say "shhh" anyway and lay his arm across me in that mute gesture of comfort. And I would gladly take his comfort and lie close to the dark warm bear of his chest. In moonlight, I could just make out the small crescent scar below his nipple where the apple corer had gone in. I did that, I thought in wonder. *I* did that. And no one knew about it but Howard and me. If I ever told Judy, she would probably make something Freudian out of it, tell me how sexual it was, how it was a true reversal of roles, with *me* penetrating *Howard* for a change. Sherry would have said that my hand was guided by Mars or by an outraged Venus.

But I had no accomplices, celestial or otherwise. It was an inside job.

42

*T*HE PAINTERS ERASED OLD COLORS AND FINGERPRINTS, those signs of the house's former life, while we wandered through it. The kitchen and laundry room came equipped with wonderful modern appliances: a stove that shuts itself off when dinner is cooked, and a washing machine with twelve finely tuned cycles. The refrigerator manufactures a steady supply of ice, and it has a blue light on the door like a soda machine in a movie lobby. With all this equipment, I thought, it will probably be a breeze to diet. I could fill the refrigerator with cottage cheese and with the fruits and vegetables we would grow in our own little garden. Maybe I could even just live on ice cubes for a while.

I went outside and saw that it wasn't really that bad. There were Eliot's lilacs right on cue. And Howard was certainly right about the clean air and the feeling of space. The children would have their own jungle gym in the backyard, and they could slide and roll on the soft summer grass. The important thing was that we were a *unit* again, that terrible but enduring eight-legged beast, a family.

Jason noticed that there were letters in the mailbox. I opened the first one and saw that it was for the woman who used to live there.

Dear Eleanor,
Bill and I are so happy to hear that you're finally getting out of that house where you've had so much rotten luck.

I didn't read any more, but folded the letter back into its envelope and wrote, *moved, please forward*. There were several advertising flyers in the mailbox too. People offered to mow our lawn and to baby-sit, to teach us belly-dancing and pottery and easy classical guitar.

I'll sign up for a poetry workshop at the New School, I decided. I'll commute to the city one night a week, just to keep a claim on that territory. The poems were starting to come anyway, just as I knew they would.

I took a walk with the children in that profound absence of traffic and other walkers. The lawn sprinklers moved back and forth with the precision of Rockettes. Women on their lawns and porches were friendly. When they saw me with Jason and Ann, who fit nicely into the mean age of all the children in the neighborhood, they waved and invited us to visit.

It was spring in the suburbs, as it was in the city, but out there it announced itself in full orchestra. During my walk I felt that I would probably be able to forgive Howard, that we could clean the whole slate and start all over again. It might take a while, I knew, but I believed we could do it. What I would have trouble dealing with was the heartbreaking leafiness of all those trees and the earth-sprung shoots of grass underfoot. What I probably couldn't ever forgive was that joyous riot of birdsong wherever I went.

We said so long to the painters and drove back to our carton-packed apartment, which had begun to look like a poor man's supermarket. At three o'clock in the morning, Raymond showed up at our door. Things hadn't worked out, he said, by way of explanation. Renee was staying in Chicago for a while to seek new horizons, but she had promised to keep in touch.

Raymond's feet hung over the arm of the sofa when I tucked him in. He snored like a diesel train approaching a crossing, and the sofa groaned in rhythm with his dreams. He looked through the want ads every day. He took our garbage to the incinerator and ran little errands. My night talks with Howard were expanded into small but amiable group sessions for a while. Raymond's stories were interesting, as I'd suspected they'd be, from his tattoos and all. He never even knew his real parents or his true history. We sent him to N.Y.U. for a battery of aptitude tests, and it was predicted he'd do well in social research or merchandising. In the meantime, we helped him find a place of his own in Sherry's current building, and we staked him to a small loan until his luck changed. We were still worried about Renee though, and a few days later there was an airmail letter. She was lonely and her body absorbed only the harmful additives in food. After all, Chicago was not her hometown.

43

This is the last stage of happiness;
the lamp still keeps one filament
of light.
And your sleeping arm, remembering
an embrace,
still circles a portion of the night.

April 30, 1962

THEN IT WAS OUR FINAL NIGHT IN THE COMPLEX. WE PUT
the children to bed, promising them good dreams, kissing
them jointly to guarantee our reunion.

"Come here," Howard said, beckoning from our bedroom door. He was unbuttoning his shirt, smiling.

"No," I said. "*You* come in here." I gestured at the living
room, that new miniature city with its cardboard skyline.

"Hey, there's no room in there."

"We'll make room." I moved some things from the sofa
and set them onto the floor and the coffee table. "It's a special occasion, you know. This is going to be our last session
here, in this place."

Howard hesitated. "We don't need *that* stuff anymore."
His smile was flickering, ready to go out.

"Don't be afraid, Howie," I said. "We're not going to go
over the recent past. It's too awful for me, anyway."

He came in then, and we lay down side by side once again,
hips touching, fingers joined. The sofa springs plunked a
small, familiar complaint.

"I want to do the future instead," I said.

Howard was relaxed, amused. "Are you a fortune-teller?" he asked. "Can you really see the future?"

But I didn't have to be a seer to do that. It was a cinch. On certain Sundays, we'll no longer look at model homes. Instead, we'll probably go to places like Plant World and Puppy Palladium. In the back of a station wagon, we'll trundle home azalea and begonia, rhododendron and spirea. One day, when Jason has outgrown his allergies, we might even bring back a puppy in a carton.

Howard will have to work longer hours to keep up the mortgage payments and all the other expenses. He'll have to spend a couple of hours every day just commuting.

As for me, at super shopping malls, I'll be a consumer, dazzled by the bounty. In bed, I'll always be a passenger ready for cosmic flight.

"Well, *can* you?" Howard asked.

"What? Oh, the future. Sure," I said. "Let me read your palm." I opened his fingers. "A lot of interesting lines here. God, it looks like Bruckner Boulevard." I sighed. "I wish I really knew what it all means."

Howard closed his hand over mine. "It doesn't mean anything," he said. "Don't look for mystical answers, love. I'll tell you what you want to know."

I didn't say anything.

"We're going to be happy," Howard continued. "*Reasonably* happy," he emended. "Peaceful. That's not so bad, is it?"

Happiness. It seemed like the most senseless and tenuous of states. "Are you happy right now?" I asked.

He paused for just an instant. "Yes," he said. "Sure. Yes, I am."

"But what's going to happen when you're not again?"

"Paulie, that's not fair. I thought we weren't going to go over the recent past."

"We're not. We're talking about the future, kiddo. Remember? But women aren't the only ones who live in cycles.

I mean, what's going to happen when you start to feel sad again, displaced, melancholy?''

"Who says I'm going to?"

"Who says you're not?"

"*I* say," Howard said. "I'm happy, damn it!" He banged his fist on the floor, and china in a nearby barrel made an answering sound. "Can't you tell? I've got everything I truly want in this world, and I know that now. You and the kids. A decent life. Nothing can affect that. Don't worry, nothing's going to change."

I smiled in the growing darkness. "Everything changes," I said.

"What are you trying to say, Paulie?"

"I'm trying to say that it wouldn't be any good if it happens again, Howard. I'm trying to say that *I've* changed."

"Yes," he said, and his hand moved cautiously to his chest. "But you'd never get away with murder in this state, baby," he said.

I let him have his little joke, thinking *he's* the one, he's the one who got away with murder.

In bed later, after we made love, Howard whispered, "Do you forgive me, Paulie? Do you forgive me?" But I didn't choose to answer; I pretended to be asleep.

It was difficult to really fall asleep, for the last time in that room. I knew that things were no longer the same between Howard and me, and we would take that burden of knowledge with us wherever we went. Maybe it was just as well, though. Obsessions never actually pay off, even in Bette Davis movies. It was more balanced now: equal passion, equal terror.

Toward morning I woke to find Howard's face, a dimly illuminated planet, suspended above mine. "But do you still love me?" he asked, and his breathing was anxious.

I looked at his shadowy features, rediscovering their dear planes. I inhaled that known odor, the heavenly stink of a well-used bed. *Love*, I thought sadly. But I felt committed to the truth. "Yes," I said. "I still love you."

"And I still love you!" he cried joyfully, letting himself

down again, crushing me under the weight of his relief. "And we're going to start all over, a new life in a brand-new place. So everything's going to be fine! Isn't it?"

44

ON MOVING DAY SEVERAL NEIGHBORS CAME IN TO SAY good-bye. I was surprised because we had never spoken to some of them. "I always meant to come in," a woman from down the hall said. "But you know how these things are. Something always came up." She wished us the best anyway, while she looked around at the packed cartons and the naked beds with an ecstatic gleam. I imagined it was the same curiosity one might feel at the funeral of a stranger; a perverse longing to see the body without any desire to have known the person.

The superintendent of our building came up too, and he said we had been very desirable tenants. We had never destroyed property that didn't belong to us, and we had been good sports about power failures and failure of water pressure. He was usually such a dour and inarticulate man. In almost five years he had hardly said anything to me. He had changed washers and knocked furiously on pipes and had always seemed to look just past me with his terrible eyes. For a moment I thought he might be trying to say something else, that I had perceived the desperate look of a man in love. But when I thanked him and offered my hand, he turned quickly away and left the apartment.

Jason and Ann ran wildly about, excited by all the activity, and for a while I sat them in front of the television set just to keep them quiet and out of the way. Cartoons flickered and squealed. They sat as close as they could, as if they drew nourishment from its milky light, until they were abruptly weaned by a mover who pulled the plug and carried the set away. They both screamed in protest and Howard took them downstairs for a final ride on the playground swings. I wondered if Mrs. X would happen to look through her window and catch her last sight of him, fixed forever in this world as a family man.

The moving men were like Chinese acrobats I had once seen in a circus: squat and powerful and communicating in wordless grunts. They worked perfectly in teams, our furniture on their backs, until the rooms were completely bare.

I went on a brief tour of inspection. A rusted steel wool pad on the kitchen counter, a collapsed pacifier in the dust where the baby's crib had been, and, in the shower stall, delicate curls of pubic hair, gender unknown.

Howard, always mindful of ceremony, came upstairs again with the children in his arms, and we all took one last look together. The baby, because she was hungry or tired, or from some deep, intuitive knowledge, began to cry, and we left quickly, leaving the door open, and we didn't look back.

About the Author

Hilma Wolitzer has taught at the Bread Loaf Writer's Conference and in the writing programs of the University of Iowa and Columbia University. Her short stories have appeared in *Esquire* and *New American Review* and she has written four novels for adults and four books for young readers. She is currently living in Long Island with her husband, a psychologist. They have two daughters, Nancy and Meg.